Alfred de Musset, E. P. Robins

Tales of Today and Other Days, from the French of ..

Alfred de Musset, E. P. Robins

Tales of Today and Other Days, from the French of ..

ISBN/EAN: 9783743444324

Printed in Europe, USA, Canada, Australia, Japan

Cover: Foto ©Andreas Hilbeck / pixelio.de

More available books at **www.hansebooks.com**

TALES OF TO-DAY

TALES OF TO-DAY

AND OTHER DAYS

FROM THE FRENCH OF

Alfred de Musset	François Coppée
Alphonse Karr	Paul Bourget
Théophile Gautier	Guy de Maupassant
Prosper Merimée	Jules Claretie
	Émile Zola

TRANSLATED BY

E. P. ROBINS

NEW YORK

CASSELL PUBLISHING COMPANY

104 & 106 Fourth Avenue

THE MERSHON COMPANY PRESS,
RAHWAY, N. J.

A WORD FROM THE TRANSLATOR.

A FEW words of explanation seem in order anent the aim and purport of this small volume, otherwise the tales of which it is composed may seem to the critical so many *disjecta membra*, without form and void, fit subjects for the waste-basket.

Briefly, then, it is a collection of those short stories that the French so excel in; the "Tales of To-day" being selected from among the most famous of our modern *raconteurs*, while the "Tales of Other Days" are some of those that served to amuse and delight our fathers and grandfathers forty, fifty, sixty years ago, the intention being to give some faint idea of the difference (if any) that characterizes the literary methods of the two epochs.

Versatile Paris witnessed in 1830 two revolutions, of which it is hard to tell which was the more important in its results: one was the fall of the Bourbons, the other the emancipation of French literature from the bondage in which it had until then been held by the Classicists. Victor Hugo, the highpriest of the new cult, produced his *Hernani* on the stage in 1830;

he was quickly surrounded by a band of young and enthusiastic followers, whose productions in the next thirty years were the delight of France and the world. The band comprised, in addition to their illustrious chief, Balzac, Dumas, George Sand, De Vigny, Sou- lié, and, last but not least, the four charming, inimit- able authors whose names appear on the title-page of this volume—De Musset, Karr, Gautier, and Merimée. They were all born in the years between 1803 and 1811; Musset was the first to die, in 1857; Karr sur- vived until 1890, forming a link between the past and present; his "Visit to the Arsenal," however, bears the date 1842. Of course there were others besides, less famous, but men of mark in their day, and they all united to form a galaxy that has hardly been equaled in any literature for delicacy, taste, and bril- liancy.

Of the five names selected to represent the writers of to-day Émile Zola, the apostle of the realistic school,—which is not realism more than the work of a painter would be who should depict the slums of a great city and assert his picture to be a faithful repre- sentation of that city, ignoring its parks and palaces, its museums, gardens, and works of art,—Émile Zola is the most popular writer of the day, if judged by the sale attained by his books. But that proves—what? According to a recent statement, of "Nana," the most prurient of his books, 155,000 copies have been sold in France; of "La Faute de l'Abbé Mouret," the cleanest, some 40,000. The inference seems to be, as Mr. Saintsbury says, that there are a great many (apparently) decent men and women who avail themselves of an opportunity to purchase publicly and carry away with them indecent literature; the difference between the greater figure and the less may be taken as the indication of the extent to which M. Zola's popularity is ascribable to depraved tastes and instincts; and while the tremendous sales of such books may put money in the author's pocket in the present, it will hardly help his reputation in the future. Argue as we may, art and beauty are closely allied; the union between art and deformity is an unholy one and the progeny will be tainted and short-lived.

Will Zola and his imitators occupy fifty years hence the place in the affection of their countrymen that Hugo and the members of his school occupy to-day? The "Great Man" recently failed to secure the election to the *Académie* that he had solicited; like Piron, he may write his own epitaph, *mutato nomine :*

> Ci-gît Zola, qui ne fut rien,
> Pas même Académicien.

Very antithetic to Zola in style, habit of thought, character, disposition, everything, is François Coppée, the poet of the people. Gifted with a singularly melodious and tenderly poetic style, intensely sympathetic with humanity in all its aspects, he selects his charac-

ters for the most **part** from among the lowlier walks
of life and pictures their troubles and sufferings and
their infrequent joys with loving fidelity. A vein of
gentle melancholy pervades his writings, varied by an
occasional indignant denunciation of the shams and
frauds of society, but without maudlin sentimentality.
It is to be doubted, however, if he will ever receive
the recognition that his tender grace and **manly**
humanitarianism entitle him to, for he neither blows
the trumpet **nor beats the big drum,** as some of his
confrères **are not** above doing; and although he pipes
so pleasantly, he does it, rather, *cum tenui avena.*

De Maupassant, who seemed likely at one time **to**
run Zola close in the race for popularity, **is** pretty
well known **on** this side of **the Atlantic;** Bourget and
Claretie, both **adepts in the** story-teller's art, are less
so. It may **be** said that the Zola school is by no
means omnipotent in the country of its birth; there
are many excellent men and eminent writers who dep-
recate its influence on morals and on literature, and
French authors, unconsciously to themselves perhaps,
permit themselves **to** be swayed to **a much** greater
extent than they did a short time ago by the influence
of English and American **writers.** They appreciate
more justly than they used to do **the** traits, habits,
and character of their neighbors across the water;
there is less (though even **now too much) of** that contempt for the outer barbarian **that they** formerly took

such small pains to conceal. For this better understanding we are indebted to no one more than to the
talented lady who, under the pseudonym of Théo.
Bentzon, contributes an occasional appreciative review
to the pages of the *Revue des Deux Mondes*.

I should have been glad could I have afforded those
who are so kind as to read my translation a better
version of the great originals, but it is my experience
that any attempt to use "fine language" is only too
apt to result in a perversion of the sense. A translation should follow its original as closely as may
be without degenerating into servility: otherwise it
ceases to be a translation and becomes an adaptation.
There is a quotation that we often hear used: "O
Liberty, what sins are committed in thy name!"
Mme. Roland did not say that in her apostrophe;
she said: *O liberté, comme on t'a jouée!* "O Liberty, how men have cheated thee!" Doubtless the
version that is more familiar to our ears rolls from off
the tongue more glibly, but it is not the same. *C'est
magnifique, mais ce n'est pas la guerre.* The old simile
occurs to me of decanting champagne, but it is trite;
the only resource that I know of that will enable the
reader to enjoy the style and sense of any foreign
author is to get down his grammar and dictionary and
master the language.

CONTENTS.

STORY OF A WHITE BLACKBIRD.

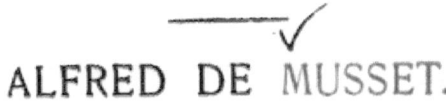

ALFRED DE MUSSET.

I

IT is a great thing, in this workaday world of ours, to be something a little above the common run of ordinary blackbirds, but then, too, the eminence is not without its inconveniences. I am not a bird of fable ; Monsieur de Buffon has written my description, but woe is me ! I am rare and but seldom met with. Would to Heaven I had never emerged from the lowly state in which I was born !

My father and mother were a couple of honest people who had lived for many years in the seclusion of a quiet old garden in the Marais. It was a model. household. While my mother, in the depths of some bushy thicket, laid three times a year regularly and hatched out her brood, gently slumbering most of the time, my father, very neat in his attire and very fussy still, notwithstanding his great age, would be pecking, pecking about her all day long, with patriarchal devotion, bringing her nice little insects that he was always careful to seize by the tail, very daintily, so that his wife's delicate stomach might not be offended, and at nightfall he never failed, when the weather was fine, to treat her to a song that delighted all the neighbor-hood. Never was there such a thing as a quarrel, never had the smallest cloud arisen to darken this sweet union.

I had hardly made my appearance in the world when, for the first time in his life, my father began to display bad temper. Although as yet I was of only a doubtful shade of gray, he failed to recognize in me either the color or the form of his numerous progeny Sometimes he would cock his head and look at me askance and say :

"There is an untidy child for you ; it would seem as if the little blackguard took pains to go and wallow in every mud-hole and plaster-heap that he came to, he is always so ugly and filthy."

" Eh ! Mon Dieu, my friend," my mother would answer, looking like nothing so much as a little round ball of feathers in the old earthenware porringer where she had made her nest, " don't you see that it is owing to his age ? And you yourself, in your early days, were you not a charming little scapegrace ? Give our little blackbirdling time to grow, and you will see how pretty he will be ; I don't think that I ever hatched out a finer one."

My mother was not deceived while pleading my cause in this manner ; she saw the growth of my ill-omened plumage, which appeared to her a monstrosity ; but she acted as all mothers do, who allow themselves to become more strongly attached to their offspring for the very reason that nature has ill-used them, as if the responsibility rested on the maternal shoulders, or as if they rejected in advance the injustice of their un-kind destiny.

With the approach of my first moulting season my
father became extremely thoughtful and watched me
attentively. He continued to treat me with considerable kindness so long as my feathers kept falling
out, and would even bring me something to eat when
he saw me shivering, almost naked, in my corner, but
as soon as the down began to come out on my poor
little half-frozen wings, he would fly into such a tearing rage at every white feather he saw that I
greatly feared he would leave me featherless for the
remainder of my days. Alas! I had no looking-
glass; I did not know the cause of his anger, and I
wondered why it was that the best of fathers could
treat me so cruelly.

One day when a glimpse of sunshine and my growing plumage had cheered me and warmed my heart a
little in spite of myself, as I was hopping about an
alley I began, tempted by my evil genius, to sing. At
the very first note that he heard my father flew up into
the air like a sky-rocket.

"What do I hear there?" he shouted. "Is that the
way a blackbird whistles? Do I whistle that way?
Do you call that whistling?"

And perching beside my mother with a most terrific
expression of countenance:

"Wretched bird!" he said, "what stranger has
been sharing your nest?"

At these words my mother indignantly threw
herself from her porringer, severely injuring one
of her claws in doing so; she endeavored to
speak, but her sobs choked her; she fell to the
ground in a half-fainting condition. I beheld her
at the point of expiring; terrified and trembling

with fear, I threw myself upon my knees before my father.

" Oh, father ! " I said to him, " if I whistle but poorly and if I am meanly clad, let not the punishment fall upon my mother. Is it her fault if nature has not graced me with a voice like yours ? Is it her fault if I have not your beautiful yellow bill and your handsome black coat *à la Française,* which give you the appearance of a churchwarden about to swallow an omelette ? If Heaven has seen fit to make me a monster and if someone must pay the penalty, grant, at least, that I alone may bear the burden of misery."

" That has nothing to do with the case," said my father ; " what do you mean by taking the liberty of whistling in that ridiculous manner ? Who was it that taught you to whistle thus, contrary to every known rule and custom ? "

" Alas ! sir," I humbly replied, " I whistled as well as I knew how ; for I was feeling in good spirits because the weather is fine, and perhaps I had eaten too many flies."

" That is not the way they whistle in my family," my father rejoined, quite beside himself with anger. " We have been whistling for centuries from generation to generation, and let me tell you that when I raise my voice at night there is an old gentleman here on the first floor, and a young *grisette* up there in the garret, who throw up their windows to listen to me. Is it not enough that my eyes are constantly offended by the horrid color of those idiotic feathers of yours, which make you look like a whitened jack-pudding at a country fair ? Were I not the most long-suffering of blackbirds I should have stripped you naked long before this and reduced you to the condition of a barnyard fowl prepared for the spit."

" Very well ! " I cried, unable longer to submit to such injustice, " if that is the case, sir, never mind ! I will relieve you of my presence ; your eyes shall no more be offended by the sight of these poor white tail-feathers by which you are continually pulling me about.   I will go away, sir, I will take refuge in flight ; since my mother lays thrice a year there will be other children in plenty to console your declining years ; I will go and hide my wretchedness in some distant country, and it may be," I added, with a sob, " it may be that along the gutters or in the neighbors' kitchen-garden I shall find some earth-worms or a few spiders to enable me to eke out my miserable existence."

" As you please," replied my father, far from melting at this speech of mine ; " only let me never set eyes on you again.   You are not my son ; you are not a blackbird."

" What am I then, sir, if you please ? "

" I have not the slightest idea ; but you are not a blackbird."

With these crushing words my father strode slowly away.   My mother sadly arose and went limping to her porringer to have her cry out, while I, for my part, confounded and disconsolate, stretched my wings and took my flight as well as I could, and went and perched upon the gutter of an adjoining house as I had said I would do.

II

My father was so inhuman as to leave me several days in this mortifying situation.   Notwithstand-

ing his violent disposition his heart was in the right
place, and I could see by his way of looking at me
askant that he would have been glad to forgive and
recall me to my home ; my mother, too, was constantly gazing upward at me with eyes that were full
of tenderness, and now and then she would even venture to address me with a plaintive little chirrup ; but
my horrible white plumage inspired them, despite their
better feelings, with a fear and a repugnance against
which I clearly saw there was no remedy.

"I am not a blackbird !" I kept repeating to myself; and, in truth, as I was preening myself one
morning and contemplating my form reflected in the
water of the gutter, I saw only too clearly how little
resemblance there was between me and the rest of the
family. "Kind Heaven !" I said again, "teach me
what I am ! "

One night when the rain was coming down in bucket-
fuls and I was getting ready to go to bed, quite worn
out with grief and hunger, a bird came and sat down
near me, wetter, paler, and more emaciated than I had
believed bird could be. He was of something the
same color as I, as nearly as I could judge through
the torrents of rain that were streaming down on us ;
he had scarcely sufficient feathers on his body to
clothe a sparrow respectably, and yet he was a bigger
bird than I. At first I took him to be some poor, needy
wanderer, but notwithstanding the storm that pelted
pitilessly upon his almost naked poll he maintained
a loftiness of demeanor that quite charmed me.   I
modestly made him a deep bow, to which he replied
with a dig of his beak that nearly sent me tumbling off
the roof.   When he saw me scratch my ear and

meekly edge away from him without attempting to answer him in his own language, he asked in a hoarse, thick voice, to correspond with his bald pate :

" Who are you ? "

" Alas ! my noble lord," I replied (fearing that he might give me another dig), " I cannot tell. I thought that I was a blackbird, but I am convinced now that I am not."

The strangeness of my answer, and my apparent truthfulness, seemed to interest him. He approached me and made me relate my history, which I did in all sadness and humility, as befitted my position and the unpleasantness of the weather.

" If you were a carrier-pigeon like me," he said to me when I had finished, " the pitiful trifles that you are bewailing so would not disturb your mind an instant. We travel—that is the way we make our living—and we have our loves, indeed, but I don't know who my father is. Cleaving the air, making our way through space, beholding plains and mountains lying at our feet, inhaling the pure ether of the skies and not the exhalations of the earth, hastening to an appointed destination that we never fail to reach, therein lie our pleasures and our life. I travel further in one day than a man can in ten."

" Upon my word, sir," said I, plucking up a little courage, " you are a bird of Bohemia."

" That is something that I never bother my head about," he replied. " I have no country ; I know but three things : travel, my wife, and my little ones."

" But what is it that you have hanging about your neck there ? It looks like an old twisted curl-paper."

" They are papers of importance," he answered,

bridling up. "I am on my way to Brussels and I have a piece of intelligence for the celebrated banker . . . that will send the price of *rentes* down one franc and seventy-eight centimes."

"Great Heavens!" I cried, "what a delightful life yours ought to be, and Brussels, I am sure, must be an extremely interesting city to visit. Can't you take me with you? Perhaps I am a carrier-pigeon, since I am not a blackbird."

"If you had been a carrier-pigeon," he rejoined, "you would have paid me back for the clip of the beak that I gave you a while ago."

"Well! sir, I will pay you; we won't quarrel over a little thing like that. See! the day is breaking and the storm is passing away. Let me go with you, I beseech you! I am undone, I have not a penny in the world—if you refuse me there is nothing left for me to do but drown myself in this gutter."

"Very well! *en route!* follow me, if you can."

I cast a parting glance upon the garden where my mother was slumbering. A tear fell from my eye! it was swept away by the wind and rain. I spread my wings and started forth.

III

As I have said, my wings were not very strong as yet. While my guide pursued his flight with the speed of the wind I was puffing and panting at his side; I held out for some time, but soon was seized with such an attack of dizziness that I thought I should faint.

"Have we far to go yet?" I asked in a weak voice,

"No," he replied," "we are at Bourget ; we have but sixty leagues to go."

I tried to muster up courage, for I did not wish to show the white feather, and flew along for a quarter of an hour longer, but it was of no use, I was quite knocked up.

" Monsieur," I again stammered, "might we not stop for a moment ? I am tormented by a horrible thirst, and if we were just to perch upon a tree——"

"Go to the devil ! you are nothing but a black-bird ! " the pigeon responded in a rage and, without so much as turning his head, he continued his mad flight. As for me, everything grew dark before my sight and I fell, senseless, into a field of wheat.

How long my unconsciousness lasted I know not. When I came to, my first recollection was the carrier-pigeon's parting remark : " You are nothing but a blackbird," he had said to me. " Oh ! my dear parents," I said to myself, " then you are mistaken, after all ! I will return to you ! you will recognize me as your true and lawful son and will let me have my place again in that dear little bed of leaves down beneath my mother's porringer."

I made an effort to rise, but the fatigue of the journey and the pain resulting from my fall paralyzed my every limb. Scarcely had I got upon my feet when my strength failed me again and I fell over on my side.

Hideous thoughts of death were now beginning to arise before my mind, when I beheld two charming creatures advancing toward me on tip-toe through the poppies and cornflowers. One was a little magpie, very stylishly speckled and of extremely coquettish appearance, and the other was a turtle-dove of a rosy complexion. The turtle-dove stopped when she had approached within a few feet of me, with a great display of modesty and compassion for my misfortune, but the pie came skipping up with the most pleasing manner in the world.

"*Eh! Bon Dieu!* my poor child, what are you doing there?" she inquired in a merry, silvery voice.

"Alas! Madame la Marquise," I replied (for I thought that she must be a marquise at the very least), "I am a poor devil of a traveler whom his postilion has abandoned here at the roadside, and I am ready to die of hunger."

"Holy Virgin! what is that you tell me?" said she. And forthwith she began to flit about among the surrounding bushes, hopping from one to another and bringing me a great provision of berries and small fruits, which she deposited in a little pile at my side, continuing her fire of questions meanwhile.

"But who are you? Where do you come from? The story of your adventure sounds incredible! And where were you going? To think of your traveling alone, at your age; why, you are only just over your first moulting! What is your parents' business? Where do they belong? How can they let you go about in the condition that you are in? Why, it is enough to make one's feathers stand on end!"

I had raised myself a little upon my side while she was speaking and was eating with a ravenous appetite. The turtle-dove had not stirred from her position and continued to eye me with a look of pity; she re-

marked, however, that I would turn my head every
now and then in a feeble sort of way, and saw that I
was thirsty.   Upon a leaf of chickweed there remained
a drop of the rain that had fallen during the night ;
she took it in her beak and timidly brought it and
offered it to me ; it was deliciously cool and refresh-
ing.   Had I not been as ill as I was, a person of her
modesty would certainly not have ventured thus to
transgress the rules of propriety.

As yet I knew not what it was to love, but my
heart was beating violently ; I was divided between
two conflicting emotions and an inexpressible charm
pervaded my being.   My clerk of the kitchen was so
lively, and my butler showed such gentleness and feeling, that I would gladly have protracted my breakfast to all eternity, but everything has an end, unfortunately, even the appetite of a convalescent.   When
the meal was ended and my strength had in a measure
returned to me I appeased the little pie's curiosity,
and related the story of my woes with the same candor
that I had displayed the day before in telling them to
the pigeon.   The pie listened with a deeper interest
than the recital seemed to call for, and the turtle-dove
evinced a degree of sensibility that was most charming.
When, however, I came to touch upon the final cause
of all my sufferings, that is to say, my ignorance as to
my own identity :

" Are you joking ? " screamed the pie.   " What you,
a blackbird ! a pigeon, you ! Nonsense ! you are a
pie, my dear child, if pie there ever was, and a very
pretty pie, too," she added, giving me a little tap with
her wing, as if it had been a fan.

" But, Madame la Marquise," I replied, " it seems to

me, respectfully begging your pardon, that I am not
of the right color for a pie."

"A Russian pie, my dear, you are a Russian pie!
Don't you know that they are white? Poor child,
how innocent you are!"

"But how could I be a Russian pie, madame," I
rejoined, "when I was born down in the Marais in an
old broken porringer?"

"Ah! the simple child! Your folks came here
with the invasion, my dear; do you suppose that there
are not others in the same case as you? Confide in me
and don't allow yourself to worry! I mean to carry
you off with me right away and show you the finest
things in the world."

"And where to, dear madame, may it please you?"

"To my green palace, pretty one; and you shall
see the kind of life we lead there. When you shall
once have been a pie for a quarter of an hour you
will never want to hear tell of anything else. There
are about a hundred of us there, not those great,
common, village pies who make a business of begging
on the highways, but all noble and of good family,
spry and slender and no larger than one's fist. There
isn't one of us that has either more or less than seven
black and five white spots; the rule is unalterable,
and we look with contempt on all the rest of the world.
It is true that you have not the black spots, but you
will have no difficulty in gaining admission on account
of your Russian descent. Our time is spent in two
occupations: cackling and prinking ourselves. From
morning until midday we prink, and from noon till
night we cackle. Each of us selects a tree to perch
upon, the tallest and oldest that he can find. In the

midst of the forest is a great oak that is uninhabited now, alas ! It was the dwelling of the late king Pie X, and we make pilgrimages to it, heaving many a deep sigh ; but, apart from this transitory grief, our life is as pleasant as we could wish. Our women are not prudes nor are our husbands jealous, but our pleasures are pure and honest, because our hearts are as noble as our tongues are merry and unrestrained. Our pride is unbounded, and if a jay or any such common trash happens to intrude his company upon us we pluck him without mercy. For all that, how-ever, we are the most. good-natured people in the world, and the sparrows, the finches and the tomtits who live in our copses always find us ready to protect, feed and help them. Nowhere is cackling carried to greater perfection than among us and nowhere is there less scandal. There are plenty of bigoted old hen-pies who do nothing but say their prayers all day, but the friskiest of our young gossips can go right up to the severest old dowager and never get a scratch. To sum it all up, our life consists of pleasure, honor, chatter, glory, and the clothes we put on our backs."

" That is very nice, indeed, ma'am," I answered, "and it would certainly be a piece of very bad manners on my part not to obey your orders. Before doing myself the honor of following you, however, permit me, I pray you, to speak a word to this good damsel here—— Mademoiselle," I continued, ad-dressing the turtle-dove, " I adjure you, speak frankly ; do you think that I am really a Russian pie ? "

At this question the turtle-dove drooped her head and her complexion changed to a light red, like Lolotte's ribbons.

"Why, sir, I don't know if I can——"

"Speak, mademoiselle, for Heaven's sake! I con-
template nothing that can possibly give you offense;
quite the reverse. You both appear so charming to
me that I call Heaven to witness, here and now, that I
will make offer of my heart and claw to either of you
that will accept them, the very instant that I learn
whether I am a pie or something else; for," I
added, lowering my voice a little to the young
creature, " I feel an inexpressible turtle-dovish sensation as I gaze on you that causes a strange disquietude
within me."

"Why, truly," said the turtle-dove, blushing more
deeply still, "I don't know whether it is the sunlight
striking on you through those poppies, but your
plumage *does* seem to me to have a slight tint
of——"

She dared say no more.

"Oh, perplexity!" I cried, "how am I to know what
to depend on? how am I to decide to whom to give
my heart when it is divided thus cruelly between
you? O Socrates! how admirable was the precept
that you gave us, but how difficult of observance, when
you enjoined upon us: ' Know thyself '!"

I had not tried my voice since that day when
my most unlucky song had so disturbed my father's
equanimity, and now the idea occurred to me of making
use of it as a means whereby I might arrive at the
truth. "*Parbleu!*" I said to myself, "since monsieur my father turned me out of doors for the first
couplet, it seems a reasonable enough conclusion that
the second should produce an effect of some kind on
these ladies." So, making a polite bow to start with

as if appealing to their indulgence on account of the
cold that I had caught in the rain-storm, I commenced
by whistling, then I warbled, then I diverted my
audience with a few trills, and finally I set to singing
in earnest, vociferously, like a Spanish mule-driver in
a gale of wind.

The little pie began to back away from me, and the
louder I sang the further she retreated, at first with
an air of surprise, which quickly changed to one of
stupefaction, and finally terminated in a look of terror
accompanied by deep disgust. She kept walking
around me in a circle, as a cat walks around a piece
of bacon, sizzling hot, against which she has burned
her nose, but of which she thinks she would like to
try another taste, notwithstanding. I saw how my
experiment was turning out and wished to carry it
to a conclusion, so, the more the poor marquise fretted
and fumed, the more deliriously did I sing. She stood
my melodious efforts for twenty-five minutes, but at
last she succumbed and flew noisily away and retired
to her palace of verdure. As for the turtle-dove, she
had gone off into a sound slumber almost at the very
beginning.

" Delightful effect of harmony ! " I thought. " Oh,
my dear native marsh ! Oh, maternal porringer !
More than ever am I firmly resolved to return to
you ! "

Just as I was poising myself in readiness for flight
the turtle-dove opened her eyes.

" Farewell," she said, " pretty and tiresome stranger !
My name is Gourouli ; don't forget me ! "

" Fair Gourouli," I replied, " you are gentle, kind
and charming ; I would like to live and die for you,

but you are of the color of the rose ; such happiness
was never meant for me ! "

IV

THE distressing results of my singing could not
but sadden me. "Alas, Music ! alas, Poetry ! " I
said to myself as I winged my way back to Paris,
" how few are the hearts that are able to comprehend
you ! "

While pursuing these reflections I ran full tilt into
a bird who was flying in a direction opposite to mine.
The shock was so violent and so unexpected that we
both fell into a tree, which, by great good luck,
happened to be beneath us. When we had shaken
ourselves and pulled ourselves together a bit, I looked
at the stranger, fully expecting that there was going
to be a quarrel. I saw with surprise that he was
white ; his head was a little larger than mine, and
rising from the middle of his forehead was a kind of
plume that gave him an aspect half heroic, half comical. He carried his tail very erect, moreover, in a
manner that bespoke an excessive intrepidity of soul ;
he did not, however, seem to be disposed to quarrel
with me. We accosted each other very civilly and
made our mutual excuses, after which we entered into
conversation. I took the liberty of asking him what
was his name and from what country he was.

"I am surprised," he said, "that you do not know
me. Are you not one of our people ? "

"Truly, sir," I replied, "I know not of what race
I am. Every one asks me that very question and
tells me the same thing ; I think they must be carrying out a bet that they have made."

"You are joking, surely," he replied ; "your plumage sets too well upon you that I should fail to recognize a *confrère.* You indubitably belong to that illustrious and venerable race that is known in Latin as *Cacuata,* in scientific nomenclature as *Kakatoës,* and in the vernacular of the vulgar as cockatoos."

"Faith, sir, that may be, and it would be a very great feather in my cap were it so. But favor me by acting as if it were not the case, and have the condescension to tell me to whom I have the honor of addressing myself."

"I am the great poet Kacatogan," the stranger replied. "I have been a mighty traveler, sir, and many are the tiresome journeys that I have made through arid realms and ways of heaviness. I am not a rhymester of yesterday, and my muse has seen misfortune. I have sung love ditties under Louis XVI., sir ; I have brawled for the republic, sung the empire in noble strains, applauded the restoration guardedly ; even in these later days I have made an effort and bowed my neck to meet the demands of this unlettered age. I have given to the world sparkling distichs, sublime odes, graceful dithyrambs, soulful elegies, stirring dramas, blood-curdling romances, vaudevilles in powder and tragedies in wig. In a word, I may flatter myself that I have added to the temple of the Muses some garlands of gallantry, some gloomy battlements and some graceful arabesques. What would you more ? I have grown old in harness, but I keep on rhyming still with pristine vigor, and even as you behold me now I had my mind on a poem in one canto, to be not less than six pages long, when you came along and gave me that lump on my forehead. Nevertheless, I am entirely at your service, if I can be of use to you."

"To tell the truth, sir, you can," I replied, "for I am in great poetic tribulation just now. I won't venture to say that I am a poet, and, above all, a great poet like you," I added, with a low bow, "but nature has kindly fitted me with an organ that makes its existence felt whenever I am joyous or sorrowful. To be entirely candid with you I am absolutely ignorant of all the rules of poetry."

"You need not let that trouble you," said Kacatogan ; "I myself have forgotten them."

"But there is a very disagreeable circumstance connected with my case," I continued ; "my voice produces upon my hearers very much the same effect as did that of a certain Jean de Nivelle upon—— You know what I mean?"

"I know," said Kacatogan. "I have experienced that singular effect in my own person. The cause is unknown to me, but the effect is indisputable."

"Very well, sir. Could you, who seem to me to be the Nestor of poetry, think you, suggest a remedy for this painful state of affairs?"

"No," Kacatogan answered ; "speaking for myself, I have never succeeded in finding one. When I was young it worried me exceedingly that I should be constantly hissed, but now I never think of it. I think that this opposition arises from the fact that the public read other works than ours : they seem to like to do so."

"I am of your opinion ; still, sir, you must admit that it is hard on a well-meaning creature that his audience should take to their heels the very moment that he is seized by a fine inspiration. Would you do me the favor to listen to me and tell me candidly what you think ? "

" With the greatest pleasure in the world," said Kacatogan ; " I am all ears."

I began to sing forthwith, and had the satisfaction of seeing that Kacatogan neither ran away nor went to sleep. He kept his eyes fixed intently on me and, every now and then, gave a little approving nod of the head accompanied by a low, flattering murmur. I soon perceived, however, that he was not listening at all and that his mind was on his poem. Taking advantage of a moment when I had stopped to breathe, he suddenly interrupted me.

" Ah, that rhyme ! I have found it at last ! " he said, with a smile and a toss of the head ; " that makes the sixty thousand seven hundred and fourteenth that has emanated from this brain ! And yet people dare to say that I show the effects of age ! I am going to read that to those good friends of mine ; I am going to read it to them, and we'll see what they have to say ! "

So saying he took flight and disappeared, seemingly oblivious of the fact that he had ever met me.

V

LEFT thus solitary with my disappointment, there remained nothing better for me to do than profit by the daylight while it lasted and reach Paris in a single flight, if possible. Unfortunately I did not know the way ; my journey with the carrier-dove had been attended with too much discomfort to leave a distinct impression on my memory, so that instead of keeping straight on I turned to the left at Bourget, and, the darkness descending suddenly upon me, I found myself obliged to look for a night's lodging in the woods of Morfontaine.

When I reached there every one was making ready to retire for the night. The pies and jays, who, as is well known, are the worst sleepers on the face of the earth, were squabbling and wrangling on every side. The sparrows were squalling among the bushes, swarming and treading one another underfoot. On the bank of the stream two herons, the George Dandins of the locality, were stalking gravely to and fro, perched on their tall stilts, patiently waiting for their wives in an attitude of profound meditation. Huge crows, already more than half asleep, settled heavily upon the tops of the tallest trees and commenced to drone out their evening prayer. Below, the amorous tomtits were pursuing one another through the copses, while a disheveled woodpecker, marching in rear of his little household, endeavored to marshal it into the hollow of an old tree. Battalions of hedge-sparrows came in from the fields, whirling in the air like smoke-wreaths, and threw themselves upon a shrub which they quite concealed from sight ; finches, blackcaps and redbreasts perched airily upon the projecting branches in little groups, like the crystal pendants on a girandole. From every side came the sound of voices that said as plainly as could be : " Come, wife !—Come, my daughter !—This way, pretty one !—Come here, darling !—Here I am, my dear !—Good-night, dear mistress !—Farewell, friends !—Sleep soundly, children ! "

Imagine what a predicament it was for a bachelor

to have to take up his quarters in an inn like that! I
thought that I would go to some birds of station similar to my own and request their hospitality. All
birds are gray in the dark, I said to myself, and
besides, what harm can it do people to have a young
fellow sleeping beside them if he behaves himself?

I first bent my steps toward a ditch where there was
an assemblage of starlings. They were just making
their toilet for the night and were devoting the most
scrupulous attention to it, and I observed that most of
them had their wings gilded and wore patent-leather
claws : they were evidently the dandies of the forest.
They were good enough fellows in their way and did
not notice me, but their conversation was so shallow,
they displayed such fatuousness in telling one another
of their broils and their love affairs, and they crowded
together so coarsely that I could not stand it.

Next I went and perched upon a limb where half-a-
dozen birds of different kinds were sitting in a row.
I modestly took the last place, away out on the end of
the limb, in the hope that they would suffer me to
remain there. As my ill-luck would have it my
neighbor was a dove well on in years, as withered and
juiceless as a rusty weather-cock on a church steeple.
At the moment of my approach she was devoting an
affectionate solicitude to the scanty feathers that
covered her old bones ; she pretended to be smooth-
ing them, but she was too much afraid that she might
pull one out to do that : she was only counting them
over to see if they were all there. I barely touched
her with the tip of my wing when she drew herself up
as majestically as you please.

"What are you doing here, sir?" she cried, with a

modesty that would not have disgraced the severest
of British prudes, and giving me a great poke with
her elbow she sent me tumbling from the branch with
a vigor worthy of a railway baggageman.

I fell into a brake where a big wood-hen was sleeping.   My mother herself, in her porringer, never wore
such a beatific air.   She was so plump, so rotund and
comfortable, with her well-filled stomach and her fluffy .
feathers, that one would have taken her for a pâté
from which the crust had been eaten off.   I crept
furtively up to her.   "She won't wake up," I said to
myself, "and even if she does, such a jolly, fat old
lady can't help but be good-natured."   She did not
turn out as I expected, however.   She lazily opened
her eyes half-way, and heaving a faint sigh, said :

"You are crowding me, young fellow ; clear out of
here."

At the same instant I heard my name called ; it
was a band of thrushes up in the top of a mountain-
ash who were making signals to me to come to them.
"There are some charitable souls, at last," thought I.
They made room for me, laughing as if they were
crazy, and I slipped into the midst of the feathered
group as expeditiously as ever you saw a billet-doux
disappear in a muff.   It soon became evident to me,
however, that the ladies had been partaking of the
fruit of the vine more liberally than was good for
.them ; it was as much as they could do to keep themselves from falling off their perches, and their equivo-
cal pleasantries, their uproarious bursts of laughter
and their indecent songs compelled me to leave their
company.

I was beginning to despair, and was about to search

for some lonely corner where I might lay my head when a nightingale began to sing. Instantly silence reigned throughout the grove. Ah! how pure was her voice! Her very melancholy, how sweet did it appear! Far from disturbing the slumbers of others, her tuneful strains seemed to soothe them. No one thought of bidding her be silent, no one took it ill that she selected that hour for singing her song; her father did not beat her, her friends did not fly from her presence.

"It is I alone, then," I cried, "to whom it is not given to be happy! Let us go, let us fly from this cruel world! Better is it to seek my way amid the shades of night and run the risk of making a meal for some wandering owl, than to linger here and have my heart lacerated by the spectacle of others' happiness!"

Upon this reflection I started forth, and for a long time wandered without definite aim. The first light of breaking day revealed to me the towers of Notre Dame. Quick as a flash I reached them and from them scanned the horizon; it was long before I recognized our garden. I winged my way to it, swifter than the wind. Alas! it was empty. It was in vain that I called upon my parents: no one responded. The tree where my father had his seat, the bush, my mother's home, the beloved porringer, all had disappeared. The fatal ax had leveled all, and in place of the verdant alley where I was born there remained only a pile of firewood.

VI

THE first thing that I did was to search through all the gardens of the neighborhood for my parents, but it was only labor lost ; they had doubtless taken refuge in some distant quarter and I never heard of them more.

Sick at heart, I went and perched upon the gutter that had been my first place of exile when driven from my home by my father's cruelty. There I spent days and nights bewailing my sad existence ; I could not sleep, I ate scarcely anything ; my grief had nearly caused my death.

One day when, as usual, I was giving way to my sorrowful meditations, I thought aloud and said :

"So, then, I am not a blackbird, since my father pulled out my feathers ; nor a pigeon, since I fell by the way when I tried to fly to Belgium ; nor a Russian pie, since the little marquise stopped her ears as soon as I opened my beak ; nor a turtle-dove, since Gourouli, even that good, kind Gourouli, could not help snoring like a trooper while I was singing ; nor a parrot, since Kacatogan would not condescend to listen to me ; nor a bird of any kind whatever, in fine, since they allowed me to sleep by myself at Morfontaine. And yet I have feathers on my body ; those appendages are claws, those are wings. I am not a monster, witness Gourouli and the little marquise herself, who seemed to look on me with eyes of favor. To what inscrutable reason is it owing that these feathers, wings, and claws compose a whole that is nothing more nor less than a nameless mystery ? I wonder if I am not——"

I was pursuing my lamentations in this strain when I was interrupted by two women quarreling in the street.

"Ay ! parbleu ! " one of them said to the other, " if

you succeed in doing it I will make you a present of a white blackbird !"

"Great Heavens !" I exclaimed ; "that decides it. I am the son of a blackbird and I am white ; I am a white blackbird !"

This discovery, as may well be imagined, modified my ideas considerably. I at once ceased to bewail my fate and began to hold up my head and strut about the gutter, looking out on the world with the air of a conquerer.

"It is no small matter to be a white blackbird," said I to myself ; "you don't find them growing on every bush. It was a fine thing for me to do, forsooth, to grieve myself to death because I could find no one like me ; it is always so with genius ; it is my case ! It was my wish to fly from the world ; now I will astonish it ! Since I am that peerless bird whose existence is denied by the vulgar herd, it is my duty, as it is my intention, to bear myself accordingly and look down on the rest of the feathered tribe, with a pride as great as their vaunted Phœnix. I must buy myself Alfieri's memoirs and Lord Byron's poems ; those noble works will inspire in me a towering haughtiness in addition to that which God has endowed me with. Yes, if so it may be, I mean to add to the prestige which is mine by birth. Nature has willed that I should be rare, I will make myself mysterious. It shall be a favor, a glory, to look on me—— And why not, indeed," I added, lowering my voice, "exhibit myself, just simply for money ?

"Fie on it ! What an ignoble thought ! I will write a poem, like Kacatogan, not in one canto, but in twenty-four, like other great men ; that is not

enough ; there shall be forty-eight, with notes and
an appendix ! The whole universe must know of my
existence. I will not fail to make my verse tell the
pitiful tale of my loneliness, but it shall be done in
such a way that the happiest shall envy me. Since
Heaven has denied me a mate I will defame most
horribly the mates of all my acquaintance ; I will
demonstrate that all the grapes are green except
those that are for my eating. Let the nightingales
look out for themselves ; I will prove, as sure as two
and two make four, that their complainings give rise
to heart disease and that their wares are worthless.
I must go and find Charpentier. First of all I want
to make for myself a strong literary position. I mean
to have a court around me, composed not of journal-
ists alone, but of real authors, and even of literary
women. I will write a rôle for Mlle. Rachel and, if
she declines to act it, I will trumpet it through the
land that there are old actresses in the provinces who
are her superiors in talent. I will go to Venice, and
there, on the banks of the Grand Canal, in the heart
of that fairy-like city, I will hire the beautiful Mocenigo
Palace that costs four livres and ten sous a day ; there
I will drink in the inspiration of all the memories that
the author of " Lara " must have left there. From the
depths of my solitude I will inundate the world with
a deluge of *terza rima*, copied from the verse of
Spenser, in which my great soul shall find solace ;
the grove shall do me reverence, tomtits shall sigh,
turtle-doves coo, woodcocks shed bitter tears, and all
the old owls shriek enviously. As regards my per-
sonal being, however, I will be inexorable and permit
no amorous advances. Vainly will the unfortunate

females, who shall have been seduced by my sublime strains, approach me with prayers and supplications to have pity on them ; my only answer to it all will be : ' Pshaw !' Oh, glory without end ! My manuscripts shall sell for their weight in gold, my books shall cross the sea ; fame and fortune shall pursue me everywhere ; I alone will appear indifferent to the murmur of the multitude that shall crowd about me. In a single word, I will be a perfect white blackbird, a veritable eccentric author, feasted, petted, admired, and envied, but always grumbling and ever insupportable."

VII

It took me only six weeks to bring out my first work. It was, as I had determined it should be, a poem in forty-eight cantos. It is true that there were some passages that showed marks of hasty composition, but that was owing to the prodigious rapidity with which it had been written, and I thought that the public, accustomed as it is to the fine writing that it finds in the feuilletons of the newspapers nowadays, would overlook such a trifling defect.

My success was such as accorded with my merit, that is to say, it was unparalleled. The subject of my work was nothing other than myself ; in that I conformed to the ruling fashion of our time. The egotistic unreserve with which I told the story of my late sufferings was charming ; I let the reader into the secret of a thousand domestic details of most absorbing interest ; the description of my mother's porringer alone filled no less than fourteen cantos. The description was perfect ; I enumerated every

dent, chink, and cranny, every spot and stain, the
places where it had been mended and its varying
appearances under different lights ; I exhibited it
inside and out, top, sides, and bottom, curves and plain
surfaces ; then, passing to what was within, I made a
minute study of the blades of grass, sticks, straws, and
bits of wood, the gravel-stones and drops of water, the
remains of dead flies and broken cockchafers' legs
that were there ; the description was simply charming.
Do not think, however, that I sent it to the press as
an unbroken whole ; there are readers who would
have known no better than to skip it. I cunningly
cut it up into fragments which I interspersed among
the episodes of the story in such a way that no part
of it was lost, so that, at the most thrilling and dramatic
moments, one suddenly came to fifteen pages of
porringer. Therein, I think, lies one of the great
secrets of our art, and as there is nothing mean about
me, let anyone who is inclined to do so profit by it.

All Europe was in a commotion upon the appearance
of my book ; it greedily devoured the details of pri-
vate life that I condescended to reveal to it. How
could it have been otherwise ? Not only had I
enumerated every circumstance that had the slightest
bearing on my personality, but I gave to the public in
addition a finished picture of all the idle reveries that
had passed through my head since the time when I
was two months old ; nay, I even inserted at the most
interesting part an ode composed by me when in the
shell. It may be supposed that I did not fail to
allude cursorily to the great theme that is now occupy-
ing the attention of the world ; to wit, the future of
humanity. This problem had seemed to me to have

something of interest in it, and in one of my leisure moments I had roughly drafted a solution of it, which seemed to give general satisfaction.

There was not a day that I failed to receive complimentary verses, congratulatory letters, and anonymous declarations of love. As to callers, I adhered unflinchingly to the resolution that I had formed for my protection : my door was rigorously barred against all the world. Still, I could not help receiving two foreigners who had announced themselves as relatives of mine ; they were blackbirds both, one from Senegal, the other from China.

" Ah ! sir," said they, with an embrace that nearly drove the breath out of my body, " what a great blackbird you are ! How well have you depicted in your immortal lay the pangs of unrecognized genius ! If we were not already as uncomprehended as possible, we should become so after having read you. How we sympathize with you in your sorrow, in your sublime scorn for the vulgar ! We, too, dear sir, have reason to know something, of our own knowledge, of the secret griefs that you have sung so well. Here are two sonnets that we composed while coming hither and that we beg you will accept."

" Here also is some music," added the Chinese, "that my wife composed on a passage in your preface. It is marvelous in its illustration of the meaning of the author."

" Gentlemen," I said to them, " so far as I can judge, you appear to me to be endowed with great depth of feeling and great brilliancy of intellect ; but pardon me for asking you a question. Why are you so sad ? "

"Eh, monsieur!" replied the traveler from Senegal, "just look at me and see how I am constructed.
My plumage is pleasing to the eye, it is true, and I am
dressed in that beautiful shade of green that shines so
lustrously on the neck of the duck, but my beak is too
small and my foot is too big, and just look at the
ridiculous tail that I am tricked out with! It is a
great deal longer than my whole body Is it not
enough to tempt one to use profane language?"

"And look at me, too," said the Chinaman; "my
pitiable state is even worse than his. · My *confrère*
sweeps the streets with his tail, but at me the little
street urchins point their fingers because I have no
tail at all."

"Gentlemen," I rejoined, "I pity you from the
bottom of my heart; it is always inconvenient to have
too much or too little of anything, be it what it may.
Allow me to suggest to you, however, that there are
several persons very like you in the Jardin des Plantes,
where they have been living very quietly for some
time past, in a stuffed condition. Even as it does
not suffice a woman of letters to cast her modesty to
the winds in order to write a good book, so no blackbird can command genius merely by manifesting dis-
content. I am the only one of my kind, and I am
sorry for it; I may be wrong, but I can't help it. I
am white, gentlemen; do you become white, too, and
then we'll see what you have to say."

VIII

NOTWITHSTANDING all my resolutions and my
affected calmness, I was not happy. My isolation
seemed none the less hard to bear for being glorious,

and I could never think without a shudder of the cheerless prospect that lay before me of living all my life unmated. The return of spring, in particular, brought with it a mortal feeling of disquietude, and I was beginning to fall back into my old morbid state of mind, when an unforeseen circumstance occurred that shaped my future for me.

It is unnecessary here to state that my writings had crossed the Channel, and that the English were quarreling among themselves for copies. The English quarrel over everything except that which is comprehensible to them. One day I received a letter from London, from a young hen-blackbird.

"I have read your poem," she said, "and the admiration that it inspired in me has induced me to make you the offer of my hand and person. God made us for each other! I am like you; I am a white blackbird!"

My surprise and delight may be readily imagined. "A white hen-blackbird!" I said to myself; "can it be possible? So, then, I am no longer alone upon the earth!" I made haste to answer the fair unknown, and I did it in such a strain as showed how acceptable her proposition was to me. I urged her to come to Paris, or else permit me to fly to her. She responded that she preferred to come to me, because her parents were plaguing her to death, that she was putting her affairs in order, and would be with me almost immediately.

She arrived, in fact, a few days after her letter. Oh, joy! she was the prettiest little blackbird in the world, and was even whiter than I was.

"Ah! mademoiselle," I cried, "or madame, rather,

for from this moment I look upon you as my lawful wedded wife, is it possible that so charming a creature can have been a dweller upon earth and the tongue of fame have never told me of her existence? Blessed be the ills that I have endured and the peckings that my father gave me with his beak, since kind Heaven has had in store for me a compensation so unhoped-for! Until this day, I believed myself condemned to eternal solitude, and to speak you frankly, the burden was a heavy one to bear, but now that I look on you, I feel within me all the qualities requisite for a good father and husband. Let us not delay; accept my hand; we will be married in English style, without ceremony, and start at once for Switzerland."

"I don't look at the matter in that light," replied the young lady blackbird. "I mean that our espousals shall be celebrated in magnificent style and that all the blackbirds in France that have a drop of good blood in their veins shall be present in solemn conclave. People of our quality owe it to their station not to marry like a couple of cats in a coal-hole. I have a store of banknotes with me; get out your invitations, go to your tradesmen, and see that you don't skimp the refreshments."

I followed implicitly the instructions of my white Merlette. Our wedding-feast was on a scale of unparalleled luxury; ten thousand flies were consumed at it. We received the nuptial benediction at the hands of a reverend Cormorant father, who was archbishop *in partibus*. The day was brought to an end by a splendid ball; in a word, there was nothing wanting to complete my felicity.

My love for my charming wife increased as I became

better acquainted with her character and disposition ; in her small person all accomplishments of mind and body were united. The only blemish was that she was a little prudish in her notions, but I attributed that to the influence of the English fog in which she had been living until then, and I doubted not but that this small cloud would quickly melt away in the genial atmosphere of France.

A matter that was cause to me of more serious uneasiness was a sort of mystery in which she would at times enshroud herself with strange inflexibility, shutting herself away under lock and key with her maids, and thus passing, *as she pretended*, whole hours in making her toilet. Husbands are not generally inclined to look with favor upon whims of this description in their family. Twenty times it had happened that I had gone to my wife's apartment and knocked and she had not opened the door. It tried my patience cruelly. One day, however, I was so persistent and in such a horribly bad temper that she was obliged to yield and unlock the door rather hastily, at the same time reproaching me for my importunity. As I entered my eyes alighted on a great bottle filled with a kind of paste made of flour and Spanish white. I asked my wife what use she put that ointment to. She replied that it was a lenitive for frost-bites that she was troubled with.

It struck me at the time that there was something more about that lenitive than she chose to tell, but how could I distrust such a sweet, well-behaved creature, who had bestowed her hand on me with such gladness and perfect candor ? I had been ignorant at first that my wife was a literary character, but she

admitted it after a while, and even went so far as to
show me the manuscript of a novel for which she had
taken Walter Scott and Scarron as her models.   It
may be imagined how pleased I was by such an agreeable surprise.   Not only did I behold myself possessed
of a beauty beyond compare, but I was now also fully
assured that my companion's intellect was in all
respects worthy of my genius.   From that time forth
we worked together.   While I was composing my
poems she would bescribble reams of paper.   I used
to read my poetry aloud to her, and that did not in
the least disturb her or prevent her from going on
with her writing.   She hatched out her romances with
a facility that was almost equal to my own, always
selecting the most dramatic subjects, such as par-
ricides, rapes, murders, and even small rascalities, and
always taking pains to give the government a slap
when she could and inculcate the emancipation of
female blackbirds.   In a word, there was no obstacle
of sufficient magnitude to daunt her intelligence, and
she allowed no scruples of modesty to keep her from
saying a brilliant thing ; she never erased a line and
never sat down to her work with a plot arranged be-
forehand.   She was the perfect type of the feminine
literary blackbird.

She was working away one day with rather more
than her usual industry, when I noticed that she
was perspiring violently, and at the same time I was
surprised to see that she had a great black spot right
in the middle of her back.

"Good gracious !" I said, " what ails you?   Are
you ill ?"

She seemed a little frightened at first, and I even

thought that there was a guilty expression on her face, but her habit of familiarity with the world quickly enabled her to regain the wonderful control that she always exercised over herself.

"Is my wife losing her color?" I asked myself in a frightened whisper. The thought haunted me and would not let me sleep. The bottle of paste arose before my memory. "Oh, heavens!" I exclaimed, "what a suspicion! Can it be that this celestial creature is nothing more than a painting, a thin coat of white-wash! Can she have made use of such a trick to deceive me! When I thought that I was pressing to my heart the twin-sister of my soul, the privileged being created for my behoof alone, can it be that I was holding in my embrace but so much flour?"

Haunted by this horrible suspicion, I devised a plan to relieve myself of it. I purchased a barometer and eagerly awaited the advent of a rainy day. My idea was to select a Sunday when the mercury was falling, take my wife to the country, and see what effect a good washing would have on her. We were in mid July, however, and the weather remained disgustingly fair.

My apparent happiness and my constant habit of writing had wrought my sensibilities up to a very high pitch. While at work it sometimes happened to me, artless being that I was, that my feeling overmastered my reason, and then I would abandon myself to the luxury of tears while waiting for a rhyme to come to me. These infrequent occasions were a source of much pleasure to my wife; masculine weakness is a spectacle that always affords pleasure to feminine pride. One night when I was busy filing and polishing, in obedience to Boileau's precept, the flood-gates of my heart were opened.

"O thou!" said I to my dear Merlette, "the only and most fondly loved one! thou, without whom my life is but an empty dream, thou, in whose look, whose smile, the universe is as another world, life of my heart, knowest thou how I love thee? It were easy for me, with a little study and application, to express in verse the hackneyed ideas that have already been employed by other poets, but where shall I find the glowing words in which to tell thee all that thy beauty inspires within my heart? Can the memory even of the suffering that is past supply me with language fitly to portray to thee the bliss that is present? Before thou camest to me my lonely state was that of a homeless orphan ; to-day, it is that of a king. Knowest thou, my beautiful one, that in this weak frame whose form I bear until it shall be stricken down in death, in this poor, throbbing brain where fruitless ideas are ceaselessly fermenting, knowest thou, dost understand, my angel, that there is not one atom, not one thought that is not wholly thine? List to what my intelligence can say to thee and feel how infinitely greater is my love. Oh! that my genius were a pearl and thou wert Cleopatra!"

While doting in this manner I was shedding tears over my wife, and her color was fading visibly. At every tear that fell from my eyes a feather became, not black, indeed, but of a dirty, rusty hue (I believe that she had been playing the same trick before some-where else). After thus indulging my tenderness for a few minutes I found myself in presence of an unfloured, unpasted bird, in every respect exactly similar to a common, everyday blackbird.

What could I do? What could I say? What course was left open to me? Reproaches would have been futile. I might, indeed, have considered the marriage as void on the ground of false representations and secured its annulment, but how could I endure to make my shame public? Was not my misfortune great enough as it was? I took my courage in my two claws, I resolved to quit the world, to abandon the literary career, to fly to a desert, could I find one, where never again might I behold living creature, and, like Alcestis, seek

some lonely spot
Where leave is granted blackbirds to be white.

IX

THEREUPON I flew away, still dissolved in tears, and the wind, which is to birds what chance is to men, landed me on a branch in Morfontaine wood. At that hour every one was a-bed. "What a marriage!" I said to myself, "what a catastrophe! That poor child certainly meant well in getting herself up in white, but for all that I am none the less to be pitied, and she is none the less mangy."

The nightingale was singing still. Alone in the silence of the night he was recreating himself with that gift of the Almighty that renders him so superior to the poet, and was pouring out, unhindered, his secrets upon the surrounding stillness. I could not resist the temptation of drawing near and speaking to him.

"What a lucky bird you are!" said I. "Not only

can you sing as much as you wish—and very well you
do it, too, and every one is pleased to listen to you—
but you have a wife and children, your nest, your
friends, a comfortable pillow of moss, the full moon,
and never a newspaper to criticize you. Rubini and
Rossini are nothing compared to you ; you are the
equal of the one and you interpret the other. I, too,
sir, have been a singer, and my case is pitiable.
While you have been here in the forest I have been
marshaling words like Prussian soldiers in array of
battle and dovetailing insipidities. May one know
your secret ? "

"Yes," replied the nightingale, "but it is not what
you think. My wife is tiresome ; I do not love her.
I am in love with the rose : Saadi, the Persian, has
mentioned the circumstance. All night long for her
sake do I strain my throat in singing, but she sleeps
and hears me not. Her petals are closed now and she
has an old scarabee sheltered there——and to-morrow
morning, when I seek my bed, worn out with fatigue
and suffering, then, then she will open them to receive
a bee who is consuming her heart ! "

A Visit to the Arsenal.

ALPHONSE KARR.

IN a spacious atelier are two young men ; one is standing before an easel and taking advantage of the last of the fading daylight, the other, stretched at length upon a great red divan, is nonchalantly smoking a long pipe and twirling in his fingers a letter of which the seal is yet unbroken. Both have their hair long and wear mustaches. To-morrow, perhaps, you will see them with close-cropped heads and lips, and the day after they will be starting a beard again beneath the chin.

"I don't know why it is," said the smoker, "that I hesitate to include this letter in the fate to which I have been condemning my other letters for the last two months. I can't help feeling sorry to burn it unread, the more that it is in my father's handwriting. I can guess very nearly what were the contents of the two missives that he addressed to me previously to this one. The first contained, necessarily, reproaches and threats, the second, probably, reproaches and good advice. I should not be surprised to find a money-order in this one. Parbleu !" he added, after having glanced over the opening lines, " I was not mistaken : my banker is authorized to pay me a hundred francs."

"A hundred francs !" exclaimed the other, laying down his brush.

"A hundred francs," replied the smoker.

"Well, well, fathers are not so black as they are painted ; as for me, I shall never have my daily bread until I can say : *Our Father who art in Heaven.*"

"In the mean time he gives me a very important bit of advice. My uncle at the Arsenal is ill, and he urges me to go and see him. It is an uncle with an inheritance to dispose of, and I have only been there once in the last three years."

"That was not doing right."

"It is an easy matter to be wise when other people are concerned. I will try to go to-morrow. I don't know the way very well, though."

"I will make a map for you."

"That will be nice."

The morrow comes.

"I am not going without my breakfast."

"I would not advise you to."

"Who is going out to get the breakfast ?"

"Not I ; I am in slippers."

"Nor I ; I don't want to soil my boots before I start. Eugène, you are not a bit accommodating."

"And *you* are not a bit just ; I did all the chores yesterday. To-day it is your turn."

"See here, let us take the foils; the first one touched shall go out for the breakfast."

They take down the foils, they fence ; Arthur is touched. It is settled that it is he who is to go for the breakfast, but since they have been at the trouble of taking down the foils, the masks and the gloves, they decide that they will not stop at a single bout. They fence for an hour. When they quit they are blown and as weak as two cats.

"We must heat some water so that I can shave."

"Yes, and you have let the fire go out."

"It is easily lighted again. But we have no water."

"What! is the cistern empty already?"

"Yes; I forgot to close the faucet last night."

"The kitchen must be afloat?"

"It is but too true. I am glad that I noticed it before going downstairs."

They breakfast, they put some water on the fire. While it is warming Eugène resumes work on his picture, Arthur takes his pipe and sprawls supine upon the divan.

"Just see, Eugène," says he, "the time that I have wasted to-day; I ought to be far on my way by this. This dawdling is decidedly a bad business; no one would believe the injury that the habit has caused me. Well did the philosopher say : 'Do that which you would wish to have done rather than that which you wish to do.'"

"That is all the more true in your case," said Eugène, taking a pipe and seating himself beside his chum, "that what you would wish to do, of all things in the world, would be to do nothing."

"It is true that I look with scorn upon that uneasy restlessness which makes certain persons exert themselves merely for the sake of exertion ; do something that is better than repose, or else keep yourself quiet."

;" Just at present it would be better for you to finish dressing than to ' keep yourself quiet.' "

" My water is not hot."

The two friends puffed away at their pipes in silence for a moment ; then Arthur continued :

" Not that I wish to say anything in defense of dawdling ; for, if you will remember, the exordium of my discourse was wholly opposed to it."

" I shall not speak ill of it, either, for

" Idleness is a gift that comes from the Immortals."

The two friends had stored away in their noddles a stock of quotations which they used as aphorisms, producing them as the exigencies of the case seemed to demand.

" But," continued Arthur, " laziness, in order to be pleasant, must be unattended by remorse and by dread of future consequences ; it must be without fear and without reproach ; one must have conquered the right to abandon himself to it, body and soul ; for the only true laziness, what you may call *loafing*, pure and unadulterated, is that to which the body yields itself while the mind is chiding and reproving it."

He arose and commenced his toilet. For a visit so rare as the one that he was about to make and where such important consequences were at stake, he thought it was his duty to lay aside the black cravat that he had worn uninterruptedly for several years. He accordingly folded a white one and laid it in readiness across the back of a chair, but when he had washed his hands he calmly wiped them on his cravat, never dreaming that that bit of white linen could be aught else than a towel. When he perceived what he had done it was too late ; the neckcloth was all rumpled and soiled. He had to go and get another one ; he seated himself to fold it across his knee. But he was so comfortable, there upon the divan ! He resumed his pipe and began to smoke ; his head rested luxuriously upon the cushions.

His state was one of languid torpor that fills the head with flitting thoughts, light and fanciful, that change their form or are dissipated into air at the slightest breath, like puffs of smoke ; that gives free rein to the imagination, which goes gadding, leaving the numbed body without strength either to follow or control it, like the bird which, escaping from the net, flutters about it and seems to mock the fowler, who looks amazedly upon its flight.

Delightful state in which the *I* disappears, in which one stands by and looks upon his own life, its sensations, its joys and sorrows, as if at a play, with the pleased unconcern of a comfortably seated spectator; in which one cannot evoke a melancholy thought that, in spite of his efforts to retain it, will not escape him, as water slips through one's fingers, and transmute itself into some ridiculous image which will dance before him in the curling smoke-wreaths of his tobacco, laugh him in the face and compel him to be merry, whether he will or no.

Arthur sets out at last, however. A man stops him on the staircase.

" Is M. Arthur at home ? "

" No, he is dead."

The man descends the stairs before him, dumfounded.

"Come, I'm mighty glad that that chap doesn't know me."

He steers his course along the boulevards. There are many things to be seen on the boulevards on a day in March. The florists have the first hyacinths exposed upon their stalls, and they exhale an odor of spring. The women, at the first warm rays of sunshine, emerge from their furs, as the early flowers emerge from their green calices.

He stops before a juggler; the juggler is just commencing a trick that is more wonderful than all other tricks, but he does not finish it : he has some others that he wants to show first ; then he is presenting, gratis, cakes of Spanish white to clean brass-work with to those who purchase a box of his charcoal paste for the teeth for twenty sous.

" This odontalgic and balsamic specific is a sovereign cure for decayed teeth. I propose to make a test of it in your presence, ladies and gentlemen. The first person that presents himself—come here, little boy. See, the teeth of this child are perfectly black ; you put a little of the powder upon a brush : you moisten it with water ; and don't think that this is prepared water ; just plain water, the first that comes along, the water of the gutter ; you rub the teeth and the gums with it."

Still there is no sign of the trick that has been announced in such glowing terms ; Arthur, who has been waiting half an hour, loses patience and starts to go, but the juggler runs after him and calls to him :

" Monsieur ! Monsieur ! "

Every eye is directed upon Arthur. He becomes red in the face and stops.

" Monsieur," says the juggler, "why do you carry away my globes ! I cannot earn my living without the implements of my profession."

The people form a ring about Arthur, who, purple with rage, exclaims :

" I have not got your globes ; go about your business."

" I beg Monsieur's pardon a thousand times, but he has my globes in his hat."

The juggler takes off Arthur's hat and extracts from it three immense balls. The trick is adroitly done ; the people look on admiringly. Arthur feels like thrashing the conjurer, and takes to his heels. The skeptically inclined smile and say :

" He is an accomplice ! "

Further on is a man peddling phosphorus boxes.

" Here you have the genuine inflammable paste. You have no need of ready-made matches ; all you have to do is to take the least little bit of my paste on the end of a knife, on the end of your cane, on the end of anything you please, no matter what ; the least contact with a lamp-wick serves to light it at once.

" To say nothing of its utility, my inflammable paste is a source of innocent and entertaining amusement, an incentive to merriment and enjoyment in society. You are out spending the evening—at a minister's house, we will say ; an awkward fellow attempts to snuff the candle and puts it out ; result, Egyptian darkness. Every one has something funny to say ; the young men take advantage of the obscurity to kiss the pretty girls, but what do you do ? You take out your little box, that you always carry about with you in your pocket ; you bet the mistress of the

house a quart of wine, red or white, that you will light
the candle.''

Arthur goes his way ; a man seizes him by the coat-
collar and stops him. This man has before him a
screech-owl and three harmless little adders ; venomous
serpents, he says they are, that he has domesticated.
Several small birds, lying stiff and motionless upon
their backs, have been taught to simulate death. If
he allowed you to touch them you would see how easy
it is for them to do the trick. This man is selling soap
for taking out grease-spots. Vainly does Arthur try
to get away from him, his enemy will not let go his
hold ; a crowd collects about them.

" I never set eyes on such a disgusting grease-spot
as that which disfigures the collar of monsieur's overcoat.''

Arthur gives the grease-spot-man a thump in the
stomach that sends him and his table rolling on top
of the birds and reptiles, animate and inanimate, and
then gives leg-bail again ; to evade the inquisitive
looks that pursue him he enters, at hazard, a street
that is unknown to him ; it takes him into another
street, and that into still another. Arthur is lost ; he
wanders aimlessly, he turns this way and that; finally
he asks a *commissionaire* where he is ; he finds that he
has traversed half the distance on his way back to his
lodging.

" It is my uncle's dinner hour ; I won't go there
to-day, I will go home.''

The next day Arthur arose very early. He lost a
frightful amount of time, the day before, in heating
water to shave with ; to-day he will shave with cold
water. He has on his feet two slippers, one his, the

other Eugène's, one yellow, the other red; his costume is completed by an old pair of black trousers covered with stains of paint and a nightshirt.

The soap does not dissolve readily in the cold water; it becomes sticky and slippery, and when he tightens his grasp in order to hold it, it flies from his fingers just as one discharges a cherry-pit from between the thumb and index.

Arthur stoops and places his hand upon it; the soap slips from his fingers and disappears beneath the sofa. He takes a cane and pokes about with it under the sofa; the cane hits the soap and sends it out flying; the door is open and the soap makes its way out; Arthur follows in hot pursuit, but it skips across the landing and slipping, slipping all the time, hops downward from floor to floor; twice Arthur overtakes it and tries to stop it with his foot, but it only descends the faster. Arthur makes his way down as quickly as his slippers will permit; he passes a woman and child and comes near upsetting them; he tears one of the sleeves of his shirt completely off against a clothes-hook. The soap has brought up in the court at last; Arthur is about to seize it when a servant-girl, who has been washing clothes at the pump, empties her pail, and the minature flood carries the soap out beneath the *porte cochère.*

"Door, if you please!"

Arthur steps outside and picks up his soap from between a horse's legs, but people in the street stop and stare at him. He makes haste to re-enter the house; on every landing he encounters neighbors who have come out of their rooms to learn the cause of the racket that he made in descending. Some of them laugh, others shrug their shoulders. When at last he reaches the top floor, he finds the door of the studio closed. He is about to knock, but hears a child crying and a woman scolding within.

" Be quiet ; it will all be over in an hour and we will go away."

" Ah ! Good Heavens ! it is that frightful little boy whose portrait Eugène is painting. I can't show myself in this condition. What is to be done ? An hour in a ragged shirt, and in such weather as this ! If I only had a pipe ! "

Arthur almost walks his legs off, tramping up and down. When he has exhausted this slightly monotonous pleasure he climbs out at a window, gets upon the roofs, and goes and warms himself at the smoke of a neighboring chimney. The hour passes wearily, but it is too late to go to see the uncle ; there is another day wasted.

Arthur scarcely sleeps at all during the night so that he may be sure of awaking bright and early the next morning. He reflects upon the excuses that he will make to his uncle for not having been to see him for so long a time. At morning he awakes ; the daylight enters his room, dark and rainy.

" Come, it is raining ; I will not go out."

When one is warm and snug in bed the least thing seems to be a sufficient excuse for remaining there. And still Arthur is mistaken ; it is not raining. His misapprehension is caused by a blue curtain that Eugène has hung before the window. There is nothing so depressing and so deceptive as light passing through a blue curtain ; one should never have blue curtains.

It does not rain ; quite to the contrary, it is clear. When Arthur gets up it is late. The sun is beginning to be more powerful ; his rays give color to the roofs, which seem to rob them of their brilliancy.

From the terrace in front of the studio a few square feet of sky are visible, but the little that the friends do see is of a beautiful, transparent blue ; the air that they breathe is balmy and penetrating ; that is as much as people who dwell in cities know of spring. The most magnificent festivals of nature, to the townsman, are no more than what the distant harmonies of the ball would be to the poor wretch dying of cold and hunger at the door of a splendid mansion.

It is enough, however, to set them thinking that the trees must be commencing to put forth their leaves, that the beeches and the maples, together with the hawthorn, are the first to assume their cloaks of green, that the cherry trees, by this time, must be nodding their rich plumes of white blossoms and that the birds of winter have hushed their thin, sharp notes, and the linnet, in the young foliage of the lilacs, is giving utterance to his full, resounding melodies. Upon the banks of the brooks the yellowish catkins of the willows must be bourgeoning, while around them are buzzing the first bees of the season.

Says Arthur to Eugène :

"We must be thinking what we shall do about our garden."

Their garden consists of three long wooden boxes stationed upon the terrace.

" What shall we plant in our garden this year? "

"I don't want any more vegetables, for my part ;

your salad last year was detestable ; besides, we ought
to have a little shade."

" How would you like a few full-grown trees and
some shrubbery ? "

" That wouldn't be so bad."

" Then why shouldn't we set out some firs ? That
would be splendid."

" Joking apart, it seems to me that we live high
enough up that no one can dispute our right to have
a few cedars here ; the cedar takes kindly to the mountains."

" I want flowers ; I shall plant some pinks and red
roses that René d'Anjou was the first to exhibit in his
gardens."

" He was also the first one who cultivated the
Muscat grape."

" If you believe what I say, we are just as likely to
have vines as we are to have forests."·

" Have it your own way."

" Do you know that to have one's name handed
down to posterity in connection with a flower is as
great a glory as the best ? "

Eugène is alone in the atelier, alone, that is, with
a model who neither speaks nor stirs. Arthur has
started out early ; there is every reason to hope that
this time he will succeed in reaching the Arsenal.

Eugène is talking to himself. While painting away
industriously he gives himself bits of good advice,
heaps reproaches on himself, occasionally indulges
himself with a few words of approval ; he imitates
the words and tones of the master under whom he

pursued his studies and intersperses this monologue with moral reflections.

" Be careful how you use your bitumen. Why are you painting without a hand-rest ? Where the devil are my hand-rests, any way ? I shall never find my hand-rests. I ought to have an apprentice to bring me my rest. One is never so ill served as when he serves himself. Ah ! you call that a hand-rest, do you ? Why don't you take the axle of a cart and have done with it ? There is a lighted candle, very well ; but what does your precious candle serve to illuminate? Why don't you put in some lights, then ? You dare not, you are afraid. There, there, a little bit more. Ah ! now your candle lights things up. Don't be too free with the bitumen. A little vermilion here. Come, come ; where is my vermilion ? Who has taken my vermilion ? Tell me, George," he says to the model, "have you been eating my vermilion ? I *must* have some vermilion. There is green, but that is not the same thing. If I had an apprentice he would hunt for my vermillion for me. Really and truly, I must have an apprentice. Economy is the mother of all the vices. Ah ! here is my vermilion ! I wonder who the devil conceived the idea of putting it into a helmet ? Nothing is ever in its place here, everything is always topsy-turvy. Who the devil took it in his head to put my vermilion in a helmet ? The idea of looking for it in a helmet ; I know very well that I placed it in a riding-boot. Come," says he, still talking to himself, " perhaps you call that an eye ; if you were to look at the model you would not disgrace yourself with such idiotic blunders. What does that great imbecile eye mean ? Bring

down the eyeball a little ; there, so ; a little
more."

Then he sings :

> " What a difficult thing it is to paint !
> I shall never be more than a tyro.

" If your picture as a whole is anything like that leg,
to give you your due, it will be the very worst picture
in the salon, and you might as well subscribe it :
Grocer pinxit. Don't abuse the bitumen, I say again.
Come, George, you may take a rest ; I am going out.
I will be back in an hour and a half ; if any one comes
and inquires for me, tell him I have gone to discover
the sources of the Niger."

Eugène leaves the house. A few minutes after he
has gone a commissionaire comes up the stairs and asks
for Eugène. George, who is smoking Levant tobacco
in a Turkish pipe, sends him away with his letter.

That letter is from Arthur. This is what has happened him :

He left the house, as we have said, bright and early ;
he felt hungry and went into a café ; when he came to
leave he found that he had no money. He gave an
order for something to be served him and wrote to
Eugène to look for his purse and send it to him.

The commissionaire returns, bringing back his letter.
How is he to pay for what he has eaten and drunk at
the café ? He cannot leave the café without settling
his check, he cannot discharge the commissionaire
without paying him. His only course is to keep the
commissionaire under pay and remain at the café ; he
sends the man to a friend and calls for his fifth glass
of sugar and water.

" What am I to do if the commissionaire does not find Robert at home? I must pay the man, I must pay my bill here. It is extremely embarrassing."

A woman passes along the street before the windows of the café; Arthur rushes to the door, hat in hand; this woman that he has just caught sight of has a strange hold upon his imagination. The reason why is this:

Coming out of a bric-à-brac dealer's shop into the street one day, carrying in his arms two plaster figures, an antique helmet and a Chinese parasol, Arthur had encountered face to face a woman whose beauty had produced a deep impression on him. These sudden impressions are more than an empty dream. A single glance served to render Arthur enamored, miserable, jealous. He came near letting the plaster figures fall from his arms; he wished to follow the fair unknown, but loaded as he was like a porter and his clothes filthy with dust and plaster, he was quickly compelled to abandon this project.

For three days he was melancholy and thoughtful. There was one thing that particularly annoyed him; the impression that he had produced on that woman's mind must have been diametrically opposite to that which he had received from her. His equipment had been ridiculous, the expression of his admiration stupid. For two weeks he never went out without being dressed to kill; if a new play was brought out he would go to witness it, if a ray of sunshine pierced the gray clouds of November he would go and walk in the Tuileries gardens, peering under all the bonnets in quest of the blue eyes of his fair one. He wished to correct the unfavorable impression that he thought he must have produced and place himself in her **eyes** on a level, at least, with indifferent acquaintances and **persons** whom she had never seen.

Two months after that **he had** caught sight of her **a second** time at a concert, **but she** was seated at a distance from him and **with all** his efforts he had not been able to **attract** her attention to his person, which **on** that occasion was magnificently attired and **per-fectly** seductive. Upon returning home he **had drawn** her portrait from memory, and **the** constant contemplation **of this picture** had contributed in no small degree to the nourishment of a passion that had begun to assume extravagant proportions. Since then he had **never met her again,** although he had spent much time prowling in **quest** of her. At times he had followed **strange women for hours** on end, believing that **he discerned some** resemblance in form or carriage to his inamorata, or else because they chanced to wear a blue shawl. On the only two occasions when he had seen her she had sported a great cashmere of that color.

He **was very assiduous** in paying his court **to the** likeness, **however, and every time that he came in** would place **a handsome bouquet before it.** Through constantly **seeking and never** finding her **he had** reached **such a degree of** adoration that, **had he** chanced **to meet her and** succeeded in gaining her love, his **love for her would not** have lasted long. He **had placed his idol upon** such a lofty pedestal **that she could not** have come down **from her eleva-tion** without doing herself a harm. Given a certain **amount** of imagination **and a sufficiency of** obstacles, it is always **possible** to adore a woman ; to **love her** is not so easy a matter. The majority of women are adored only because they cannot make themselves loved.

Not that we would decry illusions, far from it ; we have often thought that there is nothing beautiful and exalted in life but that which has no existence there ; that is to say, life in its naked reality, stripped of the bright hues that are thrown on it through the prism of the imagination, is not worth the living and is like the butterfly whose wings, rudely crumpled by some rough hand, have lost their brilliant golden dust.

To destroy illusion is to limit the world to our own narrow horizon, it is to restrict the circle of our sensations within the grasp of our outstretched hand ; it is as if we should follow the example of the Spartan ephor and cut two strings from the lyre, or that of the tyrant of Syracuse and throw our most costly ring into the sea, or disfigure ourselves like Origen.

So, then, when Arthur recognized the great blue eyes of his fair unknown beneath a black hat and through a veil of the same color he had dashed to the door of the café, but just as he was on the point of passing out he suddenly remembered that he had not paid, and could not pay, for what he had consumed, and he reflected that were he to leave the place, particularly in that hurried manner, he would inevitably be taken for a Jeremy Diddler who had endeavored to make his breakfast at the expense of the restaurateur.

He returned to his place, called for a sixth glass of sweetened water and made believe to read a newspaper.

At last a man came into the café with a laughing

face ; it was the friend to whom Arthur had written to come and get him out of his scrape. He offered his purse, and Arthur paid off the *commissionaire* and settled for his countless glasses of sugar and water.

"My dear friend," says the newcomer, "since I have paid for your breakfast you must let me set up the grub for the rest of the day as well, and come and sup with us."

Circumstances resulting from the encounter with this friend, an amour which ended in a journey, a journey which ended in a quarrel, a quarrel which ended in a return home, all these things consumed a great deal of time.

.   .   :   .   .   .   .

After these events, while *en route*, Arthur devotes his thoughts to his unknown, and upon returning to his studio removes the bouquet, long since faded, that adorned her portrait and replaces it by a fresh one of pink heather and golden broom.

"Parbleu !" says Arthur, "I *must* go and see my uncle."

Eugène was going out to his solitary dinner just as Arthur came in.

"Well ?"

"Well ?"

"Have you seen your uncle ?"

"No."

"How is that ?"

"The boulevard has been playing its old tricks on me. I stopped to see a giantess ; she was a Pole at the time of the Polish war, a Belgian during the siege of

Antwerp. Here's what I read upon the hand-bills :
' The king, having heard tell of her marvelous beauty,
desired to see her, and declared that she was rightfully
entitled to her surname of Queen of the Giants.'
Encouraged by the royal suffrage, I entered the show
and had the honor of receiving the distinguished
notice of the Queen of the Giants."

" Ah ! "

" In presence of all the assembled spectators she
said to me : ' If monsieur, who is of goodly stature,
will kindly come and stand beside me, it will be seen
that he does not reach my shoulder.' I scrambled to
her platform and gravely perched myself at her side
as long as she saw fit to keep me there. Ah ! " says
Arthur, with a sigh, " I saw something that interested
me more than that. I had stopped where a juggler
was carrying on his industry ; he was in need of a
watch for a transformation. I loaned him mine, and
I assure you that the trick was a very comical one,
but as I was watching his operations a woman passed,
wrapped in a camel's-hair shawl. That woman was
my unknown ; I determined to follow her ; she was
proceeding along the boulevard in just the same
direction that I should have to take to go to my uncle's,
but I could not leave my watch in the juggler's hands.
I stepped up to him :

" ' My watch——— '

" ' In one moment, sir.'

" ' I want to go.'

" ' It is only a matter of five minutes.'

" ' I have not one to spare.'

" The ring of spectators murmur and inveigh
against me.

"'Are you afraid that I am going to steal your watch?"

"'You are a rascal.'

"'Well, I placed it in that cup; take it.'

"I put my hand into the cup and extract a great onion. Every one laughs; I turn all the colors of the rainbow and again demand my watch; I secure it and take to my heels, but the unknown has disappeared. If she had kept to the boulevard I should have seen her, for the street pursues a straight course; a cab has just started, I follow it, I run after it. I must be born to ill-luck; the horse was a perfect trotter. At last I came up with it, quite spent and breathless, but it contained only a man in blue spectacles!"

Arthur received a letter from his father; in it was the following passage:

"Send me word how your uncle is, who was said to be in such a bad way; I do not ask if you have seen him, for your feelings, our interests, common humanity, not to mention my reiterated instructions to you, all combined to make that visit an imperative duty."

"I will go to-morrow even if it should rain old women!" exclaimed Arthur.

．　　．　　．　　．　　．　　．　　．

Six weeks afterward, Arthur managed to reach the Arsenal; his uncle's house was draped with black, the corpse had just been deposited in the hearse, the people were entering the mourning-coaches. Arthur was thunderstruck; still, a few moments' reflection showed him that what had happened was only a very ordinary occurrence, and entirely in accordance with the natural course of events.

Three persons, whose countenances were not unknown to him, signaled him an invitation to enter the
last coach with them ; Arthur took his seat and followed the procession, first to the church, then to the
cemetery, without uttering a word ; he could not,
however, master some remorseful feelings that he had
not been with his uncle in his last moments.   They
reached the burial-place ; after that ceremony, that is
ever a sad one, even for those not directly concerned,
after they had lowered the coffin into the grave and
had strewn upon it a few shovelfuls of earth that fell
with a hollow sound upon the box of pine, a gentleman dressed in black came forward, blew his nose, and,
in a voice that trembled, as much from the embarrassment of speaking in public as from grief, pronounced
the eulogy of the deceased.

This face also was not unfamiliar to Arthur ; it
occurred to him that this young man, more fortunate than he, or less hare-brained, was his uncle's
heir.

" Gentlemen," said the orator, " when we speak of
death, it may be said that it is those who remain that
feel the affliction most keenly ; the friend whose loss
we mourn is gone above to occupy that place in
heaven that his virtues have earned for him, while *we*
remain here below to shed our tears for him."

" There is no doubt about it," thought Arthur ;
" my uncle has left him his Bayeux property."

" No one," continued the heir, " obeyed more implicitly this precept of the Gospel : ' Let not thy left
hand know that which thy right hand doeth.'   It is for
that reason that the poor, not knowing whence came
the numerous benefactions that he scattered with

a lavish hand during his lifetime, have not trooped hither to bedew this earth with their tears."

" He has got the Paris mansion, too," said Arthur to himself.

" To some his mental faculties appeared to be deteriorating ; the reason was that his life upon this earth was ended and he was entering upon the childhood of another life."

" I would not give five sous," Arthur mutters, " for all that my uncle has left me of his government bonds."

" It was the childhood of immortality."

" Even the canal shares have been taken from me."

They climbed into the carriage again. Arthur's three companions conversed about their business affairs ; Arthur said not a word. He was saddened by the funereal scene, and also, if the truth was to be told, by the consideration that the labor of a lifetime would not replace the inheritance that he had lost through his own folly. He left the coach and continued his way on foot. As he was crossing the boulevard some persons had stopped (and who has not sometimes stopped for a more trifling circumstance ?) to watch a postilion mending a broken trace. Arthur mechanically halted like the others. As he was surveying the operation a man tapped him on the shoulder ; he turned his head ; it was his uncle. Arthur turned pale and for a moment was frozen with terror and incapable of motion ; then he threw his arms about his dear uncle's neck and embraced him.

" I would rather have you embrace me more frequently and less violently," said the uncle.

Arthur embraced him again, but there was something convulsive in his action.

"What! it is you, you that I have here in my arms! But it can't be!"

"It is as plain as can be; I am on my way to Bayeux to spend the summer."

"But, uncle, I am just come——"

"From a visit to me, you were going to say? They have been burying poor Dubois, my neighbor, whom you have seen at my house so many times."

"What! then it was not you?"

"I? What do you mean?"

"I have been lamenting you and shedding tears for you for the last four hours."

The uncle burst out into a great fit of laughter.

"I am going to Bayeux to attend the wedding of your cousin!"

"Which cousin?"

"The daughter of your mother's sister, my second sister; she has been living with me during the past year."

"Aunt Marthe's daughter?"

"Exactly; she does not know her future husband, but I have arranged it all by letter; she will be very happy."

The postilion had finished his repairs; the uncle took his place in the chaise and said:

"Kiss your cousin's hand, whom you will never see again, in all probability, for her husband means to live upon his property, where he is making improvements."

Arthur kissed a little hand that emerged from the window of the chaise upon the bidding of the uncle,

then raised his **eyes and beheld** the pretty face of the
stranger of the blue cashmere.   She was still **wrapped**
in the folds of the blue shawl ; the chaise started and
Arthur   **remained standing   there, seeing**   nothing,
hearing nothing, until it **was lost** among the mists
that rise from the ground with the decline of day.

THE
THOUSAND AND SECOND NIGHT.

THÉOPHILE GAUTIER.

I HAD given orders that day to deny my door to every one ; having made a solemn resolution that morning that I would do nothing, I did not wish to be disturbed in that important occupation. With a feeling of confidence that I should not be bothered by bores (there are some left yet besides those in Molière's comedy), I had concerted all my measures to enjoy the pleasure of my predilection at my ease.

A bright fire was blazing in my chimney, the curtains were drawn and admitted a dim mysterious light, some half-a-dozen Ottoman cushions were scattered about the carpet, here and there, and, comfortably reclining at exactly the right distance from the cheering blaze, I was balancing upon my toes a roomy Moroccan baboosh of quaint shape and the yellow of the Orient ; my cat was cuddled upon my sleeve, like that of the prophet Mohammed, and I would not have changed my position for all the riches of the universe.

My wandering glances, already more than half vanquished by that delicious drowsiness that succeeds the voluntary suspension of thought, were straying, rather

apathetically, from Camille Roqueplan's charming
sketch of the *Magdalen in the Desert* to the severe pen-
drawing of Aligny and the great landscape of the
four inseparables, Feuchères, Séchan, Diéterle, and
Despléchins, the joy and glory of my poor poet's
domicile ; the sensation of real life was gradually
slipping away from me, and I was sinking deeper and
deeper beneath the unfathomable waves of that ocean
of oblivion in which so many dreamers of the East have
left their reason, already weakened by the use of
opium and hasheesh.

The most intense silence prevailed in the apartment ; I had stopped the clock so that I might not
hear the ticking of the pendulum, that pulse-beat of
eternity ; for when I am in one of my idle moods I
cannot endure the feverish and idiotic restlessness of
that yellow disk of brass that is constantly swinging
from one corner of its cage to the other, and is always
in motion without taking a step forward.

All at once, kling-klang, there comes a ring at my
bell, sharp, nervous, and reverberating with an insuf-
ferably silvery tone, and falls upon my repose as a
drop of molten lead might plunge, spluttering, into the
bosom of a peaceful lake ; unmindful of my cat,
curled up like a ball upon my sleeve, I started and
jumped to my feet as if impelled by a spring, consign-
ing to all the devils the imbecile of a porter who had
allowed some one to enter in spite of my strict orders ;
then I resumed my seat. Still under the influence of
the shock that my nerves had sustained, I settled the
cushions beneath my arms and bravely awaited the
upshot of the affair.

The door of the salon opened a little way, and the

first object to present itself to my view was the woolly pate of Adolfo Francesco Pergialla, a sort of Abyssinian land-shark in whose service I then was, while flattering myself with the delusion that I had a negro servant. The whites of his eyes rolled and glistened in his black face, his broad, flat nose was dilated to an enormous size, his thick lips, expanded in a smile as broad as a barn-door, disclosed a row of teeth as white as a Newfoundland dog's ; he was bursting in his black skin with the desire to speak, and making all sorts of grimaces to attract my attention.

"Well, Francesco, what is it ? How much the wiser would I be if you should keep on rolling those crockery eyes of yours for an hour, like that bronze darky with a clock in his stomach ? A truce to pantomime, and try to tell me, in the best gibberish you are master of, what the matter is and who is the person who is come to start me from the covert of my idleness."

It is incumbent on me to inform you that Adolfo Francesco Pergialla Abdallah-ben-Mohammed ; Abyssinian by birth, formerly a Mohammedan, but now a Christian for the time being, knew every language and could not speak one intelligibly ; he would commence in French, continue in Italian and wind up with Turkish or Arabic, and this was more notably the case when the conversation took an embarassing turn for him, as when some bottles of Bordeaux wine or of liqueurs of the isles, or other good things, had mysteriously disappeared before their allotted time. Luckily for me I have some polyglot friends : we would first drive him out of Europe ; after he had exhausted his stock of Spanish, Italian and German he would take refuge in Constantinople, in Turkish, whence Alfred would chase him out in short order; finding himself in the toils he would skip over into Algeria, where he would have Eugène at his heels pursuing him through all the dialects of upper and lower Arabia; when he had reached that point he would seek shelter in the Bambara, the Galla and other jargons of the interior of Africa, where it required d'Abadie, Combes or Tamisier to force him out of his intrenchments. This time he answered me firmly in Spanish that was not very pure but was very distinct.

"Wna mujer muy bonita con sú hermana quien quiere hablar á usted." (A very pretty woman and her sister, who wish to speak to you).

"Introduce them if they are young and pretty; otherwise tell them that I am busy."

The rascal, who was something of a judge in such matters, disappeared for a short space and presently returned, followed by two women wrapped in great white burnooses with the capuchons pulled down over their eyes.

I offered the ladies a couple of easy-chairs with the most gallant air that I had at my command, but noticing the piles of cushions, they made me a little sign with the hand to indicate that they thanked me and, throwing aside their burnooses, seated themselves cross-legged upon the floor, after the Oriental fashion.

The one who was seated facing me, in the ray of sunlight that came into the room through the opening between the curtains, was apparently about twenty years old; the other one, who was not nearly so pretty, seemed to be a little older ; we will confine our attention to the prettier one.

She was richly attired in Turkish style ; her wasp-like waist was incased in a vest of green velvet heavily loaded with ornaments ; her chemisette of striped gauze, fastened at the neck by two diamond buttons, was parted in such a manner as to afford a glimpse of a white and well turned bosom ; a kerchief of white satin, studded with starry spangles, did duty as a belt. Wide, voluminous trousers came down to her knees ; her slender, shapely legs were protected by Albanian gaiters of embroidered velvet as far down as her little bare feet, that were imprisoned in tiny slippers of stamped and colored morocco, quilted and stitched with gold thread ; an orange caftan, embroidered with flowers of silver, and a scarlet fez, set off by a long silken tassel, completed this costume, certainly a rather fantastic one to go paying visits in at Paris in that year of evil omen, 1842.

As to her face, it had that regularity of beauty that characterizes the Turkish race : her eyes, those beau-tiful Oriental eyes, so clear and so deep beneath their long lids stained with henna, seemed to open mys-teriously, like two black flowers, in the dull, creamy pallor of her complexion that was like unpolished marble. She looked about her with a troubled air and seemed embarrassed ; to set her mind at ease, no doubt, she held one of her feet in one of her hands and with the other hand toyed with the end of one of her tresses, which were all loaded with sequins pierced with a hole in the middle and with ribbons and strings of pearls.

The second woman, attired in pretty much the

same way, only not so richly, preserved the same silence and immobility. Mentally referring to the appearance in Paris of the *bayadères,* I had an idea that they were dancing-girls from Cairo, some Egyptian acquaintances of my friend Dauzats, and that, encouraged by the favorable notice I had given in my paper to pretty Amany and her brown friends, Sandiroun and Rangoun, they had come to seek my favor in my quality as a *feuilletoniste.*

"What can I do for you, ladies?" I said, raising my hands to my ears in such a way as to produce a salamalec that should be adequate to the occasion.

The fair Turk raised her eyes to the ceiling, cast them down to the floor, finally looked at her sister with an air of profound meditation. She did not understand a word of French.

"Halloa, Francesco! scoundrel, blockhead, ragamuffin; come here, you misshapen monkey, and make yourself useful for once in your life, at least."

Francesco approached with an important and majestic air.

"As you speak French so badly, you must speak Arabic very well, and you are going to play the part of dragoman between these ladies and me. I promote you to the position of interpreter; in the first place ask these fair strangers who they are, whence they come, and what they want."

I will relate the conversation that ensued as if it had been carried on in French, without attempting to reproduce the various contortions and flowers of rhetoric of the aforesaid Francesco.

"Sir," said the pretty Turk, through the organ of the negro, "although you are a man of letters, you must have read the *Thousand and One Nights,* a collection of Arab tales, translated, more or less faithfully, by good M. Galland, and the name of Scheherazade should be familiar to you ?"

"Beautiful Scheherazade, wife of Schahriar, that sultan fruitful in resources who, that he might not be deceived, married a wife overnight and sent her to be bowstrung in the morning ? I know her very well."

"Well ! I am the Sultana Scheherazade, and this is my good sister Dinarzarde, who has never a single night missed saying to me: 'Sister, if you are not sleeping, tell us, I pray you, before it is day, one of those nice stories that you know.' "

"Delighted to see you, I am sure, although your visit appears a little singular ; but tell me, what is it that procures me the distinguished honor of receiving in my abode, poor poet that I am, the Sultana Scheherazade and her sister Dinarzarde ? "

"I have told so many stories that I have reached the end of my repertory ; I don't know another single one. I have exhausted the personages of fairy-land ; the ghouls, the djinns and the magicians, male and female, have been of great service to me, but nothing lasts forever, not even the impossible. The most glorious sultan, shadow of the padishah, light of lights, sun and moon of the middle empire, is beginning to yawn portentously and trifle ominously with the handle of his ataghan ; I told my last story this morning, and my sublime lord has condescended to leave my head upon my shoulders yet for a while. I have made my way hither in all haste, with the assistance of the magic carpet of the four Facardins, to hunt up a tale, a story, a romance ; for to-morrow morning, at the accustomed

summons of my sister Dinarzarde, I must have something in readiness to relate to the illustrious Schahriar,
arbiter of my destiny ; Galland, the idiot, has deceived
the universe by asserting that the sultan, surfeited
with stories, had granted me a pardon after the thousand and first night ; there is not a word of truth in
it ; he is more ravenous for stories than ever, and his
curiosity alone can countervail his cruelty."

"Your sultan Schahriar, my poor Scheherazade, is
dreadfully like our public ; if we fail for a single day
to afford it its usual amusement, it does not cut off
our head, it is true, but it forgets us, and that is pretty
nearly as · bad. Your sad fate grieves me, but what
can I do ? "

" You must have some novel, some feuilleton, in
your portfolio ; let me have it."

" Do you know what you are asking, charming
Sultana ? I have nothing finished ; I never work
except when compelled by the last extremity of famine,
for, as Persius has well said : *Fames facit poetridas
picas.* I have still enough to keep myself from starving
for three days ; go and find Karr, if you can get to
him through the swarms of wasps * that are all the
time buzzing and fluttering around his door and
against his windows ; he has his head stuffed full with
the most delightful love-stories that he will relate to
you in the interval between a boxing lesson and a
tune on his French horn ; or wait and catch Jules
Janin as he turns the corner of some feuilleton, and
he will walk along at your side and improvise such a
story as the sultan Schahriar never heard in all his
life."

* An allusion to Alphonse Karr's work, *Les Guêpes.*

Poor Scheherazade hereupon raised her long henna-stained eyes upward toward the ceiling with a look so soft, lustrous, melting, and suppliant that my heart was softened and I made up my mind to do a great thing.

"I did have a subject, such as it is, that I was intending to spin into a feuilleton ; I will dictate it to you and you can translate it into Arabic, adding the embroideries, the flowers and pearls of poesy, in which it is deficient ; there is a title ready made for it : we will christen our story the *Thousand and Second Night.*"

Scheherazade took a block of paper and began to write from right to left, in the Oriental way, with great swiftness. There was no time to lose : she had to be in the capital of the kingdom of Samarcand that same evening.

There once lived in the city of Cairo a young man named Mahmoud-Ben-Ahmed, who had his residence on the place of the Esbekick.

His father and mother had died some years before, leaving him a moderate fortune, but one which sufficed to yield him a living without having recourse to the toil of his hands ; others would have essayed the venture of loading a ship with merchandise, or sending a few camels laden with precious stuffs to accompany the caravan which traffics between Bagdad and Mecca, but Mahmoud-Ben-Ahmed chose rather to live tranquilly, and his pleasures consisted in smoking tombeki in his nargile, in drinking sherbets and eating the dried confections of Damascus.

Although he was of attractive presence, with regular

features and a pleasing expression, he held himself
aloof from affairs of love, and to those who did urge
him to marry and proffer him wealthy and suitable
alliances, he had several times made answer that the
time was not yet come and that he felt no inclination
to take unto himself a wife.

Mahmoud-Ben-Ahmed had received a good educa-
tion; he could read with ease the most ancient works,
wrote an elegant hand, knew by heart the verses of
the Koran and the remarks of the commentators, and
could have rattled you off the Moallakats of the
famous poets that were nailed against the doors of the
mosques without missing a verse; he was himself
something of a poet, and took delight in composing
sonorous rhymed couplets that he would declaim to
airs fashioned by himself, with much grace and
elegance.

Now, through much smoking of his nargile and
dreaming in the coolness of eventide upon the marble
pavement of his terrace, Mahmoud-Ben-Ahmed had
come to have exalted ideas in his head; he had determined that he would bestow his love only upon a
peri, or, at the very least, upon a princess of royal
birth. Therein lay the secret motive that made him
look with such indifference upon the offers of marriage that were made him and refuse the proposals of
the slave-merchants. The only companion who found
favor in his eyes was his cousin Abdul-Malek, a gentle
and timid youth, whose tastes seemed to be of a
modesty equal to his own.

Mahmoud-Ben-Ahmed, one day, was wending his
way to the bazaar to purchase some flasks of attar-gul
and other conserves of Constantinople that he stood

in need of. In a very narrow street he met a litter inclosed by curtains of rose-red velvet, borne by two milk-white mules and preceded by mutes and chaoushes in sumptuous raiment. He drew back against the wall to make way for the cortége, but not so quickly as to avoid catching a glimpse, through the parting of the curtains, which were just then raised by a truant breath of air, of an exceedingly handsome woman, reclining on cushions of gold brocade. The lady had trusted in the thickness of her curtains and raised her veil on account of the heat, believing that she was beyond the reach of any audacious eye. It lasted but the space of a lightning-flash, but it was sufficient to turn poor Mahmoud-Ben-Ahmed's head ; the lady's complexion was of dazzling whiteness, her eyebrows one might have deemed traced by the pencil of a painter, her mouth was like a pomegranate, and the lips, when parted, disclosed a double row of pearls, of purer water and more lustrous than those that form the bracelets and the necklace of the favorite sultana ; she possessed an agreeable and lofty mien, and from all her person there seemed to exhale an inexpressible air of nobleness and majesty.

Mahmoud-Ben-Ahmed remained a long time motionless where he stood, as if dazed by such perfection, and forgetting that he had come forth to make some purchases, returned to his dwelling empty-handed, bearing the radiant vision imprinted on his heart.

All night long he dreamed only of the fair unknown, and was no sooner risen than he applied himself to composing a long poem in her honor, on which he lavished all his most flowery and impassioned comparisons.

When his piece was finished and a fair copy made upon a noble sheet of milk-white papyrus, with great initial letters in red ink and flourishes of gold, he knew not what to do, so put it in his sleeve and went forth to show his production to his friend Abdul, from whom he had no secrets.

On his way to Abdul's abode he passed the bazaar and entered the shop of the perfumer to obtain the flasks of attar of rose ; there he found a beautiful lady, wrapped in a long white veil that concealed all her person excepting her left eye. That left eye incontinently betrayed to Mahmoud-Ben-Ahmed the lady of the palanquin. His emotion was so great that he was compelled to support himself against the wall.

The lady of the white veil remarked Mahmoud-Ben-Ahmed's trouble, and courteously inquired what ailed him and if, peradventure, he were unwell. Thereupon the merchant, the lady and Mahmoud-Ben-Ahmed withdrew to the back-shop. A little negro brought a glass of snow-water upon a salver, of which Mahmoud-Ben-Ahmed quaffed a few swallows.

" Why, pray tell me, hath the sight of me produced such an impression upon you ? " the lady said in a sweet voice that betrayed a passably tender interest.

Mahmoud-Ben-Ahmed told how he had beheld her near the mosque of Hassan the Sultan just as the curtains of her litter had been parted a little, and that since that moment he had been dying with love for her.

" Of a verity," said the lady, " and your passion was of such sudden birth as that ? I had thought that love grew not so quickly. I am indeed the woman whom you met yesterday; I was hieing me to the bath in my litter, and as the heat was stifling, I had put up my veil. But you did see amiss, and I am not as beautiful as you say."

As she said these words she put aside her veil and disclosed a face radiant with beauty, and so perfect that Envy herself could not have discovered in it the least defect.

The reader may imagine what were Mahmoud-Ben-Ahmed's transports upon receiving such a mark of favor; he overwhelmed the fair one with compliments, and, which is a rare thing with compliments, they all had the merit of being truthful and devoid of exaggeration. As he proceeded, infusing great fire and animation into his words, the scroll upon which his verses were transcribed escaped from his sleeve and rolled upon the floor.

"What is that scroll?" said the lady. "The writing appears to me of passing elegance, and tells of a skilled hand."

"It is a copy of verses," the young man made answer, blushing deeply, "that I did compose last night, being unable to slumber. I have essayed in them to do honor to your transcendent charms, but the copy is far inferior to the original, and my verse has not the brilliancy that it should have worthily to describe the brilliancy of your eyes."

The young lady read the verses attentively, and placing them in her belt, said :

"Though they contain many flatteries, they are truly not ill turned."

Thereupon she arranged her veil and left the shop negligently letting fall these words, with an ac-

cent that went straight to Mahmoud-Ben-Ahmed's
heart :

" I sometimes visit Bedreddin's shop on my way
home from the bath, to purchase essences and boxes
of perfume."

The merchant, conducting Mahmoud-Ben-Ahmed
to the most remote recess of his shop, congratulated
him upon his good fortune and whispered mysteriously in his ear:

" That young lady is no other than the princess
Ayesha, daughter of the Caliph."

Mahmoud-Ben-Ahmed returned to his abode utterly
bewildered by his happiness and scarce daring to
believe that it could be true. And yet, modest as he
was, he could not be blind to the fact that the princess
Ayesha had looked on him with an eye of favor.
That great busybody, Chance, had exceeded his most
audacious dreams. How he congratulated himself
now that he had not yielded to the advice of those
friends of his who had urged him to marry, and that
he had not been seduced by the alluring descrip-
tions that old women gave him of marriageable young
girls, who, as is well known by every one, invariably
have the eyes of the gazelle, a face like the full moon,
hair longer than the tail of Al Borack, the prophet's
favorite mare, a mouth as red as jasper, with a breath
sweet as ambergris, and a thousand perfections beside which disappear at the same time as the haick and
the nuptial veil : how he rejoiced that he was untram-
meled by any vulgar tie, and free to abandon himself
entirely to his new passion !

It was all to no purpose that he turned and twisted
on his divan, he could not sleep; the image of the

princess Ayesha kept passing and repassing before
his eyes, flashing like a bird of flame upon a background of sunset sky. Unable to secure repose, he
ascended to one of his cabinets of cedar, marvelously
carved, that in eastern cities are built out from the
exterior walls of the houses, in order to profit by the
coolness of the breeze that never failed to draw
through the street ; still sleep visited him not—for
sleep is like happiness, it flies from us when we seek it—
and to soothe his mind by the spectacle of the serenity
of the night, he took his nargile and went out upon
the highest terrace of his mansion.

The cool air of night, the splendor of the heavens,
more thickly set with golden spangles than a peri's robe,
and in which the moon was displaying her silvery face
like a sultana, pale with love, bending over the trellis
of her kiosk, brought joy and content to Mahmoud-
Ben-Ahmed, for he was a poet and could not but be affected by the glorious spectacle that offered itself to
his vision.

From that height the city of Cairo lay stretched
before his eyes like one of those birds-eye plans in
which the giaours trace the outlines of their fortified
places. The terraces adorned with luxuriant plants
in pots and gay with multi-colored tapestries ; the
spots where the waters of the Nile shone in the moonlight, for it was then the time of the yearly inundation;
the gardens, from whence rose clusters of palms and
groves of locust and fig-trees ; the blocks of houses
intersected by narrow streets ; the brazen domes of the
mosques ; the slender minarets, pierced with carvings
until they were like a toy of ivory ; the palaces, bril-
liantly lighted or else lying in deepest obscurity, all

formed a *coup d'œil* than which there could have been
found nothing more magnificent to delight the eye.
In the far distance the ashy hues of the desert sands
blended away into the milky tints of the firmament,
and the three pyramids of Ghizeh described their huge
triangular masses of stone, vaporous and unsubstan-
tial as shadows in the blue moonlight, against the line
of the horizon.

Reclining on a pile of cushions with the long, flex-
ible tube of his nargile enwrapping his form in its
coils, Mahmoud-Ben-Ahmed endeavored to make out
through the transparent darkness the shape of the
distant palace where slumbered the fair Ayesha. A
deep silence reigned over this picture that one might
have taken for the work of the painter's brush, for not
a breath, not a sound was there to reveal the presence
of a living being : the only noise perceptible was that
made by the smoke of Mahmoud-Ben-Ahmed's nargile as it passed through the ball of rock-crystal that
contained water designed to cool its white wreaths.
All at once this tranquillity was broken by a piercing
cry, a cry of supreme distress, such as the antelope at
the border of the spring must utter when it feels the
lion's paw upon its shoulder, or its head buried deep in
the wide-extended jaws of the crocodile. Mahmoud-
Ben-Ahmed, terror-stricken at this cry of agony and
despair, sprang to his feet at a single bound and instinctively placed his hand upon the pommel of his
yataghan and partially drew it so as to assure himself
that it was free in the scabbard, then bent his ear in
the direction whence the sound had seemed to him to
proceed.

Far away in the darkness he descried a strange,

shadowy group, composed of a white-robed figure pursued by a horde of black, fantastic, monstrous forms in disorderly array and with maniacal gestures. The white shadow seemed to fly over the house-tops, and the distance between it and its enemies was so small that there was reason to fear that it would soon be overtaken should the chase be protracted or should nothing happen to favor it. Mahmoud-Ben-Ahmed at first believed that it was a peri beset by a pack of ghouls, who munch the flesh of the dead with their huge tusks, or of djinns, with flabby, membranous wings and long nails like those of bats, and, drawing from his pocket his comboloio of beads of ruddy aloe-wood, he began to recite the ninety-nine names of Allah by way of exorcism. He had not yet reached the twentieth when he desisted. It was not a peri, a supernatural being, who was flying thus, leaping from terrace to terrace and bounding across the streets, four or five feet in width—which, in eastern cities, bisect the close-built blocks of houses—but a woman of flesh and blood, and the djinns were only mutes, chaouses, and eunuchs, who were after her in hot pursuit.

Only two or three terraces and a street now lay between the fugitive and the platform where Mahmoud-Ben-Ahmed was standing, but her strength seemed to be abandoning her ; she turned her head convulsively for a look backward, and, as a spent horse that feels the spur tearing his flank, beholding the hideous band so close upon her trail, she made a supreme effort, and with a desperate leap placed the street between her and her foes.

She grazed Mahmoud-Ben-Ahmed in her headlong

flight without perceiving him, for the moon was now obscured by clouds, and flew to the extremity of the terrace, which fronted on that side upon a second street, wider than the first. Distrusting her ability to leap it, she seemed to be casting her eyes about for some nook in which to conceal herself, and noticing a great marble vase, she hid within it, like the genie who re-enters the cup of a lily.

The raging troop came upon the terrace with the impetuosity of a flight of demons. Their black or copper-colored faces, either with long mustaches or else hideously beardless, their flashing eyes, their clenched hands, brandishing kandjars or blades of Damascus, the ferocity expressed upon their degraded and cruel countenances, inspired Mahmoud-Ben-Ahmed with a feeling of terror, although he was personally a brave man and well skilled in the use of arms. They gave a rapid glance over the unoccupied terrace and, not beholding the fugitive there, doubtless thought she had passed the second street, and continued onward in their pursuit without paying further attention to Mahmoud-Ben-Ahmed.

When the clash of their weapons and the noise of their babooshes upon the flagstones of the terraces had died away in the distance, the fugitive first raised her pretty, pale face above the edge of the vase and looked about her with the air of a frightened antelope, then her shoulders emerged and she stood erect, a charming pistil rising from the depths of that great flower of marble ; perceiving that there was no one there but Mahmoud-Ben-Ahmed, who was smiling upon her and making signs that she had no cause for fear, she leaped lightly from the vase and came toward the young man with an aspect of humility and hands extended in supplication.

"I beseech you, my lord, for sweet pity's sake, have mercy on me and save me; hide me in the darkest corner of your mansion, protect me from those demons who are pursuing me."

Mahmoud-Ben-Ahmed took her by the hand, led her to the staircase of the terrace, of which he lowered and carefully closed the trap-door, and conducted her to his apartment. When he had lighted his lamp he saw that the fugitive was young, which the silvery tone of her voice had already given him reason to suspect was the case, and very pretty, which did not astonish him, for the light of the stars had sufficed to reveal the elegance of her form. She seemed not to be more than fifteen years old. Her excessive pallor contrasted strongly with her big, black, almond-shaped eyes, the corners of which were prolonged so that they reached the temples; her thin and delicately moulded nose gave distinction to a profile that might have inspired envy in the most beautiful maidens of Scio or of Cyprus, and eclipsed the marble beauty of the idols that were once worshiped by the old pagan Greeks. Her neck was perfect in form and charming in its whiteness; only there was visible at the back a thin streak of scarlet, thin as a hair or the finest thread of silk, and a few tiny drops of blood were oozing from this red line. Her attire was plain, and consisted of a silk-embroidered jacket, muslin trousers and a belt with gayly colored stripes; her bosom was heaving tumultuously beneath her tunic of striped gauze, for she was still breathless and scarcely recovered from her alarm.

When she was rested and reassured somewhat, she kneeled before Mahmoud-Ben-Ahmed and told him her story in well-chosen language. " I was a slave," said she, "in the seraglio of the wealthy Abu-Becker, and I was guilty of conveying to his favorite sultana a selam, or floral letter, that had been sent her by an extremely handsome young emir with whom she was carrying on a correspondence. Abu-Becker, having surprised the secret and thereon fallen into a terrible rage, caused the sultana to be sewn up in a leather bag along with two cats and thrown into the river and sentenced me to have my head cut off. The execution of the sentence devolved upon the kislar-aga; but, taking advantage of the fright and consternation that poor Nourmahal's terrible punishment had caused in the seraglio, and finding the trap-door leading to the terrace open, I made my escape. My flight was discovered, and forthwith the black eunuchs, the zebecs and the Albanians in my master's service started in pursuit of me. One of them, Mesrour by name, whose advances I have many a time repelled, was so close at my heels that he barely missed catching me; I once even felt the edge of the blade that he was brandishing graze my neck, and it was then that I gave utterance to that dreadful cry that you must have heard, for I confess that I thought my last hour had come; but God is God and Mohammed is his prophet, and the angel Azrael was not yet ready to carry me away to the bridge Alsirat. My only hope now rests in you. Abu-Becker is powerful, he will send out men upon my track and, should he succeed in taking me, Mesrour's hand will be steadier next time and his kandjar will not be satisfied with grazing my neck," said she, smiling and passing her hand over the faint red mark that the eunuch's blade had left behind it. "Take me for your slave; I will devote to you the life for which I am indebted to you. You will always have a shoulder on which to rest your elbow, and my hair will serve to wipe the dust from your sandals."

As is the case with all men who devote their attention to poetry and literature, Mahmoud-Ben-Ahmed was of a very compassionate disposition. Leila, as the fugitive slave was called, used choice language to express her thoughts and was young and beautiful, and had this not been so, humanity would not have allowed him to drive her from his door. He designated to the young slave a corner of the room where there were a Persian carpet and some silken cushions, and upon the edge of the estrade a little collation of dates, candied cedrats and conserve of roses of Constantinople which he, distraught as he was and busied with his reflections, had not touched, and further, two jars of the porous clay of Thebes for imparting coolness to the water, standing in saucers of Japanese porcelain and covered with pearly beads of dew. Having thus provided temporarily for Leila's comfort, he mounted again to his terrace to finish his nargile and find the concluding rhymes for the ghazel that he was composing in honor of the princess Ayesha, a ghazel in which the lilies of Iran, the flowers of Gulistan, the stars and all the constellations of the heavens were quarreling among themselves to be allowed the honor of a place.

The next morning, as soon as it was day, Mahmoud-Ben-Ahmed reflected that he had no sachet of benzoin, that he was quite out of civet, and that the silken pouch, embroidered with gold and studded with spangles, in which he kept his latakia, was frayed and that it was high time to replace it by another, richer and in better taste.   Barely giving himself time to perform his ablutions and say his morning prayer, turning his face the while toward the rising sun, he went forth from his abode, first having re-copied his verses and placed them in his sleeve, as he had done the other time, not, however, with the intention of showing them to his friend Abdul, but of giving them to the princess Ayesha in person should he be so happy as to meet with her at the bazaar, in the shop of the merchant Bedreddin.   The muezzin, perched aloft upon the balcony of the minaret, had only called the fifth hour, and the streets were unten-anted save for the fellahs driving before them their asses loaded with watermelons, frails of dates, chick-ens tied together by their claws and quarters of mut-ton, which they were carrying to the market.   He was in the quarter where Ayesha's palace was situ-ated, but all that he could see was crenelated and whitewashed walls.   Nothing was to be seen at the three or four small windows, obstructed by wooden lat-tices with narrow openings, which allowed the people of the house to see what was going on in the street, but were provokingly disappointing to the inquisitive glances of the Paul Prys who were outside.   The palaces of the East, unlike the palaces of Frankestan, save their glories for the interior, and, so to speak, turn their back to the wayfarer.   So Mahmoud-Ben-Ahmed did not profit greatly by his investigations. He saw three or four richly appareled negro slaves

going out or coming in, whose insolent and haughty
bearing attested their consciousness of making part
of a prominent family and belonging to a person of
the highest quality.   Our love-struck swain made
fruitless efforts, by gazing at those thick walls, to discover in what quarter Ayesha's apartments lay.   He
gazed in vain : the main entrance, an arch describing
the shape of a heart, was protected by an inner wall ;
access to the court was by means of a lateral door
which suffered no impertinent glance to enter.¹   Mahmoud-Ben-Ahmed was obliged to retire without having made any discovery ; it was getting late and he
might have attracted attention.   He therefore bent
his steps toward Bedreddin's shop, to gain whose favor
he made considerable purchases of things of which
he was not in the slightest need.   He seated himself
in the shop, cross-questioned the merchant, examined
him upon his trade, inquired if the silks and carpets
brought in by the last caravan from Aleppo had met
with a good sale, if his ships had got into port without damage ; in a word, he had recourse to all the
contemptible tricks that lovers habitually make use
of ; he was in hopes to see Ayesha come into the
shop, but he was disappointed in his anticipation ;
she did not come that day.   He went away home with
a heavy heart, already branding her as cruel and per-
fidious, as if she had actually promised him that she
would be at Bedreddin's and had broken her word.

When he returned to his room he deposited his
babooshes in the niche of sculptured marble that was
hollowed in the wall beside the door for that purpose,
laid aside the caftan of costly stuff that he had donned
with the idea of making himself attractive and appear-

ing to the best advantage before Ayesha, and stretched himself upon his divan in a state of dejection that bordered on despair. It seemed to him that all was lost, that the world was about to come to an end, and he solaced himself by railing bitterly against fate ; and all because he had failed to meet, as he had hoped to do, a woman whom, two days before, he was entirely unacquainted with.

As he lay there with the eyes of his body closed that he might the better behold the dream of his soul, he was conscious of a gentle breeze blowing refreshingly upon his brow ; he raised his eyelids and beheld Leila, seated on the floor at his side, waving one of those little streamers made of the bark of the palm tree which in Eastern countries serve as a fan and a fly-flap. He had quite forgotten her existence.

"What is the matter with you, dear master?" she said, in a voice that was as soft and melodious as sweetest music. "Some care is troubling you ; your peace of mind seems to have deserted you. Were it in the power of your poor slave to disperse that cloud of melancholy that rests upon your brow, she would deem herself the happiest woman upon earth, and not even upon Ayesha, rich and beautiful though she be, would she look with the eye of envy."

The mention of that name caused Mahmoud-Ben-Ahmed to start upon his divan, like a sick man upon whose sore a hand is unintentionally laid ; he raised himself partially upon his elbow and cast an inquiring look upon Leila, who maintained a perfectly unruffled countenance, expressive only of a tender solicitude. For all that he blushed as if she had read his heart and surprised the secret of his passion. Leila, with-

out remarking upon this tell-tale and significant
signal, continued to soothe her new master with con-
soling words :

" What can I do to drive from your mind the dark
thoughts by which it is haunted ? Peradventure a little
music might serve to dissipate that melancholy. I
was taught the secrets of composition by an old slave
who was an odalisque of the former sultan ; I can
improvise poetry and accompany myself upon the
guzla."

So saying she took from the wall the guzla with its
sounding-board of lemon-wood, its ivory keys and
handle inlaid with mother-of-pearl and ebony, and
with rare address performed upon it the tarabuca and
some other Arab airs.

The purity of her voice and the sweetness of the
music would have gladdened Mahmoud-Ben-Ahmed
at any other time, for he was extremely susceptible
to the charm of poetry and harmony, but now his
brain and heart were so full of the woman whom he had
seen at Bedreddin's that he gave no attention to Leila's
songs.

The next day was kinder to him than the preceding
one had been, for he met Ayesha at Bedreddin's shop.
To attempt to describe his joy would be a hopeless
undertaking ; only those who have loved are capable
of understanding it. He remained for a moment
speechless, breathless, seeing things dimly, as through
a cloud. Ayesha, who perceived his emotion, was
gratified by it and addressed him very affably, for
there is nothing that so flatters the pride of those
of noble birth as the disturbance that they cause.
Mahmoud-Ben-Ahmed, once he was master of himself

again, strained every nerve to make himself agreeable,
and as he was young and good looking, had studied
poetry and expressed himself in the most elegant
language, he thought he could see that he was not
displeasing to her eyes and made bold to ask the
princess for a rendezvous in a more suitable and more
retired place than was afforded by Bedreddin's shop.

" I know," he said, " that at best I am but fit to be
the dust beneath your feet, that the swiftest horse in
the stable of the prophet, even should he gallop at
his highest speed, could not traverse the distance that
parts me from you in a thousand years ; but love
begets audacity, and the worm enamored of the rose
may not refrain from telling his passion."

Ayesha listened to it all without the slightest indication of anger, and fixing full upon Mahmoud-Ben-
Ahmed her languorous eyes, said to him :

" Be in the mosque of the sultan Hassan, beneath
the third lamp, to-morrow at the hour of prayer ; you
will encounter there a black slave attired in yellow
damask. Follow him whither he may lead you."
That said, she covered her face with her veil and left
the shop.

Our swain, as may well be supposed, did not fail to
be punctual at the rendezvous ; he stationed himself
beneath the third lamp and did not dare to stir from
it for fear of not being found by the black slave, who
was not yet at his post. It is true that Mahmoud-Ben-
Ahmed was there two hours ahead of the appointed
time. At last he saw the negro in yellow damask approaching ; he came straight to the pillar against
which Mahmoud-Ben-Ahmed was leaning. When the
slave had observed him closely he made a sign to indi-

cate that the young man was to follow him, and they
left the mosque together. The black walked rapidly,
and led Mahmoud-Ben-Ahmed, with many a twist and
turn, through the tortuous tangle of the streets of
Cairo. Once our young man would have entered into
conversation with his guide, but the latter, opening
wide his mouth that bristled with sharp, white teeth,
showed that his tongue had been cut away at the
roots. This circumstance would have rendered it
difficult for him to commit an indiscretion.

At last they reached a portion of the city that
seemed entirely deserted and to which Mahmoud-
Ben-Ahmed was a stranger, although he was born in
Cairo and thought that he knew every quarter of it :
the mute stopped before a whitewashed wall in which
there was no indication of a door. He measured off
six paces from the corner of the wall and then looked
very carefully among the interstices of the stones,
doubtless for a spring that was concealed there.
Having discovered it he pressed the lever and a
column revolved upon its axis, disclosing a dark and
narrow passage which the mute entered, followed by
Mahmoud-Ben-Ahmed. First they descended a flight
of steps, over a hundred in number, after which they
pursued their way along a dark corridor that seemed
to be of interminable length. Mahmoud-Ben-Ahmed,
as he groped his way along the walls, covered with
sculptured hieroglyphics, knew that they had been
cut through the living rock, and perceived that he was
among the subterranean passages of an ancient Egyptian necropolis which some one had utilized by trans-
forming them into this concealed exit. There was a
glimpse of bluish daylight visible in the remote dis-

tance, at the end of the corridor. This light came to them through the lace-work of a carving that evidently made part of the room in which the corridor terminated. The slave again touched a spring, and Mahmoud-Ben-Ahmed found himself in a great hall paved with white marble, with a basin and fountain in the middle, columns of alabaster, walls covered with mosaics of glass and sentences from the Koran, interspersed with flowers and other decorations, while over all was a vault, intricately and laboriously carved, like the interior of a beehive or of a grotto roofed with stalactites ; the decoration was completed by huge scarlet poppies growing in great Moorish vases of blue and white porcelain. Seated upon an estrade piled with cushions, in a sort of alcove that had been excavated in the thickness of the wall, was the princess Ayesha, unveiled, radiant with beauty and surpassing in loveliness the houris of the fourth heaven.

"Well! Mahmoud-Ben-Ahmed," she said, addressing him in a most gracious tone and signing to him to be seated, " have you been making more verses in my honor ?"

Mahmoud-Ben-Ahmed cast himself at Ayesha's feet and, drawing the papyrus from his sleeve, recited his ghazel in most impassioned tones; in truth it was a remarkable piece of poetry. As he read the princess's cheeks brightened and flamed like a lamp of alabaster that has been newly lighted. Her eyes shone like stars and emitted rays of surprising brightness, her form seemed to become transparent, and there was a faint apparition as of butterfly-wings growing from her pretty, vibrating shoulders. Unfortunately Mahmoud-Ben-Ahmed, too deeply engrossed in reading

his piece of poetry, did not raise his eyes and so saw
nothing of the transformation that had been going on.
When he reached the end he had only before him the
Princess Ayesha, who looked at him with an ironical
smile upon her lips.

Like all poets, who are too much wrapped up in their
own creations, Mahmoud-Ben-Ahmed had forgotten
that the finest lines are of no worth as compared with
a sincere word or a look that is illumined by the light
of love. Peris are like women, it behooves one to
read them and grasp them just at the very moment
when they are about to wing their way back to
heaven, to descend to earth no more. Opportunity
is to be seized by the forelock, and the spirits of air,
by their wings; it is by such methods alone that they
are to be subjugated.

" Of a truth, Mahmoud-Ben-Ahmed, you possess a
poetic talent of the rarest, and your verses are worthy
of being displayed upon the doors of the mosques,
written in letters of gold, beside the most celebrated
productions of Ferdusi, Saadi and Ibnn-Ben-Omaz.
It is a pity that you were so absorbed but now in the
perfection of your alliterative rhymes that you did
not look at me : you might have seen—something that
perhaps you will never see again. The dearest wish
of your heart was fulfilled right before your eyes without your being aware of it. Adieu, Mahmoud-Ben-
Ahmed, who would marry none but a peri."

Thereupon Ayesha arose with an extremely majestic
air, raised a portière of gold brocade and disappeared.

The mute came to seek Mahmoud-Ben-Ahmed and
conducted him by the same road back to the same
place whence he had taken him. Mahmoud-Ben-

Ahmed, shocked and grieved at having been dismissed in such summary fashion, knew not what to think, and lost himself in conjectures without being able to discover any reason for the princess's abrupt leave-taking: his reflections resulted in attributing it to the caprice of a woman who would be ready to veer around again at the first opportunity, but it was to no purpose that he visited Bedreddin to purchase benzoin and skins of the civet cat, he saw nothing more of the Princess Ayesha ; he made countless pilgrimages to the mosque of the sultan Hassan and wasted much time standing by the third pillar ; the black slave in yellow damask did not appear, and the result of it all was that he sank into a deep, black fit of melancholy.

Leila taxed her ingenuity in inventing a thousand things for his diversion : she played for him on the guzla ; she told him most wonderful tales, adorned his chamber with festoons and garlands of flowers of which the colors were so agreeably mated and diversified that the sense of sight was as much gratified as was that of smell ; sometimes she even danced before him, displaying as much agility and grace as the most skilful almée ; any other than Mahmoud-Ben-Ahmed would have been touched by such attention and good will, but his thoughts were elsewhere and the longing to find Ayesha again left him no repose. Many a time he had gone and wandered about the princess's palace, but had never succeeded in catching a glimpse of her ; nothing was visible behind the tightly closed lattices ; the palace was like a tomb.

His friend Abdul-Malek, alarmed by his condition, frequently came to see him, and on such occasions could not help observing Leila's beauty and accom-

plishments, which, to say the least, equaled those of
the princess Ayesha, even if they did not surpass them,
and he was astonished to see how blind Mahmoud-
Ben-Ahmed was ; had it not been that he feared to
violate the sacred laws of friendship he would gladly
have made the young slave his wife. Still, however,
Leila, without suffering any loss of beauty, grew paler
and paler day by day ; her great eyes were suffused
with languor, and the roseate hues of dawn upon her
cheeks were displaced by the pallor of the moonlight.
One day Mahmoud-Ben-Ahmed perceived that she
had been weeping and asked of her the reason.

"Oh ! dear master," she said, "how can I tell it?
I, the poor slave, received and sheltered by your
compassion, have dared to love you ; but what am I
in your eyes? I know that you have made a vow to
love none but a peri or sultana : others might be
content to have the sincere love of a pure young heart
without longing for the daughter of the caliph or the
queen of the genii. Look at me ; I was fifteen years
old yesterday, and it may be that I am as beautiful as
that Ayesha whose name you are constantly mention-
ing in your dreams ; it is true that my brow is not
adorned by the magic ruby or by the aigrette of heron-
plumes, I am not accompanied in my walks by soldiers
bearing muskets inlaid with silver and coral. I can
sing, however, I can improvise airs upon the guzla,
and I dance like Emineh herself. I am to you as a
devoted sister ; what, then, is wanting to enable me
to reach your heart?"

Mahmoud-Ben-Ahmed felt a disturbance in the
region of his heart as he listened to these words of
the fair Leila ; he said nothing, however, and seemed

to be buried in profound meditation. His mind was divided between two conflicting considerations : on the one hand he could not renounce his cherished dream without a pang ; on the other, he told himself that he would be a madman to bestow his affections upon a woman who had trifled with him and left him with mocking words, when right there in his house there was a being who was, at least, the equal in youth and beauty of her whom he had lost.

Leila, as if awaiting her doom, remained kneeling before him, and two great tears coursed silently down the poor child's pale cheeks.

"Ah ! why did not Mesrour's blade complete the work that he had begun !" she exclaimed, raising her hand to her white, slender neck.

Moved by her despairing accent, Mahmoud-Ben-Ahmed raised the young slave and imprinted a kiss upon her forehead.

Leila drew herself up as a dove does when it is caressed, and taking a position in front of Mahmoud-Ben-Ahmed took both his hands in hers and said to him :

"Look at me closely ; don't you think that I am very like some one whom you know ? "

Mahmoud-Ben-Ahmed could not help uttering a cry of surprise :

" The face is the same, the eyes are the same ; in a word, all the features are those of the princess Ayesha. How is it that I have never noticed the resemblance until now ? "

"The looks with which you have favored your poor slave up to the present time have been very unobservant," Leila replied in a tone of gentle raillery.

" The princess Ayesha herself, now, might send me her blackamoor in his yellow damask robe with the selam of love ; I would refuse to follow him."

" Do you mean it ? " said Leila, in a voice more melodious than that of Bulbul telling his tale of love to his dear rose. " And yet it won't do to be too scornful toward that poor Ayesha, who is so like me."

The only answer that Mahmoud-Ben-Ahmed made was to press the young slave to his heart. Imagine his astonishment, though, when he beheld a gentle light emanating from Leila's face, the magic ruby glittering upon her brow, and wings, shot with the hues of the peacock, sprouting from her lovely shoulders ! Leila was a peri !

" Dear Mahmoud-Ben-Ahmed, I am not the princess Ayesha, neither am I Leila, the slave. My true name is Boudroulboudour. I am a peri of the highest rank, as you may see by my ruby and my wings. As I was passing through the air one night, over your terrace, I heard you express the wish that you might be loved by a peri. The daring aspiration pleased me ; ignorant, vulgar mortals, abandoned to terrestrial pleasures, are not visited by such dreams of rare delights. I determined to make trial of you, and I assumed the disguise of Ayesha and of Leila to see if you would recognize me and love me in my human garb. Your heart was more clear-sighted than your mind and your goodness was stronger than your vanity. The devotedness of the slave made you prefer her above the sultana ; it was what I wished to see you do. At one time I was seduced by the beauty of your verse and was on the point of betraying myself, but I feared that you were but a poet enamored of

your own imagination and your rhymes, and I left you
with an affectation of haughty disdain. It was your
wish to marry Leila, the slave : Boudroulboudour,
the peri, takes it upon her to replace her. I will be
Leila for all the world beside and peri for you alone,
for I have your happiness at heart and the world would
never forgive you the enjoyment of a felicity greater
than its own. Fairy though I be, it would tax all
my powers to protect you against the envy and the
wickedness of mankind."

These conditions were rapturously accepted by
Mahmoud-Ben-Ahmed, and the wedding-feast was
celebrated just as if he had really married little Leila.

Such is substantially, the story that I dictated to
Scheherazade, with the assistance of Francesco.

"How did the Sultan like your Arab story, and
what has become of Scheherazade ?"

"I have never seen her since."

I am afraid that Schahriar did not like the story
and gave orders, in earnest, this time, to chop off the
poor Sultana's head.

Friends of mine, returning from Bagdad, have told
me that they saw a woman sitting on the steps of a
mosque, whose craze it was to think that she was
Dinarzarde of the *Thousand and One Nights*, and that
she kept repeating these words over and over :

"Sister, if you are not sleeping, tell us, I pray you,
one of those pretty stories that you know so well."

She would wait a few moments, turning her head
and listening intently, and as she received no answer
would begin to weep, then would dry her eyes with a
gold-embroidered handkerchief, all stained with spots
of blood.

IL
VICCOLO DI MADAMA LUCREZIA.

PROSPER MERIMÉE.

I WAS twenty-three years old when I set out for
Rome. My father gave me a dozen letters of
introduction, one alone of which, that was no less
than four pages long, was sealed. It bore the address :
"For the Marquise Aldobrandi."

"I wish you to write," my father said to me, "and
let me know if the marquise still retains her good
looks."

Now, ever since childhood I had been accustomed
to see a miniature that hung in my father's study,
over the fireplace, the portrait of a very pretty woman,
wearing her hair in powder and crowned with an ivy-
wreath and with a tiger-skin thrown over her shoulders.
At the bottom was the inscription : "*Roma*, 18—."
Attracted by the singularity of the costume, I had
many a time inquired who the lady was. The
answer always came :

"It is a bacchante."

But this answer was not at all satisfactory to me ;
I even suspected the existence of a secret, for at that
question, innocent as it was, my mother would purse

her lips and my father's countenance assume an
aspect of seriousness.

On this occasion, as he handed me the sealed letter,
he cast a furtive look at the portrait ; I involuntarily
followed his example, and the idea came into my head
that that powdered bacchante might be no other than
the Marquise Aldobrandi.   As I was beginning to
have some insight into the things of this world, I drew
all sorts of conclusions from my mother's manner and
from that glance of my father's.

When I reached Rome, the first of my letters that I
presented was the marquise's.   She lived in a handsome palace near the place Saint Marc.   •

I handed my letter and my card to a servant in yellow livery, who ushered me into a large, dark and
gloomy drawing-room, rather scantily furnished.   In
Rome, however, in all the palaces there are paintings
by distinguished masters.   This salon contained quite
a number of such pictures, several of which were
well worthy of attention.

The first that I remarked was a portrait of a
woman, which seemed to me to be a Leonardo da Vinci.
The richness of its frame and of the ebony easel upon
which it stood showed conclusively enough that it was
considered the gem of the collection.   As the marquise was slow in making her appearance I had time
to make a leisurely examination of it.   I even carried
it to a window so as to get a more favorable light on it.
It was evidently a portrait and not a product of the
imagination, for fancy never conceives such physiog-
nomies as that : a beautiful woman, with rather thick
lips, eyebrows that almost met, and an expression
that was lofty and at the same time caressing.   In the

bottom corner was an escutcheon surmounted by a ducal coronet. What struck me most, however, was that the costume, with the exception of the powder, was the same as that of my father's bacchante.

I still had the portrait in my hand when the marquise entered the room.

"Just like his father!" she exclaimed, as she came toward me. "Ah! those Frenchmen! those Frenchmen! Scarcely inside my door, and he already has his hand on *Madame Lucrèce!*"

I was vehement in apologizing for my temerity and involved myself in a long eulogistic disquisition upon the *chef d'œuvre* of Leonardo that I had had the boldness to remove from its place.

"It is in fact a Leonardo," said the marquise, "and it is the portrait of the too famous Lucrezia Borgia. Your father used to admire it more than all the rest of my collection. But, good heavens! what a resemblance! It seems to me as if I were looking on your father as he was twenty-five years ago. How is he? What is he doing? Won't he come to Rome to see us some day?"

Although the marquise had neither powder in her hair nor tiger-skin upon her shoulders, I recognized in her my father's bacchante at the very first glance, by sheer force of genius. Twenty-five years or so had been unable completely to efface the traces of what had once been a great beauty. Her expression alone had changed, like her toilette. She was dressed all in black, and her triple chin, her sedate smile, her mingled air of cheerfulness and solemnity, told me that she was become devout.

Her reception of me, however, was as affectionate

as it well could be.   In three words she placed at my
disposal her house, her purse, her friends, among
whom she named several cardinals.

"Look upon me as your mother," she said.   "Your
father charges me to keep an eye on you and advise
your inexperience."

To prove to me that she did not consider her charge
a sinecure, she began forthwith to put me on my
guard against the perilous attractions that Rome has
for a young man of my age and exhorted me strenu-
ously to avoid them.   I was to shun bad company,
artists in particular, and associate only with such persons as she should recommend to me.   In a word, she
gave me a sermon under three heads.   I replied respectfully and with the proper amount of hypocrisy.

As I was rising to take leave :

"I regret," she said, "that my son the marquis is
just now absent at our country-place in the Romagna,
but I wish to make you acquainted with my second
son, Don Ottavio, who will soon be a monsignor.   I
hope that you will like him and that you will be
friends together, as you should be——"   And she
added hurriedly : "For you are of nearly the same
age, and he is a quiet, steady young man, like yourself."

She sent at once to summon Don Ottavio.   I beheld a tall, pale young man of melancholy aspect, who
never took his eyes from the floor, already exhaling an
odor of monkish hypocrisy.

The marquise, without giving him a chance to say
a word, made me the most courteous proffers of service in his name.   He confirmed every one of his
mother's words with a low bow, and it was agreed that

he should come and take me next morning for a ramble about the city and bring me back to the Palace Aldobrandi for a family dinner.

I had scarcely taken twenty steps in the street. when some one behind me shouted in an imperious tone :

" Don Ottavio, where are you going alone at such an hour as this ? "

I turned my head and beheld a portly abbé who was staring at me with all his eyes.

" I am not Don Ottavio," I said to him.

The abbé bowed almost to the ground and was profuse in his apologies ; a moment later I saw him enter the Palace Aldobrandi.   I went my way, not over well pleased to have been taken for a sucking monsignor.

Notwithstanding the marquise's admonitions, perhaps even because of them, one of the first things that I did was to hunt up the dwelling-place of an artist of my acquaintance, and I spent an hour in his atelier conversing with him upon the facilities for amusement, innocent or otherwise, that Rome had to offer.   I turned the conversation upon the Aldobrandi.

The marquise, he told me, after having been very frivolous in her younger days, had devoted her attention to spiritual things when she saw that there were no more conquests in store for her.   Her elder son was a brute who spent his time in hunting and taking care of the money that was paid in to him by the tenants of his extensive property.   They were pursuing a course to make an idiot of Don Ottavio, the second son, and intended to make a cardinal of him some day.   In the meanwhile he was handed over to the Jesuits.   He never left the house unattended ; he was forbidden to look at a woman or to stir a step out of doors without having at his heels an abbé who had trained him for the . service of God and who, after having been the last *amico* of the marquise, now ruled her household with an authority that was almost despotic.

The next morning Don Ottavio, accompanied by the Abbé Negroni, the individual who the day before had mistaken me for his pupil, came with a carriage and offered me his services as cicerone.

The first monument that we stopped to inspect was a church. There Don Ottavio, following the example of his abbé, kneeled, beat his breast and made innumerable signs of the cross. Upon arising he pointed out to me the various frescoes and statues and discoursed upon them like a man of taste and good sense. I was agreeably surprised. We began to converse and his talk pleased me. We had been speaking Italian for some time ; all at once he said to me in French :

"My tutor does not understand a word of your language ; let us talk French ; we shall be more at our ease."

It seemed as if the young man in changing his idiom had suffered a change of nature. Nothing in his conversation savored of the priest. I seemed to be listening to one of our provincial politicians of a liberal turn. I noticed that he rattled off everything in one unvarying monotonous tone of voice, and that this tone was frequently in strange contrast with the liveliness of his expressions. This was apparently a habit assumed for the purpose of mystifying Negroni, who kept asking us from time to time what we were

talking about. It may be imagined that the trans-
lations which we gave him were of the freest.

We saw a young man in violet stockings pass by.

" Behold," said Don Ottavio, " our patricians of the
present day. Degrading livery ! and in a few months
I shall be wearing it ! What happiness," he added,
after a momentary silence, " what happiness to live in
a country like yours ! Were I a Frenchman, perhaps
I might some day become a deputy."

This noble ambition inspired me with a strong inclination to laugh, which having been noticed by our
abbé, I was obliged to explain to him that we were
talking of the blunder of an archæologist who had
mistaken a statue by Bernini for an antique.

We returned to the Palace Aldobrandi for dinner.
We had scarcely swallowed our coffee when the
marquise made her excuses to me in behalf of her son,
who was compelled to retire to his apartment on account of certain pious observances. I was left alone
with her and the Abbé Negroni who, buried in a great
easy-chair, slept the sleep of the just. The marquise,
meanwhile, was questioning me in detail upon my
father, upon Paris, upon my past life and my plans for
the future. She gave me the impression of being
amiable and kind-hearted, but rather too inquisitive,
and, in particular, too much interested in my religious
well-being. She spoke Italian with admirable purity,
though, and I received from her a fine lesson in pro-
nunciation, which I promised myself to repeat without
loss of time.

I often returned to see her. Almost every morning
I would go to visit the antiquities in company with her
son and the everlasting Negroni, and in the evening

would dine with them at the Palace Aldobrandi.   **The**
marquise received but little **society** and that little consisted almost entirely of ecclesiastics.

On one occasion, however, **she presented me** to a
German lady, a fresh convert to the faith and her intimate friend.   This was a Madame de Strahlenheim,
an extremely handsome person who had made Rome
her dwelling-place for a long time.   While these ladies
were discussing the merits of a famous preacher I
was scrutinizing the portrait of Lucrèce by the light
of a lamp, when I thought it incumbent on me to put
in my word.

"What eyes!"   I exclaimed;   "one would almost
swear that he saw those lids move!"

At this rather high-flown hyperbole, which I put
forth with a view to impress Madame de Strahlenheim
with an idea of my connoisseurship, she started with
affright and hid her face in her handkerchief.

"What ails you, my dear?" said the marquise.

"Ah, nothing! only what this gentleman has just
said!"

She was at once overwhelmed with questions, and
once she admitted that the expression I had made
use of reminded her of a frightful story, she was
obliged to tell it.   It was briefly as follows:

Madame de Strahlenheim had a sister-in-law named
Wilhelmine who was engaged to a young man of
Westphalia, Julius de Katzenellenbogen, a volunteer
in General Kleist's division.   (It afflicts me to have to
repeat so many barbarous cognomens, but it is a fact
that these marvelous stories never happen except to
people with unpronounceable names.)

Julius was an extremely nice young man, stuffed

full with patriotism and metaphysics. When he left
for the army he had given Wilhelmine his portrait and
Wilhelmine had given him hers, which he wore constantly upon his heart. That sort of thing is practiced
quite extensively in Germany.

On the 13th of September, 1813, at about five o'clock
in the afternoon, Wilhelmine was at Cassel, in a salon
with her mother and sister-in-law, busy with her knitting. Without interrupting her work she would
frequently glance at the portrait of her betrothed,
which she had laid upon a small work-table that stood
in front of her. All at once she uttered a fearful
shriek, carried her hand to her heart, and fainted.
It was with the greatest difficulty that they succeeded
in bringing her to, and as soon as she could speak :

"Julius is dead!" she exclaimed. "Julius has
been killed!"

She declared, and the horror that was depicted on
all her lineaments was sufficient proof of the earnest-
ness of her conviction, that she had seen the portrait
close its eyes, and that at the same moment she had
suffered an unspeakable pang, as if a red-hot iron had
been thrust into her heart.

Every one strove, to no purpose, to make it clear
to her that her vision could have no connexion with
reality and that she should attach no importance to
it. The poor child was inconsolable ; she passed the
night in tears and next day insisted on putting on
mourning, as if already assured of the misfortune
that had been revealed to her.

Two days after that the news came of the bloody
battle of Leipzic. Julius sent his betrothed a note
dated the 13th, at three o'clock in the afternoon.

He had not been wounded, had distinguished himself in the action and had just entered Leipzic, where he was expecting to spend the night at headquarters and would consequently be out of the way of all danger. This letter, reassuring as it was, did not serve to remove Wilhelmine's apprehensions, who, noticing that it was dated at three o'clock, persisted in believing that her lover had died at five.

The unfortunate girl was not mistaken. It soon became known that Julius had been intrusted with an order to deliver; he had left Leipzic at half-past four, and three-fourths of a league from the city, on the other side of the Elster, one of the enemy's stragglers had fired at him, from his hiding-place in a ditch, and killed him. The ball, on its way to the young man's heart, had pierced Wilhelmine's portrait and destroyed it.

"And what became of the poor young lady?" I asked Madame de Strahlenheim.

"Oh! she was very, very ill. She is married now to M. de Werner, the councilor, and should you ever go to Dessau she will show you Julius' portrait."

"All that is the work of the devil," said the abbé, who had been sleeping with one eye open during Madame de Strahlenheim's story. "He who used to make the old pagan oracles talk can very well cause the eyes of a portrait to move when he sees fit. It is less than twenty years ago that an Englishman was choked to death by a statue at Tivoli."

"By a statue!" I exclaimed; "and how was that?"

"It was an English *milord* who had been making excavations at Tivoli. He had dug up a statue of one of the empresses, Agrippina, Messalina,—it don't make much difference whom. The sum and substance of it was that he had her carried home to his abode and by dint of looking at her and admiring her he became mad. All those Protestant gentlemen are more than half mad, any way. He used to call her his wife, his ' milady,' and he would kiss her, all of marble though she was. He said that the statue came to life every night for his sake, and this went on until one morning they found milord stone dead in his bed. Well, you would not believe it, but there was another Englishman foolish enough to buy that statue. If it had been my case I would have had the thing burned for lime."

When people once get fairly started on the subject of supernatural adventures they never know when to stop. Every one had his story to tell. I made my own contribution to the cycle of blood-curdling tales, and the result was that when the time came for us to separate we were all pretty well worked up and im-bued with respect for the power of his satanic majesty.

I started on foot to reach my lodging, and in order to get into the Rue du Corso, took a little tortuous lane through which I had never yet passed. It was quite deserted. All that was to be seen were long garden walls and a few houses of mean appearance, in no one of which was a light visible. The bells had just struck midnight ; it was very dark. I was in the middle of the street, walking at a good round pace, when I heard a faint sound, a *st!* just above my head, and at the same moment a rose fell at my feet. I raised my eyes, and, notwithstanding the darkness, discovered a woman dressed in white standing at a

window with her arm extended in my direction. We
Frenchmen are regarded with very kindly eyes in foreign lands, and our fathers, who vanquished all Europe, have comforted us with traditions very flattering
to our national vanity. It was my pious belief that
every German, Spanish or Italian lady would kindle
up like so much tinder at the mere sight of a Frenchman. To tell the truth, in those days I was pretty
much like the rest of my countrymen, and then, besides, had not the rose spoken clearly enough ?

"Madame," said I, in a low voice, picking up the
rose, "you have dropped your bouquet."

But the woman had already disappeared and the
window had closed without making the slightest noise.
I did what any one else in my place would have done.
I sought the nearest door ; it was only two steps from
the window, and having found it I waited for someone to come and open it for me. Five minutes passed
in deep silence. Then I coughed, then I scratched
gently with my finger nails upon the wood, but the
door did not open. I examined it more closely,
hoping to discover a key or a latch ; to my great surprise I found that it was fastened with a padlock.

"The jealous husband is not come home yet," I
said to myself.

I picked up a small pebble and threw it against the
window ; it struck a wooden shutter and fell back at
my feet.

"The deuce !" I thought, "do the Roman ladies
imagine that folks go about carrying ladders in their
pockets ? That is a custom that I never heard speak
of."

I waited several minutes longer with equally fruit-

less results, only once or twice it seemed to me that
the shutter shook a little, as if someone on the inside
were trying to put it back in order to obtain a glimpse
into the street. At the expiration of a quarter of an
hour, my patience being exhausted, I lit a cigar and
went my way, not, however, until I had carefully noted
the location of the house of the padlock.

When I came to reflect upon this adventure the following morning I reached these conclusions : A young
Roman lady, probably of surpassing beauty, had
caught sight of me in my strolls about the city and
fallen a victim to my poor charms. If she had
selected no other means of declaring her flame than
the gift of a mystic flower, the reason was that she
had been restrained by her decorous modesty, or it
may have been that she was prevented by the presence .
of some old duenna, or perhaps by an accursed guardian, like Rosina's Bartolo. I made up my mind that
I would lay siege according to rule to the house in-
habited by this infanta.

With this fine project in my head I brushed my
hair so as to give myself a conquering aspect and
started forth from my lodging. I had put on my new
frock coat and a pair of yellow gloves. Thus attired,
with my hat cocked over my ear and the faded rose in
my button-hole, I turned my steps toward the street
of which, as yet, I knew not the name, but which I had
no difficulty in finding again. A signboard fastened
up over the head of a Madonna informed me that it
was called *il viccolo di Madama Lucrezia.*

The name took me aback. I immediately remembered the portrait by Leonardo da Vinci and the stories
of presentiments and diabolical doings generally that

had been told at the marquise's the night before.
Then I reflected that there are loves that are predes-
tined in heaven. Why should not the object of my
affections be named Lucrèce ? What reason was there
why she should not be like the Lucrèce in the Aldobrandi gallery ?

It was broad day, I was but a couple of steps away
from a charming young lady, and no thought of evil
intruded upon the emotion that I experienced.

I was before the house. It bore the number 13—
an omen of ill. Alas ! it did not answer in the slightest
degree to the idea that I had formed from having seen
it by night. It was not a palace, very far from it. I
beheld an inclosure of moss-covered walls, blackened
by time, behind which rose the branches of a few ill-
cared-for fruit trees. At one corner of the inclosure
stood a pavilion of a single story, with two windows
opening on the street, both of them closed by old
wooden shutters reinforced on the outside by numerous iron bars. The door was low, surmounted by an
obliterated escutcheon, and was made fast, as it had
been the night before, by a huge padlock attached to
a chain. On this door was the inscription, written in
chalk : *This house for sale or to let.*

And yet I could not be mistaken ; on that side of
the street the houses were so few in number as to
render any confusion impossible. It was my padlock,
beyond a doubt, and in addition two rose-leaves upon
the pavement, close beside the door, indicated the
very spot where my loved one had signaled me her
declaration, and at the same time bore witness to the
fact that no one ever swept the space before the house.

I questioned some poor people of the neighborhood

to learn where the custodian of this mysterious dwelling might live

"Not here," was the abrupt answer that I received.

My question seemed to be unwelcome to those whom I interrogated, and that only served to excite my curiosity still further. Keeping on from door to door, I wound up by entering a kind of dark cavern where there was an old woman who might have been suspected of being a witch, for she had a black cat and was cooking some indistinguishable mess in a kettle.

"You wish to see the house of Madame Lucrèce?" said she. "It is I who have the keys."

"Well, show it to me."

"Would you be wanting to hire it?" she asked, smiling with a rather doubtful air.

"Yes, if it suits me."

"It won't suit you. But come, will you give me a paul if I show it to you?"

"I shall be very glad to."

Upon this assurance she arose nimbly from her bench, took from its place on the wall a key that was quite covered with rust, and conducted me to the door of No. 13.

"Why," I asked her, "do they call this house the house of Lucrèce?"

The old woman replied with a sneer: "Why do they call you foreigner? Isn't it because you are a foreigner?"

"Very well; but who was this Madame Lucrèce? Was she a Roman lady?"

"What! You come to Rome and have never heard

of Madame Lucrèce? I will tell you her story when we get inside the house. But here is some more of the devil's work! I don't know what has got into this key, it won't turn. Try it yourself."

It was a long time, in fact, since the lock and the key had seen anything of each other. Still, by dint of thrice gritting my teeth very hard and indulging in profanity a similar number of times, I succeeded in turning the key in the lock, but I tore my yellow gloves and sprained the palm of my hand. We entered a dark passage-way which afforded access to several low apartments.

The ceilings, intricately paneled, were covered with spiders' webs, beneath which some traces of gilding were with difficulty to be distinguished. The smell of mold that exhaled from all the rooms demonstrated conclusively that they had been untenanted for a very long time. Not an article of furniture was to be seen. Some strips of old leather were hanging in streamers from the sweating walls. I judged from the carvings on some brackets and the shape of the chimney-pieces that the house dated back to the fifteenth century, and it is likely that in former days its decorations had had some pretensions to elegance. The windows, with very small panes, most of them broken, had an outlook on the garden, where I distinguished a rose tree in bloom, together with some fruit trees and an abundance of broccoli.

When I had inspected all the apartments of the *rez-de-chaussée* I ascended to the floor above, where I had seen my fair unknown. The old woman endeavored to prevent me, saying that there was nothing to be seen there and that the staircase was in very bad condition, but seeing that I was determined she followed me, though with visible reluctance. The rooms on this floor were very like those below, only they were not so damp ; the windows and the floor, too, were in a better state of preservation. In the room that I entered last there was a large fauteuil in black leather, which, strange to say, was not covered with dust. I seated myself in it, and finding the place a comfortable one to listen to a story in, requested the old crone to tell me that of Madame Lucrèce ; but first, in order to refresh her memory, I made her a present of a few pauls. She coughed, wiped her nose, and started off after this fashion :

"In the time of the pagans, Alexander being emperor, there was a girl who was as beautiful as the day and whom they called Madame Lucrèce. See, there she is ! "

I turned about quickly. The hag pointed to a carved bracket that sustained the main beam of the apartment. It was a siren of very clumsy execution.

" *Dame*," the old woman went on, "she liked to enjoy herself, she did, and as her father might have seen fit to make a fuss about it she had this house built for herself where we are now.

"Every night she would hasten down from the Quirinal and come here to have a good time. She would seat herself by that window, and whenever there passed along the street a handsome cavalier, like your-self, monsieur, she would call him in ; you can imagine whether he was well received. But men are talkative, some of them are, at least, and they might have done her harm with their babbling. So, she took steps to make that all right. When she had said good-night-to the gallant her bravos were there, waiting on the stairs by which we came up. They finished him off for you, then they buried him for you in those broccoli beds. *Allez*, they have turned up their bones, right there in that garden !

"This business lasted for some time. One evening, though, look you, along comes her brother, whose name was Tarquinius Sixtus, and passes beneath her window. She does not recognize him. She calls him in. He ascends the stair. At night all cats are gray. As it had been with the others, so it was with him. But he had left his pocket-handkerchief behind him, on which his name was written.

"No sooner had she seen the wickedness that they had been guilty of than she was seized with despair, so, quick she unclasps her garter and hangs herself to that beam there. Well, there you have a fine example for young folks !"

While the old woman was thus confounding the centuries, and mixing up the Tarquins and the Borgias, I had my eyes fixed on the floor. I had discovered there a few rose petals, still quite fresh, which gave me food for reflection.

"Who is it that cultivates this garden ?" I asked the crone.

"My son, sir, who is gardener to M. Vanozzi, the gentleman who owns the garden next door. M. Vanozzi is always in the Maremma ; he don't ever come to Rome nowadays. That is why the garden is not kept in better order. My son is with him—and I'm afraid that they won't return very soon," she added, with a sigh.

"So M. Vanozzi keeps him occupied, does he ?"

" Ah ! he is a strange man, and he gives my son too many things to do. I am afraid that there is something wrong going on. . . . . Ah, my poor boy ! "

She made a step toward the door as if desirous of ending the conversation.

" No one lives here, then ? " I continued, stopping her.

" Not a soul."

" And why is that ? "

She shrugged her shoulders.

" Listen," said I, giving her a piastre, " tell me the truth. There is a woman who comes here."

" Holy Jesus, a woman ! "

" Yes, I saw her last night. I spoke to her."

" Holy Madonna ! " cried the old woman, making a dash for the stairs ; " it must have been Madame Lucrèce ! Let us go, let us go, good gentleman ! I had been told that she walked by night, but I did not wish to tell you of it for fear of doing the owner a bad turn, for I thought that you were inclined to hire the house."

I could not keep her. She was in haste to leave the house, in order, she said, to carry a wax candle to the nearest church without delay. I let her go, and left the house myself, despairing of learning anything further from her.

It may be imagined that I did not tell my story at the Aldobrandi palace : the marquise was too prudish, and Don Ottavio was too much wrapped up in his politics to be a competent adviser in a love affair. I went and hunted up my painter, however, who knew all Rome, from the cedar to the hyssop, and asked him what he thought of it,

" I think," he said, "that you have seen the phantom of Lucrèce Borgia. What a risk you incurred!
Dangerous as she was while living, just think for a
moment what she must be now that she is dead! It
is enough to make one shake in his shoes."

" Joking apart, what could it have been?"

" That is to say that the gentleman is a philosopher
and an atheist and has no faith in the things most
worthy of respect. Very good; what say you then
to this other hypothesis? Let us suppose that the old
harridan lends her house to women who are not above
addressing gentlemen who pass along the street.
There have been old women depraved enough to ply
that trade."

" That sounds reasonable enough," I said, "but then
I must have a very goody-goody air for the old woman
not to have made me the offer of her services. The
supposition is offensive to me. And then, my dear
fellow, remember how the house was furnished. It
could scarcely please anyone unless he were possessed
with a devil."

" In that case it is a spook, beyond the shadow of a
doubt. Hold on, though! Here is just one hypothesis remaining: you made a mistake in the house.
Parbleu! I have it: near a garden? a little low
door? Well, it is my old friend Rosina. It is less
than a year and a half ago that she was the principal
ornament of that street. It is true that she has gone
blind, but that's a mere detail; she still has a very
handsome profile."

None of these explanations were satisfactory to me.
When evening came I walked slowly past the house of
Lucrèce. I saw nothing. I turned and passed it

again, with no better result.   Three or four evenings
in succession, on my way home from the Aldobrandi
palace, did I stop and cool my heels beneath those
windows, but always to no purpose.   The mysterious
inhabitant of the house No. 13 was beginning to
fade from my memory when, passing through the
viccolo about midnight, I distinctly heard a low
woman's laugh behind the window-shutter at the very
spot where the fair flower-girl had appeared to me.
Twice I heard that low laugh, and I could not help being a little frightened when I saw a troop of cowled
penitents, bearing wax-candles and conveying a dead
body to the grave, make their appearance at the other
end of the street.   When they were gone by I posted
myself as sentry beneath the window, but then there
was nothing more to be heard.   I tried throwing
pebbles, I even used my voice with more or less dis-
tinctness ; no one appeared, and a shower coming up
just then obliged me to beat a retreat.

I am ashamed to tell how many times I stopped in
front of that accursed house, without ever succeeding in solving the riddle that was bothering me.
Only on one occasion did I pass through the viccolo
of Madame Lucrezia in company with Don Ottavio
and his inseparable abbé.

" There is the house of Lucrèce," said I.

I noticed that he changed color.

" Yes," he replied, " an ill-defined popular tradition
has it that Lucrezia Borgia had her ' little house '
here.   If those walls could only speak what horrors
they might reveal !   And yet, my friend, when I compare that time with our own, I can scarce help regret-
ting it.   There were Romans still in the days of

Alexander VI.; to-day they have ceased to exist.
Cæsar Borgia was a monster, but he was a great man ;
it was his aim to expel the barbarians from Italy, and
had his father lived, perhaps he might have succeeded
in accomplishing that grand design.   Ah ! would that
Heaven might grant us a tyrant like Borgia to deliver
us from these human despots who are reducing us
to the level of the brutes."

When Don Ottavio once took his flight into the re-
gions of politics there was no such thing as stopping
him.   When we had reached the Place du Peuple his
panegyric upon enlightened despotism was still running its course, but we were a hundred leagues away
from my Lucrèce.

On a certain evening when I had gone at a very
late hour to pay my respects to the marquise, she
told me that her son was indisposed and requested
me to go upstairs to his room.   I found him lying
upon his bed, fully dressed, and reading a French
newspaper that·I had sent him that morning carefully
concealed in a volume of the Fathers of the Church.
For sometime past the collection of the Fathers had
served as a vehicle for those communications that had
to be kept from the eyes of the abbé and the marquise.
On those days when the French mail was due a servant would bring me a folio volume, and I would return another into which I had slipped a newspaper
that had been loaned me by the secretary of the em-
bassy.   It was the means of giving the marquise and
her director an exalted idea of my piety, and now and
then they tried to induce me to talk theology.

After I had conversed with Don Ottavio for a while,
noticing that he was greatly agitated and that even

politics failed to interest him and secure his attention, I advised him to undress and go to bed and bade him adieu. The weather was cold and I had no cloak. Don Ottavio urged me to take his, so I accepted it and received a lesson in the difficult art of draping one's self in the true Roman fashion.

I left the Aldobrandi palace, muffled up to the ears. I had barely taken a few steps along the sidewalk of the Place Saint Marc when a man of the people, whom I had observed sitting upon a bench by the palace door, came up to me and handed me a paper with writing on it.

" For the love of God," he said, "read this."

Whereupon he disappeared, running as fast as his legs could carry him.

I had taken the paper, and looked about for a light to read it by. By the light of a lamp burning before a Madonna I saw that it was a note written in pencil and apparently by a trembling hand. With considerable difficulty I managed to decipher the following words :

"Do not come this evening, or we are undone ! Everything is known excepting your name. Nothing shall ever separate us.

"Thy LucRÈCE."

" Lucrèce !" I exclaimed. " Still Lucrèce ! What diabolical mystification is there at the bottom of all this ? 'Don't come !' But I would like to know what road one has to take to reach you, my pretty one."

While ruminating upon this note I had mechanically turned my steps in the direction of the viccolo di

Madama Lucrezia, and soon I found myself in front of the house No. 13.

The little street was in its usual deserted condition and there was no sound to break the silence that reigned throughout the neighborhood save my footsteps. I halted and raised my eyes toward a window that was well known to me. This time I could not be mistaken : the shutter was thrown back.

There was the window wide open.

I thought that I could descry a human form drawn in relief against the dark background of the apartment.

" Lucrèce, is that you ? " I said in a low voice.

There was no answer, but I heard a clicking sound of which I did not at first understand the cause.

" Is that you, Lucrèce ? " I repeated, a little louder this time.

At the same moment I received a terrible blow in the chest, a loud report was heard and I found myself lying prone upon the pavement. A hoarse voice cried to me:

" Take that from the Signora Lucrèce ! "

And the shutter was closed noiselessly.

I arose immediately, reeling as I did so, and the first thing that I did was to make an inspection of myself, fully expecting to find a great hole in the middle of my stomach. The cloak was perforated, and my coat as well, but the thick folds of heavy cloth had served to deaden the force of the ball and I escaped with a severe contusion. The idea entered my head that a second shot might not be long in coming, so I forthwith dragged myself away from that inhospitable house, hugging the walls in such a way as to prevent any one from securing a fair aim at me.

I was retiring as rapidly as I was able to, quite breathless still, when a man whom I had not noticed, owing to his being behind me, came up and took my arm and inquired with much feeling if I was wounded. I recognized the voice ; it was Don Ottavio. It was not the time for asking questions, however surprised I might be at seeing him alone and in the street at that hour of the night. I briefly told him that some one had fired at me from a certain window that I described and that I had got off with a contusion.

"It was a mistake !" he exclaimed. " But I hear people coming this way. Are you able to walk ? I am lost if we are found together. Still, I will not leave you."

He took me by the arm and dragged me rapidly away. We walked, or rather ran, as long as I could go, but soon my breath failed me and I was compelled to seat myself upon a stone. We luckily chanced to be but a little way from a great mansion where there was a ball going on. There were coaches in abundance standing before the door. Don Ottavio went and procured one, helped me into it and went with me to my hotel. A large glass of water that I drank having quite put me to rights again, I proceeded to relate to him in detail everything that had happened me before that ill-omened house, from the present of a rose down to that of a leaden bullet.

He listened to my story with his head down, half hidden in one of his hands. When I showed him the note that I had received he snatched it from me, read it eagerly, and again exclaimed :

"It is all a mistake! a horrible mistake!"

"You must admit, my dear fellow," said I, "that it is a very disagreeable one for me, and for you also. I narrowly escape being killed, and you have ten or a dozen holes punctured in your handsome cloak. Heavens! what a jealous set your countrymen are!"

Don Ottavio pressed my hand with an air of compunction and read the note over again without making me any answer.

"Try and see if you can't give me some explanation of all this business," I said to him. "The deuce take me if I can make head or tail of it."

He shrugged his shoulders.

"At least," said I, "what am I to do? To whom must I address myself, in this holy city of yours, in order to obtain redress against this gentleman who blazes away at people in the street without so much as stopping to ask what their name is? I confess that it would afford me much delight to be the means of having him hanged."

"Do nothing of the kind!" he exclaimed. "You are not acquainted with this country. Say nothing of what has happened you to any one. You would be exposing yourself to great danger."

"How should I be exposing myself? *Morbleu,* I mean to have my revenge. If I had given the ragamuffin any cause for being offended it would have been a different matter, but for having picked up a rose—in all conscience, I don't deserve a bullet for that."

"Leave the matter to me," said Don Ottavio; "perhaps I may be able to clear up the mystery. But I ask you as a favor, as a signal proof of your friendship for me, don't speak of this affair to a living soul. Will you promise me that ? "

He had such an expression of sadness as he addressed this supplication to me that I had not the courage to refuse him, and so I promised all that he desired. He thanked me effusively, and after having applied a compress of eau de Cologne to my chest, clasped my hand and bade me good-night.

"Apropos," I asked him just as he was opening the door to leave the room, " tell me how it was that you happened to be on hand just at the right moment to come to my assistance ? "

" I heard the report," he replied, not without some display of embarrassment, "and left the house immediately, fearing that something might have happened you."

He left me hurriedly, after having again enjoined me to secrecy.

In the morning a surgeon came to look at me, sent, doubtless, by Don Ottavio. He prescribed an embrocation, but asked me no question as to the cause that had been instrumental in strewing violets upon the lilies of my complexion. They are close-mouthed at Rome, and being in that city I wished to conform to the usages of the inhabitants thereof.

Several days passed without my having an opportunity of conversing freely with Don Ottavio. He was preoccupied, even more gloomy than usual, and appeared, besides, to endeavor to avoid my questions ; he said not a word about the strange inhabitants of the viccolo di Madama Lucrezia during our brief and infrequent interviews. The day fixed for his ordination was drawing near, and I attributed his moodiness to his dislike for the profession that was being forced upon him.

For my part, I was making my preparations to leave Rome in order to go to Florence. When I mentioned my impending departure to the Marquise Aldobrandi, Don Ottavio, alleging some pretext or other, I have forgotten what, requested me to come up to his room. There taking me by my two hands :

"My dear friend," said he, "if you don't grant me the favor that I am about to ask of you I shall certainly blow my brains out, for I can see no other way of extricating myself from the difficulty that I am in. I am firmly resolved never to put on the hateful coat that they want to make me wear. It is my wish to fly this country. What I have to ask of you is that you will take me with you. You can pass me off as your servant ; a single word added to your passport will suffice to facilitate my flight."

At first I tried to dissuade him from his project by speaking to him of the grief that he would cause his mother, but finding him inexorable in his determination I finally promised to take him with me and to have the necessary alterations made in my passport.

"That is not all," he said. "My departure is contingent also upon the success of an enterprise in which I am engaged. You intend to set out day after to-morrow ; by that time I shall have been successful, may be, and then I am wholly at your service."

"You can't have been so mad," I asked him, not without uneasiness, "as to have gone and got yourself entangled in some conspiracy ? "

"No," he replied, "the interests at stake are of less importance than the fate of my country, but yet they

are of such weight that on the success of my
enterprise depend my life and happiness. I cannot
tell you more just now ; in two days you shall know
all."

I accepted the situation resignedly, for I was beginning to become accustomed to mystery. It was
settled that we were to start at three o'clock in the
morning and that we were to make no stop until we
had reached Tuscan territory.

Convinced that it was useless to go to bed, having
to start at such an early hour, I employed the last
evening that I was to spend in Rome in paying visits
at all the houses where I had been received. I went
to take leave of the marquise and shake hands with
her son, ceremonially and for form's sake. I could
feel his hand tremble as I took it in my own. He
said to me in a whisper :

" At this moment my life is hanging on the toss of
a penny. When you return to your hotel you will find
a letter from me. If I am not with you by three
o'clock precisely, do not wait for me."

I was struck by the changed expression of his countenance, but I attributed it to a very natural emotion
on his part at a moment when he was about to separate himself from his family, perhaps for ever.

I reached my lodging about one o'clock. I desired
once more to pass through the viccolo of Madame
Lucrèce. There was something white hanging from
the window where I had beheld two apparitions of
such different nature. I approached it cautiously. It
was a knotted rope. Was it an invitation to go and
say good-by to the signora ? It looked very much
like it, and the temptation was great. I did not give

way to it, however, remembering the promise that I had made Don Ottavio and also, if the truth must be told, the unpleasant reception that a much less audacious proceeding had earned for me a few days before.

I went my way, therefore, but slowly, vexed to lose this last occasion of penetrating the mystery of the house No. 13. At every step that I took I turned my head, fully expecting to see a human form ascending or descending by the rope-ladder. Nothing appeared. At last I came to the end of the viccolo ; I was about to enter the Corso.

"Adieu, Madame Lucrèce," said I, taking off my hat to the house that was still visible to me where I stood. "Please see if you can't find some other one than me upon whom to wreak your vengeance against the jealous husband who keeps you in bondage."

It was striking two when I returned to my hotel. The carriage was standing in the courtyard, all packed and ready. One of the hotel attendants handed me a letter. It was Don Ottavio's, and as it seemed to be a long one I thought that it would be better to read it in my room, so I told the waiter to go before with a light.

"Monsieur," he said, "the domestic that you spoke to us of, he who was to travel with Monsieur——"

"Well, is he arrived?"

"No, sir."

"He is at the post ; he will come with the horses."

"Monsieur, there came a lady a little while ago who asked to speak to Monsieur's domestic. She insisted upon going up to Monsieur's apartment, and instructed

me to tell Monsieur's domestic, the very moment that
he came, that Madame Lucrèce is in your room."

"In my room ?" I exclaimed, grasping the rail of
the staircase with all my strength.

"Yes, Monsieur. And it appears that she is going,
too, for she gave me a little bundle. I have put it in
the boot."

My heart was beating violently. I cannot describe
the mingled feeling of superstitious terror and curiosity that had taken possession of me. I ascended
the staircase, step by step. When I reached the first
story (my room was on the second), the waiter who
was preceding me made a misstep and the candle
that he was carrying fell from his hand and was ex-
tinguished. He begged a million pardons and went
down to relight it, but I kept on ascending.

Already my hand was on the handle of my door. I
hesitated. What new vision was about to greet my
sight ? More than once the story of the bleeding nun
had recurred to my memory in the darkness ; was I,
like Don Alonso, possessed by a demon ? It seemed
to me that the waiter was horribly slow in returning
with the candle.

I opened my door. Praise be to Heaven ! there
was a light in my bedroom. I passed with rapid
steps through the small sitting-room from which it
opened. A glance was sufficient to show me that
there was no one in my sleeping-room, but I immediately heard, close at my heels, light footsteps and the
rustling of a woman's dress. I think that the hair
upon my head stood straight on end. I wheeled
about abruptly.

A woman, dressed all in white, with a black mantilla

over her head, came toward me with outstretched arms.

" Here you are at last, my beloved," she cried, seizing my hand. Her own was cold as ice and her features bore the pallor of death. I retreated to the wall.

" Holy Virgin ! it is not he! Ah ! Monsieur, are you the friend of Don Ottavio ? "

At these words everything was made clear. Despite her pallor, the young woman had nothing of the air of a phantom. She cast down her eyes, a thing which ghosts never do, and held her two hands crossed before her in a modest attitude, which led me to believe that my friend Don Ottavio was not so much of a politician as I had given him credit for being, after all. In a word, the time had come for abducting the fair Lucrèce, and the only rôle that I was fated to play in the adventure was that of confidant.

Don Ottavio appeared upon the scene a moment after, disguised ; the horses came and we started. There was no passport for Lucrèce, but a woman, and a pretty woman at that, never inspires suspicion. There was one gendarme, however, who was inclined to raise difficulties. I told him that he was a brave fellow and that he certainly must have served under the great Napoleon. He did not deny it, and I made him a present of a portrait of that illustrious man, in gold. Then it was all plain sailing.

If I must give you the whole of this story, Don Ottavio, the traitor, had made the acquaintance of this charming person, who was sister to a certain Vanozzi, a wealthy farmer and a man of ill-repute as being a little of a liberal and a good deal of a smuggler. Don Ottavio was well aware that, even if his relatives had not destined him for the church, they would never have consented to let him marry a girl of a condition so far beneath his own.

Love, they say, laughs at locksmiths. The Abbé Negroni's pupil succeeded in establishing a secret correspondence with his beloved. Every night he made his escape from the Aldobrandi palace, and as it would have been too hazardous an undertaking to attempt to escalade Vanozzi's house, the two lovers made their rendezvous in that of Madame Lucrèce, the evil reputation of which, moreover, served them as a protection against intruders. A little door, concealed by a fig tree, afforded communication between the two gardens. Young, and in love as they were, Lucrèce and Ottavio never thought of complaining of the scantiness of their furniture, which consisted, as I think I have already mentioned, of a single old leather-covered armchair.

One evening, while awaiting Don Ottavio, Lucrèce mistook me for him and made me the present that I carried off in his place. It is true that there was some resemblance in height and shape between Don Ottavio and myself. . . . . Then it came to pass that the confounded brother got wind of the affair, but his threats were unavailing to make Lucrèce divulge the name of her lover. You know how he revenged himself, and how I thought to pay the scot for the whole party. It is useless to tell you how the two lovers "took the key of the fields," each in his own way.

Conclusion. We arrived safely at Florence, all three of us. Don Ottavio married Lucrèce and started immediately with her for Paris. There my

father welcomed him with the same cordiality that I
had received from the marquise. He took it upon
himself to negotiate a reconciliation between mother
and son, and was finally successful, though not without considerable difficulty. The Marquis Aldobrandi
very opportunely contracted the fever of the Cam-
pagna and died of it. Ottavio inherited his title and
fortune, and I was godfather to his first child.

THE BARREL-ORGAN.

FRANÇOIS COPPÉE.

I

WHAT mournful memories music brings up! How sad are the recollections of other days that it evokes! And how the tears rise in our eyes in the gathering twilight of November, at the wailing of the barrel-organ, as it plays some long-forgotten polka!

An old, old polka that used to set all Paris dancing fifteen years ago, when the number of your years was eighteen, madame, or thereabout! Yes! you, poor, faded blonde, who are wearing a blue velvet hat that only looks the shabbier for having new strings, and are wheeling your baby—the third, it is—in his little carriage, beneath the leafless lindens that border the cheerless boulevard of the suburban quarter where you live.

How pretty you were in the days when the band used to play that polka at all the bourgeois frolics, with their refreshments of stale cake and glasses of sweetened water! How like you were to a bright spring morning, with the pure oval of your face that would not have shamed a Correggio and your beautiful waved tresses, of the gold of ripened grain, that you lost the half of—the pity of it !—at the birth of your second child !

Portionless, you were ? Yes, you had no dowry. How could it be otherwise with the daughter of an honest, second head-clerk, whose recommendation from his superiors uniformly consisted of these blighting words: "A good man in his place, very useful and unassuming ;" a poor fellow who, when he went with you to your dances, never dared sit down to whist at ten sous the point, and was continually feeling in his waistcoat pocket to see if he had not lost the three francs that were to pay the cab-fare home ?

Portionless !—Every mirror in the room as you made your entry, hanging on your father's arm, radiant in clouds of pink, gave you assurance that no portion was needed in your case. Who would have suspected that the mother, detained at home for lack of finery, had ironed out your skirt on the dining-room table and that your dress was the result of your own labors, cut and sewed by your own hands ? Were you not gloved up to the elbows ? How could anyone have known of the needle-pricks that you had on your finger-ends ?

Listen to the old polka that the broken-winded barrel-organ is playing in the dim November twilight. Does it not remind you of the song of a crazy woman, broken by sobs ?

Many a time were you invited to dance that polka by the handsome, dark young man with the military mustache, so elegant in his well-cut evening suit, whom you used to speak of to yourself in thought as

Frédéric, his baptismal name. He used to ask you to dance that polka with him, and the mazurka, too, and the waltz. Your voice would tremble a little as you answered : " Yes, sir," and your hand would flutter, also, as you laid it in his, for he was a young man of good family, a pretty hard case, so the rumor was, who had fought a duel and whose father had twice had to pay his debts. What distinction !

How tightly his arm would clasp your waist as he led you to the floor, and when you paused for a mo-ment to take breath, leaning on his arm with a happy smile upon your lips and quickened respiration, how your poor little heart would beat as he turned and looked you in the eyes and addressed to you in low, caressing tones a compliment—upon some trifle, some slight detail of your toilette, or the flower that you had in your hair—a compliment that was perfectly re-spectful in form, but in which you felt there lurked some hidden meaning that was cause to you at once of fear and pleasure !

But a gay young fellow like M. Frédéric, alas ! had something else to do than waste his time at such milk-and-water entertainments. He took himself off to other scenes of gayety and you, is it not true ? though you refused to admit it even to yourself, were sorry. Then two, three, four, five years rolled by. You gave up wearing pink dresses, for your cheeks were growing pale, and still at the little bourgeois parties, where the repertory of dance music never changes, they kept playing that old polka that re-minded you of M. Frédéric.

At last it became necessary to look at things as they were and come to a decision, so you finally

married the bashful young man who had until then
been the dancing partner of all the scraggy young
ladies of thirty and upward.   In other days it had
more than once happened you to forget when his turn
came for a quadrille, although you had his name
written down on your little ivory tablets.   It was
rather a feeling of pity, you must admit, that this
good M. Jules inspired in you at that time, with his
stiffly starched cravats and his cleaned gloves.   You
married him, though, after all, and he has turned out
to be an industrious man and a good husband and
father.   He is now second head-clerk, like deceased
Monsieur your father, and like him he is always
characterized by his superiors in the same discourag-
ing terms : "A quiet, useful man in his place ; to be
retained in the service."   When you presented him
with his second boy the poor man was stirred by a
feeble impulse of ambition, and in the hope to secure
advancement published a couple of small pamphlets
upon special subjects, but the powers that be dis-
charged their obligation toward him by awarding him
academic honors.

Three children there are now,—first two boys
and then a little minx of a daughter who came sometime afterward,—and they are a heavy load to
carry !   The oldest, fortunately, is at college, partially assisted by state funds ; by dint of strict
economy the two ends are made to meet.   But what
a monotonous, trivial way of living !   The father
leaves home early in the morning taking with him his
breakfast—a sandwich and a little bottle of wine
and water—in the pocket of his overcoat, for he is
to give a lesson in geography at a young ladies'

boarding-school before taking possession of his leather-covered chair at the department. You, madame, have not the time to stop and think of your grievances, and the day is all too short for one who has so much to do. And withal, never the least amusement! During all the past year you have been at the play but once, and that was last September, when you went to see the *Domino Noir* on free tickets.

You have accepted the situation and are resigned to your fate, doubtless ; but that old polka that the organ keeps relentlessly playing reminds you that the other afternoon, as you were pushing before you the little carriage containing your slumbering baby, just as you are doing now, and pursuing your way along this same boulevard, you came near being run over by a spanking victoria and pair and recognized, well protected by his comfortable wraps, that identical M. Frédéric, the same as of old, with that air of unfailing youthfulness that is the property of the fortunate ones of this world, and he cast an ugly look at you as he shouted : "Stupid !" to his coachman.

Truly, that organ is insupportable, is it not?—It ceases, however, fortunately, and now the night is coming down. At the extremity of the dismal suburban boulevard, yonder, the gas-jets as they spring into light sprinkle with their pale stars the purple mist that follows close upon the sunset. It is time to return, Madame Jules. Your second son must have come in from school by this, and he never masters his morrow's lessons before dinner unless you are there. Go home, Madame Jules. Your husband will soon be back from his office, tired and hungry, and you know full well that in your absence the small maid at twenty-five francs a month would not be equal to the task of "warming over" the remains of the roast beef of yesterday with potatoes and onions.

II

WHAT mournful memories music brings up! How sad are the recollections of other days that it evokes! And how the tears rise to our eyes in the gathering twilight of November at the wailing of the barrel-organ as it plays some long forgotten galop!

Of what are you thinking, Madame la Comtesse, as you listen to it, and why do you stand thus motionless at the lofty window of your boudoir, as if some mighty hand had fallen and smitten you into stone among your musings? Happy woman that you are, in all the plenitude of your beauty of thirty years, say, what memories has it for you, that old galop that the wailing, groaning organ, compeller of dreams, is playing down there upon the bleak boulevard, behind the naked lindens of your garden?

It recalls to you the great amphitheater of " Johnson's American Circus," with its fringe of intently gazing faces, as it used to be in the days of your equestrian triumphs. The two negro minstrels have brought their comic concert to an abrupt end by smashing their violins over each other's head and the groom has brought your trick-horse out upon the sawdust track—you remember him, the huge, gentle white horse, spotted with black, who used to remind one of a raw turkey dressed and stuffed with truffles? Then you make your entrée, hand in hand with the ring-master, a resplendent being in scarlet coat and hair à

la Capoul, with whom you were a little bit in love, as
you may as well confess, as indeed were all the lady
performers of the troupe. A quick *entrechat* of twink-
ling feet by way of salutation to the public and then
at a single bound, presto, hop ! there you are erect on
your great platform of a saddle. There is a crack of
the whip, a furious storm of sound from the brasses of
the orchestra, the truffled horse falls into his mechanical little gallop and hop ! hop ! away you go !

What an Olympian creature you were in those
days, comtesse ! The number of your years was
seventeen, and you had the legs of the Capitoline
Venus. What strength and grace ! and that perfection of beauty that it takes the New World to produce
with its crossing and blending of different strains.
The murmur ran through the throng : " It is the
beautiful Adah ! the American ! " and then, carried
off your feet by this gale of triumph, you pirouetted
away more audaciously than ever.

. The first part of the performance always wound
up with a long, crackling fire of bravos. While the
assistants were climbing upon their stools with their
hoops and streamers in preparation for the next part
of the programme, and the clown was amusing the
gallery gods by knocking his comrade flat, face downward, and then picking him up delicately by the seat
of his trousers, you were making the circuit of the
ring at a walk, perched on the edge of your saddle as
lightly as a butterfly. That was the moment that
afforded the keenest enjoyment to your admirers.
Proudly erect did you hold your goddess-like head,
garlanded with flowers, and from the skirts of gauze
that eddied and swirled about your form your sublime

pedal extremities, incased in pink silk tights, emerged
as from a cloud.

It was when you were resting on one of those occasions that you first observed the comte, now your
husband, then one of the gayest of Parisian men
about town.   There he stood in the passage that led
to the stables, tall, slender, and irreproachable in his
closely buttoned overcoat and pearl-gray hat, wearing
a sprig of lilac in his buttonhole and tapping his lips
with the gold knob of his little walking-stick.   He
was there again the next day, and the day after that,
and every day ; and your eyes would sink in confusion
as their glance met that distracted gaze of his, the despairing gaze of a man who has lost his head.

He had lost his head, indeed, but you were neither
more nor less than an honest, good girl.   You had
become an orphan when five years old, your father,
the man who did the pole act, having broken his neck
in a fall.   Then the people of the troupe adopted the
little one of "the profession" and the old Parisian
clown, Mistigris, taught you your French and a little
reading and writing.   From being the plaything and
spoiled child of those honest mountebanks,—retaining
their respect, too, through it all,—you became one of
the glories of their enterprise.   You were gaining a
livelihood in an honest way, by the display of your
physical proportions, it is true, but you were virtuous
for all that, and you remember that evening when the
comte offered you the turquoise set—in pretty cynical
terms, it must be confessed—and you came near
horsewhipping him in front of the elephants' stall in
presence of all the company.

That was the spark in the powder magazine to that

man of violent passions. Johnson's American Circus
was making a tour through France at the time. The
comte followed it to Orlèans, to Tours, to Saumur, to
Angers, and finally, at Nantes, he capped the climax of
his folly, just as a Russian might have done, and having neither father nor mother living, carried you off
and married you.

Oh, dear! how dolefully that asthmatic barrel-organ keeps on grinding out that old galop in the twilight!

What was there left to do after the first weeks of
the delirious honeymoon, that you spent in a lovely
little village at the seashore? The men at the Jockey
Club, down there in the city, were laughing to split
their sides, and the women of fashion were bursting
with anger and jealousy behind their fans. The
comte did the best thing he could under the circumstances; he went into voluntary exile for a few
years. Ah! my poor comtesse, how you yawned
with ennui in that great black palace at Florence,
where your husband had you trained and taught like
a little girl, and where you had to stomach so many
lessons and endure so many instructors. Like the
grateful woman that you were—alas! it could not be
said that you were a loving one—you wished to please
the comte and make yourself worthy of him, but that,
of course, required time, and, for all his patience, how
your husband used to wound you with his continual :
" Don't speak like that—don't do that," invariably accompanied by a freezing *my dear*, that went to your
heart!

All women are teachable. "Parvenu" is a word
for which there is no feminine. At the expiration of

three years you were an unimpeachable comtesse.
The comte, who was tired to death of the museums
and had never been able to make much of the old
masters, now gave up entirely and brought you back
to Paris. The shutters of the old hôtel that had been
closed so long flew back against the wall with a bang,
and you ate your first home-coming dinner in the vast
dining-room, seated opposite the big portrait of the
comte's great-grandfather, who had been lieutenant-
general of the king's armies; a stately old gentleman
with powdered hair he was, wearing the cordon-bleu
across his red coat, and particularly remarkable by
reason of the immense nose that runs in the family,
and he seemed to look down on you from his lofty
position with somewhat of severity.

And here, again, comtesse, solitude and melancholy were your lot. What labor, and expenditure
of money in charitable works, it cost your husband
merely to create for you a small society of priests and
priestesses ! How lugubrious, those black robes of
either sex ! For the last six years you have been
spending all your mornings in visiting schools and
nurseries, and at night you shiver in your solitary box
at the Français or the Opera. No child, and no hope
of ever having one. The years are fleeting ! And,
what is worst of all, your only feelings toward the
comte are those of deep gratitude and sincere friendship, and you have your opinion concerning him.
Oh ! a perfect gentleman in every way ; no doubt of
that, but chokeful of stupid, aristocratic prejudices,
and as tiresome as a concert. He is forty-eight, now,
and quite a type of the old beau turned milksop ;
isn't that so? a sufficiently vapid mixture of impor-

tance, dyed whiskers, prejudices, gray hats, and weak
stomach.

Why will that pitiless organ persist in playing the
galop that used in other days to time your *entrechats*
on the back of the truffled horse? Now you behold
yourself again in the middle of the arena at the end
of your "act," blowing your farewell kiss to the public
and listening delightedly to the hailstorm of applause.
Are you taking leave of your senses, comtesse?
And now again you feel your heart beating, and the
first delicious emotion of your girlhood comes back
to you, when it seemed to you that the handsome ring-
master in his scarlet coat had tenderly squeezed your
finger-tips as he led you off the track!

The sound of the organ has died away at last; the
tall skeletons of the naked trees can scarcely be discerned against the dull, dark sky that grows darker
and duller still. The valet de chambre enters respectfully, bringing in a lamp. He places it upon a stand
and says in ceremonial tones:

"Monsieur le curé de Saint Thomas-d'Aquin is
awaiting Madame la Comtesse in the drawing-room."

A CASE OF CONSCIENCE.

PAUL BOURGET.

I HAD gone into the club upon leaving the opera and stopped in front of the baccarat table. I was observing matters from my perch on one of those high chairs that are placed there for the accommodation of such players as may have been unable to find room at the board and of simple onlookers like myself. It was what was called, in club parlance, a stiff game. The banker, a good-looking young man in evening dress with a gardenia in his buttonhole, had lost about three thousand louis, but his features, those of a man about town of twenty-five, were set impassibly to conceal all evidence of emotion. All was that the corner of the mouth that kept letting fall the fateful words: "I deal—cards—baccarat—That's a point" would not have chewed so fiercely the end of an un-lighted cigar had not the cold fever of the game weighed heavily on his heart. Facing him a white-haired individual, a professional gambler, was acting as croupier, and this person took no pains to conceal his vexation at the run of ill-luck which, at every deal, was reducing the dimensions of the pile of coin and counters before him. On the other hand the most

cheerful complacency illumined the visages of the
punters who were seated around the table as they
deposited their stakes on the cloth and marked the
run of the cards on bits of paper with their lead pen-
cils, that evidence of belief in the efficacy of " com-
binations " that the least superstitious cannot help
putting their trust in as soon as they touch a card.
There can be no doubt there is some inexplicable
attraction that exercises a most potent sway over the
inner nature in the spectacle of every conflict, even if
it be only a battle between a seven and eight or an
ace and king, for there we all were, forty-nine beside
myself, standing about those gamesters and watching
that game, quite unconscious that the night was wan-
ing.   What philosopher is there who will explain this
phenomenon, that every night in Paris there are so
many people stricken with immobility after the clock
has struck twelve, just where they happen to be, no
matter where, anywhere except in their own homes
where they might find rest from their labors and their
pleasures?   Speaking for myself.I do not regret that
I yielded that night to the deleterious delight of
noctambulism, for if I had been virtuous and gone
home at a respectable hour, I should not have encountered my friend Frémiot, the painter, sitting all
alone at his small table in the salon where supper is
served and about to take a cup of bouillon, and he
would not have offered to give me a seat in his carriage
and set me down at my own door, and I should not
have heard him tell a gambling story which I set down
in black and white the very next morning as well as I
knew how and which he has given me, also, permission
to tell through the medium of my pen.

" What the devil were you doing at the club at midnight and after," he asked me, " since you were not
taking supper ? "

" I was watching them play," I replied. " I left
little Lautrec in a nice way. His losses were up
among the sixty thousand——"

Just as I uttered this sentence the coupé gave a jolt.
I had a good view of Frémiot in profile, as he was
lighting his cigarette, with that air of his, à la Francis
the First,—the Francis of Titian in the Louvre,—the
beauty of which his forty-five years, good measure,
have only served to fill out, and, as it were, solidify.
Is it not singular enough that with his shoulders of
a life-guardsman, his redundancy of form and that
mask of self-indulgent, almost gluttonous, sensuality,
this giant is yet the most delicate, the most nicely appreciative of our painters of flowers ? It is proper to
add that the voice that issues from this gladiator's
chest is most musically sweet, and his hands,—I took
note of them afresh as they were manipulating the
little taper and the cigarette,—are of a slenderness
that is almost womanlike. Besides, I know by experience that this man-at-arms is a person of exquisite
feeling, and I was not greatly astonished by the mournful confidence that my remarks about gambling had
involuntarily elicited. There was abundant time, as
it fortunately happened, for him to impart this confidence to me in all its details. As we approached the
Seine the fog grew denser and our horses had to proceed at a walk, while my companion abandoned himself entirely to remembering, *viva voce*, for my benefit,
a history that was now of very ancient date. Doubtless this impression of the past, to which the artist

was yielding, was augmented by the fantastic, shad·
owy outlines of other coupés meeting ours in that
nauseous fog that was almost black, and through
which the gas-lamps cast shafts of light here and
there, for his voice gradually fell and became very
low and gentle, as if he were going back in spirit far,
very far from me, who kept interrupting him from
time to time, just sufficiently to keep his memory
on the alert.

"For my part," he began, "I never played but
once, and, if you will believe me, at this day I cannot
even stand by and watch people playing. There are
times, you know, when one's nerves are not in the
very best condition, and then, the mere sight of a
playing-card compels me to leave the room. Ah !
that one single game of mine conjures up such terrible memories. . . . "

"Who is there that has not memories of that description ?" I interrupted. "Was not I present when
our poor friend Paul Durieu engaged in a quarrel in
that very club that we have just left on account of a
doubtful trick ? and then came that absurd duel, and
we buried him four days after I had shaken hands
with him, there, right in front of that gambling-table.
Cards always carry a bit of tragedy in their train,
and crime, and dishonor, and suicide. Still, all that
does not keep people from going back to them, just
as in Spain they go back to the bull-fights, for all the
disemboweled horses, the wounded picadors and the
slaughtered bull."

"That may be so," replied Frémiot, " but no one
ought to be the cause in his own person of one of
those tragedies, and that is just what happened to me.

Oh ! the circumstances connected with it were quite simple . . . . but when I shall have told you them you will understand how it is that the most innocent round game causes me that same little chill of horror that a man who had unintentionally killed some one while cleaning his weapon would feel when passing a shooting-gallery. It was the very year that I was admitted as a member of the club, in 1875, and that was also the year of my first success at the Salon. . . . ."

" Your *Ophelia among the Flowers ?* Don't I remember it ? I can see before me now the cluster of pink roses beside the blonde tresses, roses that were so delicately, tenderly pink, and then over the heart those black roses, as if they had been dipped in blood. Who owns that picture now ? "

" An American," said the painter with a sigh, " and he paid forty thousand francs for it, while I sold it at the time for fifteen hundred. Ah ! in those days I was not the lucky artist of whom your *alter ego* Claude Larcher unkindly said ; ' Happy Frémiot ! his occupation consists in looking all day long at a bunch of lilacs which brings him in ten thousand francs.'—Between you and me he would have done as well to select some other person than an old friend as the subject of his witticisms. But if I mention money," he continued, touching me on the arm to keep me from answering him and defending my old friend Claude, " believe me that it is not with any idea of making a merit of my commercial value. No ; I only speak of it because those fifteen hundred francs have something to do with my adventure. You must consider that I had never had such a sum in my possession at once. Times were so hard with me at the beginning. I came up to Paris with a yearly allowance from my native town of a thousand francs, and for six years I lived on it contentedly, or nearly so."

"But you couldn't have done it!" I exclaimed.

"Oh! yes; it was entirely possible," he replied, with evident pride. "A few chums and I went to housekeeping together. One of our number had a little friend who had been a cook,—pardon me, but it is the truth,—and she used to get us up two meals a day for forty-five francs a month. Room rent was fifteen francs. We had no servants; I used to make my own bed. There you have it; sixty francs procured me the necessaries of life. I was togged out like a chimney-sweep, and I never thought of such a thing as taking the omnibus. My comrades lived in the same way, and we were not so very badly off, after all. There was Tardif the sculptor, Sudre the animal painter, Rivals the engraver, and then the one who was more fortunate in his belongings than any of us, the 'Cantinier' of our 'Cantinière,' as we used to call them, Ladrat."

"Ladrat? Ladrat?" said I, rummaging my memory, "I know that name."

"You have seen it in the newspapers," rejoined the painter, upon whose countenance appeared a pained look; "but I am coming to him. This Ladrat, who carried off all the prizes at the Art School, was even in those days the victim of the most horrible of vices: he drank. What would you have? In the life that we led, almost that of laborers, where there was too little restraint, mingling constantly as we did with models and workingmen, we were exposed to many low temptations, and to that particular one more than any other. Ladrat had succumbed to it. I have to tell you that in order that presently you may not judge me too severely. It was this terrible habit, indeed, that was the cause of his losing his *prix de Rome :* he got so drunk that the composition which he had begun with the hand of a master he finished recklessly, *à la diable.* In short, in 1875 he was the only one of our number who had remained an inhabitant of Bohemia, and in the lowest part of Bohemia. He had degenerated into what we call a '*tapeur*,' a man who goes from studio to studio, borrowing a hundred sous here and something more there without any intention of ever paying. A life like that often lasts for years."

"Was he accustomed, at least, to express his gratitude by insulting his benefactor a bit ?" I asked, "like a man whom I used to know and who never came to my room without asking me for 'something for the little chapel '—that was his invariable formula—and then insulting me by way of keeping on good terms with his dignity? He comes in one day and finds me busy correcting proof for an article that was about to appear. He begs. I give him something. 'Monsieur,' he says, slipping the piece of silver into his pocket, 'if you wish to know whether a writer has talent or not, all you have to do is to find out whether his copy is accepted at the newspaper offices. If it is accepted, his sentence is pronounced ; he is a man of mediocrity. Good-by.' There was a man for you."

"No," said Frémiot, "that was not Ladrat's way. He would thank you, burst into tears, swear that he would go to work and then go out to the café and get blind-drunk on absinthe. Then he would be ashamed and keep out of the way for some days. Besides, the loans that he asked for were always ridiculously small in amount. I was not a little astonished, therefore, on returning to my house one afternoon to find a letter from him in which he requested a loan of no less a sum than two hundred francs. I had not seen anything of him for six months, and he told me a long story how he had been struggling against his vice during those six months, that he had quit drinking, that he had tried to work, that his strength had given out, that his wife was ill—he was living with his cantinière still ; in a word, one of those pitiful begging letters that it makes your heart ache to receive."

"When you believe them," I insinuated, " for one receives so many communications of that description during ten years of life in Paris, and out of the whole lot there won't be two that have a word of truth in them."

"It is better to take the chance of being duped in all the other cases than to allow those two to pass unheeded," said the painter. " Moreover, I had no reason to question Ladrat's truthfulness at the time. It so happened that I had received the fifteen hundred francs for the *Ophelia* that very day. I have always been very exact in money matters. I was not in debt to the extent of a centime and I had a sum about equivalent to the amount requested lying in my drawer. My studio was equipped and my wardrobe supplied for several years to come. I remember taking mental account of my financial position as I was brushing my coat to go out to one of my first

dinners in society, a dinner where I was received as
something of a lion, and to which I brought the appetite of a famished man and the self-sufficiency of a
schoolboy. Under such circumstances the genuine-
ness of the wines and of the compliments is taken for
granted with equal confidingness. At all events, I
compared my own situation with that of my former
chum of the South and experienced one of those
benevolent impulses that are as natural to youth as
activity and good spirits ; I took ten louis and put
them in an envelope and addressed it to Ladrat, then
I summoned my concierge. If this man had only
been on hand my old comrade would have had the
money that same evening, but as it was he happened
to be out on some errand. ' It will do as well to-morrow,' I said to myself, and went out, leaving the envelope lying on my table in readiness for him. I was
so firmly resolved in mind to do the action that I experienced in advance that mean little feeling of vanity
and self-laudation that is always inspired by the consciousness that one is doing a generous deed. It is
not a very creditable sentiment, that vanity is not, but
it is very human. To this vanity was presently added
another one, and this was of an excessively gross description. At the house where I dined I found myself
seated between two very stylish women, who seemed
to endeavor to outdo each other in the flattering at-
tentions which they lavished on me. To make my
story short, I left about eleven o'clock, completely
overmastered by one of those attacks of fatuousness
which make a man think that he owns the earth, and I
brought up at our club, under the guidance of one
of my fellow-guests who had offered me his ser-

vices to do the honors, for I knew none of the members and had not set foot in the building in the six weeks since I had been elected a member. A couple of painters had put up my name, and the prospect of the approaching annual exposition was the only thing that had determined me to allow it to be voted on.

"We entered the main saloon, and so unsophisticated was I that I had to ask my conductor the name of the game that had collected such a crowd of men about the table. He laughed, and in two words explained to me the rules of baccarat. 'Doesn't it tempt you?' he asked. 'Why shouldn't it?' I laughingly replied, 'but I have no money about me.' Then he explained to me, still laughing all the while, how I might obtain any sum that I desired, upon parole, up to three thousand francs, simply by going to the cashier and signing a note, with the understanding that the note was to be taken up within twenty-four hours. Since then I have learned that the young man tempted me to play so that he might play himself upon a beginner's luck. I should have been tempted without his assistance, however; it was one of those moments for me when I might have shouted as once another man shouted to his boatman in the storm : 'You carry Cæsar and his fortunes!' Oh! a very small Cæsar it was, and a very small fortune, for I seated myself at the table, saying to my companion : 'I am going to sign a note for five louis, and if I lose, I shall go home !'"

"And you lost, and you remained. My pocket-book could tell just the same story," I replied with a laugh, "for I also remember making good resolutions like yours and then breaking them."

" The matter was not so simple as that," rejoined
Frémiot. " My tempter, who had taken a seat beside
me, tells me to wait until I get a hand. I obey him.
The hand comes to me, I throw down a nine. I had
staked my five louis. 'Go paroli,' whispers my
adviser. I follow his instructions. I throw down an
eight. Again I double, there comes a seven, and I
win. In a word, from nine to eight and from eight to
seven I win six times hand-running. At the seventh
hand, counseled by my companion still, I bet only a
louis. I lose, but I have something like sixty louis in
front of me. My friend, who is a winner to about the
same extent, rises and says to me : 'If you are wise,
you will do as I do.' But I no longer heeded what
he told me ; I had experienced a sensation that was
too strong to allow me to part with it thus. I am not
what you call a great analyst, and I do not spend my
life in taking account of my thoughts and feelings, so
you will pardon me if I do not go into details and if I
make use of metaphors to express what was passing
in my mind. During the brief moments when I had
been winning all my being had been invaded and
possessed, as it were, by a sudden access of delirious
pride. I was excited and raised aloft by a sort of
exalted notion of my own personality. I have experienced a similar feeling when swimming through a
heavy sea. That vast, moving mass of water that
threatens you, that holds you suspended on its crest,
and that you vanquish by sheer muscular strength,
yes, that is the exact counterpart of what play was to
me in this first period—the period of winning—for I
won again in the same proportions as before, and then
still again. I laid large amounts only on my own

hand, and on that of the others my stakes were insignificant, but each time that I touched the cards my luck was so marvelous that at first a deep silence prevailed about me, succeeded, when I threw down, by something like a thrill of admiration. If it had not been for that admiration, perhaps I might have had the courage to quit. Alas! I have always had the self-esteem of Satan himself, and it has got me into a hundred scrapes, and will get me into many another before I die. I know it, I confess it, but there is no use talking; when the gallery has its eyes on me, I can't endure to have people say: 'He has backed down.' To be like that when the scene is laid upon the bridge of Arcola is sublime, but at a baccarat table, while awaiting the turn of a card, it is idiotic, and yet it was owing to nothing in the world but that childish vanity that, after having cut such a dash with my good luck, I was unwilling to submit to the bad when I saw it coming my way. For I did see it; there came a moment when I understood that I was going to lose, and the sort of clear-sightedness of victory that had made me take up my cards with absolute confidence all at once grew dim. It was written that in the course of one-sitting I was to become acquainted with all the emotions that gambling affords its devotees, for after having known the intoxicating delight of winning I had the cold, cutting intoxication of losing. Ah'! it is all the same. You know the celebrated *mot*: 'At cards, after the pleasure of winning comes the pleasure of losing.' I know of no other expression that so well depicts that morbid eagerness, that mixture of hope and despair, of cool calculation and rash daring. We look to vanquish

adverse fortune and are certain of ourselves being
vanquished. Our reasoning faculties desert us and
we play a game that we know to be absurd. And the
chips disappear ; first the white, then the red. then the
blue, and we put our name to more notes.

" After having had the self-control for ten long years
to think twice before spending thirty-five sous for cab-
hire, as I had done, we make bets of five hundred
francs without hesitating. But I will sum up the
situation for you in very few words : I had entered
the club at eleven o'clock ; when I turned the key in
my door at two I had lost and owed the whole sum of
three thousand francs that I had obtained upon my
credit, and, as I told you, it was nearly all that I
possessed in the world."

" Well, well ! " said I, "if you did not become a
confirmed gambler after such a shaking up as that, it
was because you hadn't it in you. It was enough to
ruin a man forever."

" You are right," rejoined Frémiot, " when I awoke
the following morning after the lethargic slumber that
always succeeds such sensations, the scene of the preceding night arose before my mind in its entirety and
I had but two ideas in my head : to secure my revenge
that same evening and to utilize the experience that
I had acquired in the combination of my bets. I
mentally reviewed certain deals, where I had lost and
where I should have won. All at once my eyes fell
on the envelope that was lying on the table addressed
to Ladrat. An involuntary calculation passed through
my head which made it clear to me that the gift of
that money would be a foolish sacrifice. After paying
the three thousand francs that I owed I would have

scarcely anything left. To get together a stake sufficient to allow me to return to the place that evening,
and I felt that *I could not avoid returning,* I should
have to borrow from the picture-dealer ; sell some of
my studies for what they would bring. I could scrape
together fifty louis in this way, and out of those fifty
louis I was going to divert ten for that drone, that
sot, that liar !—for I wished to prove to myself that
his letter was nothing more than a tissue of falsehoods ;
I took it up and reread it. Ah ! its accents again
penetrated my heart. But no ; I would not listen to
that voice, and I jumped hurriedly from my bed to
write a note of refusal—and I made it curt and cold,
so that the breach between my old comrade and my
pity might be irreparable. Once the note was dis-
patched I experienced a feeling of shame and remorse,
but I stifled it as well as I could among the occupations that the day had in store for me. 'Besides,' I
said to myself, by way of quieting my conscience, 'if
I win there will be plenty of time to send Ladrat the
money to-morrow—and win I shall.'"

"And you won ? " I said to him as he ceased.

"Yes," he replied, in a voice that was quite unlike
his own ; "but the next day it was too late. Immediately upon receiving my note Ladrat, who had not
been lying to me, was doubtless seized with the mad-
ness of despair. He and his companion formed the
fatal resolution of suffocating themselves. They were
found dead in their bed ; and it was I—do you understand, I,—who gave the order to break down the door.
I had come there with the two hundred francs. Yes,
it was too late. That is how it is that you remember
having read that name of Ladrat in the newspapers.

Now can you understand why it is that the mere sight of a card is horrible to me?"

"Nonsense," said I, "if you had sent him the money the night before it might have saved him for a month or two, but he would have relapsed, his vice would have reconquered him, and his end would have been the same."

"That may be true," replied the painter, "but one ought never to be that last drop of water that causes the vase to overflow."

WHO CAN TELL?

GUY DE MAUPASSANT.

I

MY God! My God! At last, then, I am to commit to paper that which happened me. But can I do it? Shall I dare do it? It is all so strange, so inexplicable, so incomprehensible, so maddening!

Were I not assured of what my eyes beheld; were I not certain that there was nothing defective in my reasoning, that there was no error in my observation, no link missing in the chain of rigorous verification, I should set myself down as a mere bedlamite, the sport of a fantastic vision. After all, who can tell?

I am to-day the inmate of an asylum for lunatics, but I took up my abode there voluntarily, from caution, from fear! Only one living soul is acquainted with my story. The physician here. I am going to write it down. Why? I do not clearly know. To rid myself of it, for I feel it within me like an intolerable nightmare.

It is this:

I have always been a recluse, a dreamer, a sort of lonely, kindly disposed philosopher, content with little, without bitterness toward man and without hate

toward Heaven. I have always lived alone by reason
of a sort of incommodity that the presence of others
affects me with. How shall I explain that? I cannot. I do not shut myself entirely from the world, I
do not refuse to converse and dine with my friends,
but when I have had them by me for any length of
time, even the nearest and dearest of them, they tire
me, they weary and depress me, and I experience a
constantly increasing, tormenting desire to see them go
away, or to go away myself and be alone.

This desire is something more than a mere fancy; it
is an irresistible necessity. And should the people
with whom I chance to be continue to remain with me,
should I be compelled, not to listen and attend to, but
to hear their conversation for a long time, some acci-
dent would doubtless happen me. Of what nature?
Ah! who can tell? Perhaps a simple fainting-fit?
Yes, probably.

I love so to be alone that I cannot even endure the
propinquity of other beings sleeping beneath my roof;
I cannot live in Paris because it is infinite torture to
me. I die a moral death, and am racked, too, in
body and nerves, by that immense throng that swarms
and lives about me, even while it sleeps. Ah! the
slumber of others is even more afflictive to me than
their speech, and I can never rest when I know, when
I feel that, parted from me by a wall, there are lives
whose thread is broken by these regular eclipses of the
reason.

Why am I thus? Who can tell? The reason, perhaps, is very simple: I weary very quickly of everything that occurs outside my own individuality. And
there are many people constituted as I am.

There are two races of us here on earth. There are those who feel the need of their fellow-men, who find the company of others a distraction and a peaceful, soothing influence, and are exasperated, exhausted, crushed by solitude as they would be by ascending a terrible glacier or crossing a desert; and again there are those whom the companionship of others serves to weary, nauseate, incommode and tire to death, while isolation tends to calm and refresh them, and bathe them in repose, in the independence and the dreamland of their fancy.

In a word, there is a normal psychical phenomenon in it. Some are formed to live the outer life, others to live the inner life. For myself, my interest in external objects is shortlived and soon exhausted, and the moment that it reaches its limits I am conscious of an intolerable wretchedness in all my being, physical and mental.

From this it has resulted that I am deeply attached, that I *was* deeply attached, to inanimate objects that assume in my eyes the importance of living beings, and that my house is, or was, a world where I lived an active and solitary life in the midst of objects, furniture, familiar *bibelots*, that were as sympathetic to my eyes as human countenances. I had filled the house with those things little by little, and had made it beautiful, and within its walls I experienced content and satisfaction; I was very happy, as one is in the arms of a loving woman whose accustomed caress has become a calm and gentle portion of our existence.

I had built this house in a handsome garden which secluded it from the public roads, and close to the gate

of a city where, when I felt like it, I might have the
resource of society, for which I felt at times an inclination.   My servants all had quarters in a remote building at the bottom of the kitchen-garden, which was
surrounded by a high wall.   The silence of my dwelling that was lost, hidden, drowned beneath the leaves
of the great trees, wrapped in the obscurity of the
night, was so restful and so grateful to me that every
night I would put off going to bed for several hours in
order that I might have the longer time to enjoy it.

There had been a performance of *Sigurd* at the
opera house in the city that evening. It was the first time
that I had heard that fine and imaginative drama and
it had afforded me keen delight.

I was returning on foot at a lively pace, and sounding phrases were ringing in my ears and graceful
visions were floating before my eyes.   It was dark,
very dark, so dark that I could scarcely distinguish the
road before me, and several times I was near tumbling
into the ditch.   From the *octroi* at the gate to my
house it is about a half-mile, perhaps a little more,
say twenty minutes of easy walking.   It was one
o'clock in the morning, one o'clock or half-past one:
the sky brightened a little ahead of me and the crescent
appeared—the cheerless crescent of the moon's last
quarter.   The crescent of the first quarter, that which
rises at four or five o'clock in the afternoon, is bright,
cheerful, touched with silver, but that which rises after
midnight is red, sullen, disheartening; it is the veritable crescent of the Sabbat.   Every night-walker must
have remarked this.   The former, even if it is no
thicker than a thread, casts a joyous little light that
makes glad the heart and projects clearly drawn shad-

ows upon the earth; the latter sheds a scanty, expiring light, so dull that it scarcely makes a shadow.

I perceived in the distance the dark mass of my garden, and I know not whence arose the feeling of disquiet that I experienced at the idea of entering it. I proceeded at a slower pace. The night was very balmy. The great group of trees seemed to me like a necropolis in which my house lay buried.

I opened my gate and entered the long alley of sycamores that stretched away toward the building, arching the road like a lofty tunnel; I threaded the dense, opaque masses of shrubbery and skirted the lawn where, in the wan darkness, the flower-beds lay in oval splashes of indistinct color.

As I drew near the house a strange disturbance took possession of my mind. I stopped. There was nothing to be heard. There was not a breath of air to move the leaves. "What ails me?" I thought. For ten years I had been coming home in this way, and never until now had I known the slightest uneasiness. I was not afraid. I have never been afraid at night. The sight of a man, a depredator, a robber, would have excited my wrath, and I should not have hesitated to try conclusions with him. Besides, I was armed. I had my revolver with me. I did not lay hand on it, however, for I wished to resist that influence of dread that was gathering within me.

What was it? A presentiment? The mysterious presentiment that takes possession of the minds of men when they behold the approach of the unfathomable? Perhaps so. Who can tell?

I felt my flesh creep as I went forward, and when at last I stood in front of my big house with its tightly closed shutters, I was sensible that I should have to wait a few minutes before opening the door and effecting an entrance. I therefore seated myself upon a bench, before the windows of my salon. I remained there, slightly trembling, my head resting against the wall, my gaze fixed upon the shadowy foliage. I noticed nothing unusual about me during those first instants. I had something of a roaring in my ears, but that is a frequent occurrence with me. At times it seems to me that I hear the passing of trains, the ringing of bells, the marching of an army.

Then this roaring soon became more distinct, more clearly defined, more unambiguous. I had deceived myself. It was not the normal beating of my pulses that had caused those noises in my ears, but a nondescript, and, at the same time, very confused sound, which emanated, beyond the possibility of a doubt, from the interior of my house.

I could distinguish it through the wall, this continuous, uninterrupted noise; a tremor, it was, rather than a noise, an aimless moving about of many objects, as if all my furniture, my chairs and tables, had been shaken and moved from their places, and dragged gently to and fro.

Oh! I questioned, for quite a length of time, the reliability of my sense of hearing, but having placed my ear against the shutter in order to gain a clearer knowledge of this strange disorder in my dwelling, I was convinced beyond room for doubt that something unnatural and incomprehensible was going on within. I was not afraid, but I was—how shall I express my meaning? I was struck dumb with astonishment. I did not draw my revolver—for I knew very well that I should have no occasion to use it. I waited.

For a long time I waited, unable to decide upon what to do, my mind perfectly clear, but wildly apprehensive. I waited, standing erect, all the while listening intently to the noise that kept increasing, assuming at times a character of intense violence and rising, seemingly, into a roar of impatience, rage, and mysterious riot.

Then, ashamed of my cowardice, I seized my bunch of keys, selected the one that I required and inserted it in the lock. I gave it two turns and pushing the door with all my strength, I sent it flying back against the wainscot. The crash sounded like the report of a musket, and lo! straightway, from top to bottom of my house, responsive to the explosive sound, there arose a fearful din. It was so unexpected, so terrible, so deafening, that I recoiled a few steps and, though well aware how futile was the proceeding, drew my revolver from its case.

I waited again. Oh! only for a short time, though. I could distinguish now an outlandish trampling on the steps of my staircase, on the wooden floors, on the carpets—a trampling not of shoes and of foot-coverings such as are worn by human beings, but of crutches, crutches of wood and crutches of iron, which rang with a noise such as is made by the beating of cymbals. And behold! there upon the threshold of my door I suddenly perceived a fauteuil, my great reading-chair, go waddling out of the house. It made off through the garden. Others followed suit, those of my drawing-room first, then the low sofas, dragging themselves along like crocodiles on their short legs,

then all the rest of my chairs, bounding and leaping
like goats, and the little footstools, which trotted off
like rabbits.

Oh, what an experience! I slipped into a clump
of bushes, where I crouched down and remained watching this migration of my goods and chattels, for they
all cleared out, every one of them, one after the other,
moving at a slow or rapid pace according to their
size and weight. My piano, my grand piano *à queue*,
went by galloping like a runaway horse, with a faint
murmur of music proceeding from its depths, and the
smaller objects—brushes, glasses, cups—glided over
the sand like ants, and the moon touched them with
phosphorescent lights so that they shone like glow-
worms. The stuffs of silk and woolen crawled, spread
themselves out in sheets after the fashion of monsters
of the sea, octopi and devil-fish. I beheld my desk
approaching, a rare *bibelot* of the last century, containing all the letters that I ever received, all my heart
history—an old history that has been cause to me of so
much suffering! And in it, too, were photographs.

Suddenly I ceased to be afraid. I rushed upon the
desk and seized it, as we seize a robber, as we seize a
woman who is trying to escape us, but it pursued its
way with irresistible momentum, and despite my
efforts, and despite my wrath, I could not even so
much as retard its progress. As I was pulling backward like a madman in resistance to this appalling
force, I fell to the ground in my conflict with it; then
it rolled me over and over, dragged me upon the sandy
path, and the pieces of furniture that were following
in its train were already begininng to tread upon me,
trampling on my legs and bruising them; then, when I

had let go my hold of it, the others passed over my body, just as a charge of cavalry passes over a trooper who has lost his saddle.

Maddened with affright, at last I succeeded in dragging myself out of the main alley and concealing myself again among the trees, from thence to watch the flight of the most unconsidered, the smallest, the most trifling objects, those the very existence of which I had been unaware of, which had been mine.

Then in the distance, in my dwelling, that now had the resonancy of other empty houses, I heard a direful sound of closing doors. Downward and from top to bottom of the house they kept slamming, until the door of the vestibule, that I myself, idiot that I was, had opened for this flitting, had swung closed, the last of all.

I immediately fled, running toward the city, and only when in its streets, where I met belated wayfarers, did I regain my self-command. I went to a hotel where I was known and rang the bell. I had beaten my clothing with my hands in order to remove from it the traces of dust, and I told them that I had lost my bunch of keys, among which was that of the garden where my servants were sleeping in an isolated house, behind the inclosing wall that served to protect my fruits and vegetables from the visit of the spoiler.

I buried myself up to the eyes in the bed which they gave me, but I could not sleep and passed the time until daybreak listening to the thumping of my heart. I had given orders that my household should be apprised of my presence there at earliest dawn, and at seven o'clock in the morning my valet-de-chambre knocked at my door. His face bore an aspect of consternation.

"A great misfortune happened last night, sir," said he.

"What was it?"

"All monsieur's furniture was stolen—all, everything, even to the smallest objects."

The intelligence gave me pleasure. Why? Who can tell? It rendered me master of myself and my actions, it gave me an opportunity to dissemble, to say nothing to any one of what my eyes had seen, to conceal it, to bury it at the bottom of my consciousness like a dread secret. I made answer:

"Then those must be the same parties who stole my keys from me. The police must be notified at once. I will get up and be with you in a few moments."

The investigation lasted five months. No discovery was made; no trace of the robbers was found, nor was the least bit of my furniture recovered. Parbleu! If I had told what I knew—if I had told—they would have locked me up, *me*—not the thieves, but the man who had been capable of seeing such things.

Oh! I knew enough to hold my tongue. I did not refurnish my house, however. There would have been no use in doing that; the same thing would have happened again. I did not wish to return to it. I did not return to it. I never set eyes on it again.

I came and lived at Paris, at the hotel, and I consulted physicians upon my nervous condition, which had been the cause of much anxiety to me since that ill-omened night. They urged me to travel. I followed their advice,

II

I COMMENCED by a trip to Italy. The sunlight was beneficial to me. I spent six months in wandering from Genoa to Venice, from Venice to Florence, from Florence to Rome, from Rome to Naples. Then I made a tour through Sicily, an interesting country to visit on account of its natural advantages and its monuments, relics of the Greeks and Normans. I passed over into Africa, I traversed unmolested that peaceful, yellow desert that is trod by camels, gazelles and vagabond Arabs, where the light, transparent atmosphere harbors no haunting visions, by night more than by day.

I re-entered France by way of Marseilles, and notwithstanding the gayety of the Provençals, the paler light of their country afflicted me with sadness. In returning to the continent I experienced the strange sensation of a sick man who believes that he is cured and who is warned by a dull pain that the embers of his disease are still alive.

Then I returned to Paris. I grew tired of life there at the expiration of a month. This was in the autumn, and I felt a desire to make a trip through Normandy before the setting in of winter, a country that I was unacquainted with.

I took Rouen as my starting-point, as a matter of course, and for a week I wandered in a state of distracted, delighted enthusiasm about the streets of this middle-age city, this surprising museum of wonderful Gothic monuments.

Now, as I was picking my way one afternoon, about

four o'clock, along an outlandish street through which
flows an ink-black stream that they call the "Eau de
Robec," my attention, which had been devoted to the
fantastic and antiquated aspect of the houses, was suddenly attracted by the sight of a row of second-hand
dealers' shops that adjoined each other, door by door.

Ah! they had made good choice of their location,
those sordid traffickers in the frippery of the past, in
that quaint, narrow street, over that repulsive water-
course, beneath those peaked roofs of tile or slate on
which the old-fashioned weathercocks were still creaking as they turned with the wind!

Heaped confusedly together in the depths of the
dark shops could be seen carved chests, pottery of
Rouen, of Nevers, of Moustiers, painted statues and
others of oak, images of Christ, of the Virgin and of
the saints, ecclesiastical ornaments, chasubles, copes,
even sacred vases and an old tabernacle of gilded wood
that had ceased to be a residence of the Divinity.
Oh! those strange caverns in those lofty houses, in
those wide, deep houses that were filled, from garret
to cellar, with objects of every description that seemed
to have outlived their usefulness, that had survived
their natural owners, their age, their time, their cus-
toms, to be purchased as curiosities by new genera-
tions!

My old passion for bric-à-brac came to life again in
this antiquarian region. I went from shop to shop,
crossing in a couple of strides the bridges of four rot-
ting planks that spanned the unsavory current of the
Eau de Robec.

Miséricorde! How it upset me! At the edge of a
vault that was stuffed full with all sorts of things, and

that seemed to be the entrance to the catacombs of a
graveyard of old furniture, one of my finest armoires
greeted my eyes. I approached it trembling in every
limb, trembling to such a degree that I dared not touch
it. I put forth my hand to touch it; I hesitated and
drew it back. And yet there could be no doubt of its
identity; a unique armoire of the time of Louis XIII.,
that any one who had seen it but once would recognize without difficulty. Suddenly casting my eyes a
little further, toward the more dimly lighted depths of
this gallery, they lighted on three of my fauteuils covered with fine-stitch tapestry, then, further still, I perceived my two Henri II. tables, such rarities that people used to come from Paris merely for a look at them.

Think! just think what my feelings must have been!

And I advanced, paralyzed, in a fever of emotion;
still, I advanced—for I am a brave man—I advanced as
a knight of the dark ages might have penetrated a lair
of necromancers. As I proceeded I found everything
that had belonged to me, my chandeliers, my books,
my pictures, my stuffs of silk and woolen, my arms,
everything, excepting the desk that contained my letters, and of that I could see nothing anywhere.

I kept on and on, descending into dark galleries only
to climb out of them again immediately and mount to
floors above. I was alone. I called; no one responded.
I was alone; there was not a soul in that great house
with its labyrinthine passages.

Night came on, and I had to sit down, in the darkness, on one of my own chairs, for I would not go
away. Every now and then I shouted: "Halloa!
halloa! some one!"

I had been there, certainly, more than an hour,

when I heard footsteps, soft, slow footsteps, I could
not tell where.   I came near taking to my heels, but
plucking up my courage I called again and saw a light
in the adjacent apartment.

"Who is there?" a voice said.

"A purchaser!" I replied.

The answer came: "It is very late to enter a shop
in this manner."

I answered: "I have been waiting for you for more
than an hour."

"You can come again to-morrow."

"To-morrow I shall have left Rouen."

I dared not go forward, and he did not come to me.
I could still see the light of his lamp, shining on a
tapestry where two angels were represented hovering
over the dead of a field of battle.   It, also, was my
property.   I said: ،

"Well!   Are you coming?"

"I await you here," he replied.

I arose and went toward him.

In the middle of a great room was a little bit of a
man, very little and very fat, phenomenally fat, a
most repulsive sight to see.

He had a thin beard, composed of straggling, yellowish hairs of unequal length, and not the sign of a hair
on his head!   Not a hair!   As he held his candle up
at arm's length to get a better view of me, his cranium
appeared to me like a small moon in that immense
room crowded with old furniture.   His face was
wrinkled and swollen, and the eyes were imperceptible.

I made a bargain with him for three chairs which
were my property, and paid a large sum for them,
money down, merely giving him the number of my

room at the hotel. They were to be delivered the following day before nine o'clock.

Then I took my departure. He escorted me to his door with a great show of politeness.

After that I called upon the *commissaire central* of the police of the city, to whom I related the story of the theft of my furniture and the discovery that I had just made. He immediately telegraphed the public prosecutor who had conducted the investigation of the robbery for full particulars, requesting me to await the answer. In an hour's time it came and was satisfactory to me in every respect.

"I am going to have this man arrested and examine him at once," he said to me, "for he may suspect something and take steps to get rid of your property. You had better go and get your dinner and come back here in two hours; I will have him here and will put him through another examination in your presence."

"I shall be glad to do so, sir, and I thank you with all my heart."

I went to my hotel and dined, and ate with a better appetite than I could have believed possible. I was well pleased with the turn affairs had taken. He was in custody.

Two hours later I returned to the police official, who was waiting for me.

"Well, sir," he said, as he caught sight of me, "we have not succeeded in finding your man. My men have not been able to lay hands on him."

Ah! I experienced a sickening feeling.

"But—you found his house, did you not?" I inquired.

"Certainly. We shall put a guard over it and keep a sharp lookout until he comes back. As to the man, he has disappeared."

"Disappeared?"

"Disappeared. He generally passes his evenings with his neighbor, the widow Bidoin, who is also a second-hand dealer and a good-for-nothing fortune-teller. She has not seen him this evening and can give us no intelligence of him. We shall have to wait until to-morrow."

I went away. Ah! how sinister, how haunted and dread-inspiring the streets of Rouen appeared to me that night!

I slept so badly, awakening in a nightmare from every one of my short naps.

As I did not wish to appear unduly anxious or impatient, I waited the next morning until it was ten o'clock before going to the police-station.

Nothing more had been seen of the merchant. His shop remained closed.

The commissaire said to me:

"I have taken all the necessary steps. The public prosecutor has been fully apprised of the circumstances of the case; we will go together to that shop and have it opened, and you will point out to me your property."

A coupé conveyed us thither. There were policemen, together with a locksmith, standing in front of the shop-door, which was quickly opened.

When we had effected an entrance I could see nothing of my armoire, my fauteuils, my tables; nothing, not a thing of the furniture that had been in my house, absolutely nothing, while the night before I could not take a step without encountering some article that had been mine.

The commissaire, in his bewilderment, at first looked at me distrustfully.

"Mon Dieu, monsieur," I said, "the disappearance of that furniture and that of the merchant form a strange coincidence."

He smiled. "It is true. You made a mistake in buying and paying for your bibelots yesterday. It put him on his guard."

I replied: "What I cannot see through is, how it is that the space that was occupied by my furniture is now filled with other chattels."

"Oh!" the commissaire answered, "he had all the night to work in, and accomplices, no doubt. There must be a communication between this house and the adjoining ones. Never fear, sir; I am going to follow this matter up closely. The scamp can't escape us for long, since we have a watch at the entrance of his den."

.   .   .   .   .   .

Ah! my heart, my heart, my poor heart; how it beat and throbbed!

.   .   .   .   .   .

I remained at Rouen fifteen days. The man did not return. Parbleu! parbleu! A man like that, who could have expected to capture him, or do aught to interfere with his plans?

Now, on the sixteenth day, in the morning, I received this strange letter from my gardener, whom I had made the guardian of my pillaged and empty house:

Monsieur :

I have the honor of informing Monsieur that something happened last night that no one can understand, the police no more
than the rest of us. All the furniture was returned, all, without
exception, everything, even to the smallest article. The house is
now exactly as it was the day before the robbery. It is enough
to drive one wild. It occurred during the night between Friday
and Saturday. The roads are cut up as if everything had been
dragged from the gate to the door. It was the same on the day
of the disappearance.

We await the arrival of Monsieur, of whom I am the very hum-
ble servant.

PHILIPPE RAUDIN.

Oh! no, oh! no, oh! no. I will not go back there!
I took the letter to the commissaire of Rouen.

"It is a very adroit restitution," said he. "We
must dissemble and lay low. We will pinch the man
one of these days!"

.   .   .   .

But he has not been pinched. No. They have not
pinched him, and I am afraid of him, now, as if he
were a wild beast let loose at my heels.

Undiscoverable! he is undiscoverable, this monster with a skull like a full moon! He will never be
caught. He will never return to his home. What
matters it to him. I am the only cne that he fears to
meet, and I won't do it.

I won't! I won't! I won't!

And if he does return, if he takes possession of his
shop again, who is there that can prove that he had my
furniture there? My testimony is all there is against
him, and I feel that it is beginning to be discredited.

Ah! but no! it was no longer possible to lead such
a life. And then I could not keep the secret of what

I had seen. I could not keep on living like the rest of the world with the dread that such things might happen me again.

I came and found the doctor who has charge of this asylum and told him everything.

After he had examined me at great length, he said:

"Would you agree to remain here for some time, monsieur?"

"Very gladly, monsieur."

"You have means of your own?"

"Yes, monsieur."

"Do you wish a pavilion to yourself?"

"Yes, monsieur."

"Shall you wish to see friends?"

"No, monsieur; no, not a soul. The man of Rouen, in his desire for vengeance, might make bold to come and pursue me here."

.   .   .   .

And so I am here alone, all alone, for three months, now. My mind is at ease, nearly. I fear but one thing: If the antiquary should become crazy—and if they should bring him to this asylum—— The very prisoners themselves are not secure——

THE DROWNED MAN.

GUY DE MAUPASSANT

1

EVERY one in Fécamp was acquainted with the
story of Mother Patin. There could be no doubt
that Mother Patin had not had a happy life of it with
her man, for during his lifetime her man had used to
thrash her as they thrash the wheat on the barn-floor.

He was captain of a fishing-boat, and had married
her, long ago, although she was poor, for her good
looks.

Patin, a good sailor, but very much of a brute, was
a frequenter of Father Auban's pothouse, where, on
ordinary days, he would drink four or five small
glasses of tanglefoot, and on days when the luck was
good out at sea eight or ten, and even more, according to his gayety of heart, as he used to say.

The tanglefoot was served to the customers by
Father Auban's daughter, a comely brunette of pleasing aspect, who attracted custom to the house by dint
of her good looks alone, for she had never been the
subject of scandal.

At the commencement of Patin's visits to the pot-

house he would be content to gaze upon her, and his
remarks to her would be simply such as were demanded by common politeness, the reasonable remarks
of a modest young man. When he had taken his first
glass of tanglefoot he began to discover that she was
handsomer than before; at the second he would make
eyes at her; at the third he would say: "If you were
only so minded, Mam'zelle Désirée——" without ever
concluding his sentence; at the fourth he would be
pulling her by her petticoats and trying to kiss her;
and when he reached his tenth, then it was Father
Auban who waited on the customers.

The old wineseller, who was up to all the tricks of
his trade, used to send Désirée around among the
tables to keep the drinking up to a satisfactory pitch,
and Désirée, who was Father Auban's own worthy
daughter, would whisk her petticoats to and fro among
the drinkers and exchange pleasantries with them, a
smile on her lips and malice in her eye.

Through drinking many glasses of tanglefoot Désirée's image became so deeply imprinted on Patin's
heart that he was thinking of her constantly, even
while he was out at sea, while he was casting his nets
into the water, away out on the broad ocean, on the
nights when the wind blew and the nights when it
was calm, on the nights when the moon shone and the
nights when it was dark. He thought of her as he
held the tiller in the stern of his boat, while his four
shipmates were slumbering with their heads pillowed
on their arms. He always beheld her smiling on him,
raising her shoulder to pour out the yellow brandy,
and then going away, saying:

"There! Are you satisfied?"

And so, by reason of thus keeping her before his eyes and in his mind, he became possessed of such an inordinate desire of having her to wife that he asked her hand in marriage.

He was well to do, owning his vessel, his nets, and a house on the Retenue down by the end of the beach, while Father Auban had nothing. He was consequently accepted with avidity, and the wedding was celebrated at the earliest moment possible, both sides, for different reasons of their own, being desirous to have the matter over and ended.

When he had been married three days, however, Patin did not understand at all how he could ever have believed that Désirée was different from other women. True as gospel, he must have been a blockhead to saddle himself with a woman as poor as a church mouse, who had bewitched him with her brandy, that was as plain as a pikestaff, with brandy in which she had put some unclean nostrum to addle his brain. And he swore, and he swore, at all times of the tide, and he smashed his pipe between his teeth, and he blew up his crew; and when he had ripped and stormed, up hill and down, with all the hard words in the dictionary and against everything that he could think of, he would expectorate what bile was left in his stomach upon the fishes and the lobsters as he took them from the nets, one by one, and never consigned them to the hampers without a running accompaniment of insult and unseemly language.

Then when he got home, where his wife, old Auban's daughter, was at the mercy of his tongue and fist, it was not long before he began to treat her as the lowest of the low. Then, as she endured it all with

resignation, accustomed as she had been to the out-
bursts of the paternal abode, her calmness only exasperated him the more, and one night he gave her a
thumping. After that life became a terrible affair in
his house.

For ten years all the talk on the Retenue was of the
kicks and cuffs that Patin gave his wife, and how he
never spoke to her without swearing at her, with or
without occasion. He had, in truth, a way of swearing that was all his own, a redundancy of idiom and a
stentorian lung power such as were possessed by no
other man in Fécamp. The moment that his boat
was sighted off .the entrance of the harbor, returning
from the fishing-ground, folks waited to hear the first
volley that he would let fly from his deck upon the
wharf so soon as he should catch the first glimpse of
his helpmate's white cap.

On days when there was a heavy sea on he would
be standing at the stern managing his vessel, one eye
on the bow and one on the canvas, and notwithstanding the care that was necessitated by the narrow and
difficult passage, notwithstanding the great waves that
came rolling into the contracted channel, mountain-
high, he would manage to keep an eye on the women
who stood there, drenched by the spray of the breaking waves, waiting for their sailor lads, so that he
might recognize his own wife, old Auban's daughter,
the good-for-nothing huzzy!

Then, as soon as he set eyes on her, unmindful of
the roaring of the wind and waves, he would salute
her with a deafening bellow of abuse, which detonated
from his gullet with such explosive violence that every
one laughed, though they all felt much compassion for

her. When the boat had got up to the wharf, too, he
had a way of discharging his ballast of politeness, to
make use of his own expression, while at the same time
discharging his load of fish, that attracted about his
fasts all the blackguards and all the idlers of the harbor.

These things would pour from his mouth, at one
time terrific and of short duration, like the report of a
cannon, and again reverberating like thunder-claps,
which for five minutes at a time would keep up such a
rolling fire of bad language that it seemed as if all the
tempests of the Everlasting Father must have their
home within his breast.

When, after this performance, he had left his vessel
and was face to face with her amid the throng of gap-
ing idlers and fishwives, he would summon up from
the mysterious recesses of his memory an entirely
fresh assortment of outrages and insults, and in this
way would conduct her home to their dwelling, she
preceding, he following, she weeping, he shouting at
the top of his voice.

Then, when the doors were closed and they were
alone together, he would beat her upon the most
trifling pretext. Anything sufficed him for an excuse
for raising his hand to her, and when he had once begun he never stopped, brutally casting in her face at
such times the true reasons of his hatred. At every
slap, at every cuff he would roar: "Ah! you beggar,
you! You scarecrow, you starveling! A pretty stroke
of business I made of it the day when I washed my
mouth with the vile stuff of that rascally old father of
yours!"

She was living, now, poor woman, in a never-ceasing

state of terror, in a continuous tremor of body and of mind, in the despairing expectation of indignities and blows.

And that went on for ten years. She was so entirely cowed that she never spoke to any one, no matter whom, without changing color; she could think of nothing but the beatings with which she was constantly threatened, and she had become yellower, leaner, and drier than a smoked herring.

II

ONE night, when her husband was away at sea, she was suddenly awakened by that growling, as of wild beasts, that the wind makes when it rushes upon us like a dog that has broken his chain. She was frightened and sat up in bed, then, hearing it no more, laid down again, but almost instantly there came a roaring in the chimney that seemed to make the whole house tremble, and it extended over all the heavens, as if a drove of maddened animals had passed, snorting and bellowing, through space.

Then she arose and hurried to the harbor. Other women came flocking there from every quarter, bearing lanterns. The men came running up, and they all stood looking out to sea, watching the foam on the crest of the waves as it shone in the darkness of the night.

The storm lasted fifteen hours. There were eleven sailors who never came back, and Patin was one of them.

What was left of his vessel, the *Little Emily*, was picked up over Dieppe way. The bodies of his men were recovered in the neighborhood of Saint Valéry,

but his was never found. As the boat's hull seemed
to have been cut in two, his wife for a long time expected, and feared, to see him come home, for if there
had been a collision it might well be that the colliding
vessel had taken him aboard, him alone of all the crew,
and carried him off to distant parts.

By slow degrees she familiarized herself with the
thought that she was a widow, but would never fail to
be startled whenever a neighbor or a beggar or a
vagrant peddler unexpectedly entered her house.

As she was passing along the Rue aux Juifs one
afternoon, about four years after her husband's disappearance, she stopped in front of an old sea-captain's
house who had died a short time before, and whose
household goods were being auctioned off.

It so chanced that just at that moment they were
bidding on a parrot, a green parrot with a blue head,
who was considering the assemblage with an air of dejection and anxiety.

"Three francs!" exclaimed the auctioneer; "three
francs, for a bird that can talk like a lawyer!"

A friend of the widow Patin gave her a nudge with
her elbow:

"You've got plenty of money," she said; "you
ought to buy that bird. It would be company for
you; it's worth more than thirty francs, that bird is.
You could get twenty or twenty-five for it, any time
you wanted to sell it."

"Four francs! ladies, four francs!" the man continued. "He can sing vespers and preach as good a
sermon as M. the curé. He is a wonder—a phenomenon!"

Madame Patin raised the bid fifty centimes and the

hook-billed bird was knocked down to her, and she walked off, carrying it with her in a little cage.

When she got home she hung up the cage, and as she was opening the wire door to give the brute a drink he snapped at her finger with his beak and bit it so that the blood came.

"Ah! how cross he is," she said.

Nevertheless she gave him some hemp-seed and corn to eat and then left him to smooth down his rumpled feathers, which he did, casting meanwhile sly, stealthy glances upon his new abode and his new mistress.

The day was just breaking next morning when the widow heard a voice, as distinct as could be, a loud, ringing, resounding voice, old Patin's voice, shouting:

"Will you get up, carrion!"

Her fright was so great that she drew the sheets up over her head, for every morning, in the old days, as soon as he had fairly got his eyes open, her deceased husband had yelled in her ears those five words that were so familiar to her.

Trembling in every limb, curled up like a ball and her back made ready to receive the shower of blows that she already felt in anticipation, she murmured, sinking her face still deeper into the pillow:

"Holy Father, there he is! Holy Father, there he is! He is back again, Holy Father!"

The minutes passed; no further sound disturbed the silence of the chamber. Then, quaking still with her great fear, she protruded her head from the bedclothes in the certainty that she should behold him there, watching her, prepared to beat her.

She saw nothing, nothing but a sunbeam shining through the window-pane, and she thought:

"He has hidden himself away somewhere, depend
on 't."

She waited a long time, then, her fears being somewhat reassured, came to the conclusion:

"I must have been dreaming, since he don't come
out and show himself."

She was just closing her eyes again, a little embold-
ened by this reflection, when, close to her ear, as it
seemed, exploded the wrathful voice, the drowned
man's voice of thunder, vociferating:

"Name of a name, of a name, of a name, *will* you
get up, you——!"

She sprang from her bed, impelled by the instinct of
obedience, by the blind obedience of a woman who
has known many a beating, who remembers still, after
four years have gone by, and who will always remember and always obey that dread voice. And she said:

"Here I am, Patin; what do you want?"

But Patin answered not.

Then she looked about her wildly, distractedly;
then she searched the room through, every part of it,
the closets, the fireplace, beneath the bed, and found
no one; and at last she sank into a chair, beside herself with terror, certain that Patin's spirit, divested of
its earthly garb, was there, at her side, returned
again to earth to torment her.

All at once she thought of the garret, which could
be reached from outside by means of a ladder. There
could be no doubt of it, he had concealed himself up
there the better to surprise her. It must have been
that the savages had held him prisoner upon some distant coast and he had been unable to escape them
until then, and now he was returned, more ruffianly

than ever.   The mere ring of his voice was clear
enough evidence of that.

Raising her face toward the ceiling, she asked:

"Are you up there, Patin?"

Patin made no answer.

Then she left the house, and, with a horrible fear that
seemed to freeze her very heart, climbed the ladder,
threw back the shutter of the window, looked into the
room, saw nothing, entered, searched, and found
nothing.

Seating herself upon a bundle of straw she gave way
to tears, but while she sat there sobbing, transpierced
by a weird and breathless terror, in her chamber below
she heard Patin going over his story.   His anger
seemed to have subsided, he was calmer, and this was
what he was saying:

"Dirty weather!   High wind!   Dirty weather!
I've had no breakfast, name of a name!"

She shouted to him through the ceiling:

"Here I am, Patin; I'm going to make the soup for
you.   Don't be angry, I'm coming."   And she has-
tened down the ladder.   There was no one in the
room.

She felt her strength failing her, as if Death had
touched her with his finger, and was about to take to
her heels and ask protection from the neighbors when
the voice, right at her ear, shouted:

"I've had no breakfast, name of a name!"

And there was the parrot in his cage, watching her
with his round, sly, wicked eye.

She looked at him, too, as if her senses were leaving
her, muttering:

"Ah! it's you!"

The bird continued, with a movement of its head:
"Wait, wait, wait, I'll teach you to dawdle!"

What passed through her mind? She felt, she knew
that it was no other than he, the dead man, who had returned; who had disguised himself in the feathers of
this brute to begin afresh his old work of torment; that
he would swear at her all day long, as he had done
before, and bite her, and yell at her with taunting
words to raise the neighbors and make them laugh.
Then she made a wild rush, opened the cage, seized
the bird, which tore her flesh with beak and claws in
its struggle to defend itself; but she held him with all
her strength, in both her hands, and throwing herself
upon the floor she rolled upon him with the frenzy of
one possessed, crushed him, reduced him to a rag of
flesh, a small, green object, devoid of speech or movement and which dangled from her hand inanimate;
then, taking a dish-clout, she wrapped the shapeless
mass in it as in a shroud, went out by the door,
barefooted, in her chemise, crossed the wharf,
against which the sea was breaking in small waves,
and, shaking out the cloth, let fall into the water that
small dead object that was like nothing so much as a
handful of grass; then she returned to the house, and
throwing herself upon her knees before the empty cage,
all wrought up by what she had done, sought forgive-
ness from God the Comforter, sobbing, the while, as
if she had been guilty of some horrible crime.

THE CIGARETTE.

JULES CLARETIE.

"IT was in the time of the war of Don Carlos, the last one, yes, sir. All this Basque country, these environs of Saint Sebastian, these mountains of Guipuzcoa, they have all reeked with blood and powder—and that for months, for long, long months. You must have seen many blackened and torn walls in the country. Yes, you say? Well! those were once farms, houses, abodes of life and happiness; now they are ruins, graveyards, almost. That is war.

"They fought—you should have seen them fight! The Carlists on one side, the soldiers of the government at Madrid on the other. These roads, look you, have beheld long trains of dead and wounded, poor lads who knew that they were doomed to die, and who asked themselves why—why? Civil wars, ah! fine things those civil wars are! And when one thinks that it may commence again to-morrow—who knows? Men are such fools!

"You see how it was; they bring us word, one fine morning, that the king is there, that Don Carlos is come; then it is all plain sailing, the old leaven rises,

and you see our Basque peasants hastening to the pretender and supplying him with an army. That means
wearing a fine uniform, with the flat cap cocked over
the ear, and coming into the villages with trumpets
sounding and, when they have stacked muskets, giving
the girls a dance on the green to the accompaniment
of their singing. It means, too, that they will hear
the bullets whistle, for our Basques are brave, live
frugally and die well. But good-by to the harvests,
to the apple trees, to the daily life of their poor world!
They fought all day long; they fought for three years.
At a given moment, sir, you might have seen all these
miry roads filled with men of the same country whose
only thought it was to cut one another's throat.

"You know the story of the siege of Bilbao, that the
Carlists squeezed as if they had it in a vise. The city
had to be relieved, and Don Carlos' soldiers held the
passes between Saint Sebastian and Bilbao, repelled
the attacks that were made on them and thrashed the
columns of troops that were hurled against them with
the bayonet. The Carlist chief who commanded in
this quarter was named Zucarraga. He was a hero,
sir! An old army officer, who had returned his sword
to the government of Madrid, saying: 'Give it to some
one else and let it be turned against my breast; the
sword that I shall carry henceforth I will receive from
my rightful king.' Thirty years old he was, and handsome, tall, superb. He held the mountains about
here, and never let go his hold. They sent their best
troops against him, and every day they sent fresh
troops. We saw them come back, the poor halting,
crippled soldiers, with their decimated ranks and their
officers borne on bloody litters, shaking their heads

mournfully and saying: 'See! it is for the sake of
Spain that they are murdering Spain!'

"That Zucarraga! His reputation increased with
every reverse of the national army. Folks said to
one another: 'It is Thomas Zumalacarregui come to
life again!' Zumalacarregui, you know, the paladin
of the other Carlist war, in the old times. Even his
name reminded people of the other one, and this made
Zucarraga a hero of romance, a general whose name
was sung in the songs of the people, like the Cid.

"The general who was in command at Hernani—
yes, the little town where, as the *Gazette* told us the
other day, your great writer Hugo passed his childhood and the name of which he has made illustrious—the general, who kept sending his poor soldiers forward against the passes' that Zucarraga was
defending, was wild with rage. He had promised
himself that he would force a passage, crush the flat-
capped people and pierce their lines and relieve Bilbao. Ah! yes, indeed! Every attack was followed
by a defeat, every assault resulted in something that
was very near a rout. The dispirited troops returned
with hanging head and heavy foot, leaving their dead
lying by the roadside.

"As General Garrido one evening, up there on the
Place de l'Ayuntamiento, was watching his shattered
battalions as they slowly and sullenly re-entered their
cantonments, while in the distance, over in the direction of the mountains, Zucarraga's artillery was growling away as usual and we were looking at the smoke rising, rising from the depths of the valley along the
bloodstained mountain-side, the general, I say—his
gray hairs surmounted by his *ros*, his ros that in days

gone by had been pierced by the bullets of the Moors
—said, his fists clenched and his eyes flashing like a
mitrailleuse:

"'Ah! that Zucarraga! that Zucarraga! that
wretch of a Zucarraga! I would give my skin for
his! And there is a fortune waiting for the man that
kills him!'

"He was beside himself with rage, shedding bitter
tears to see his regiments melting away like the snow
among these defiles. It seemed to him as if all those
brave boys that lay scattered along the roadside were
children of his own whom he had lost, whom some one
had taken from him and slaughtered. And who had
done this? Zucarraga, Zucarraga's Basques, the
Carlists!

"The words were scarcely out of old Garrido's mouth
when, there on that Place that was swarming with
troops, upon which the shades of night were descending, a tall, good-looking young fellow stepped forward
and planted himself in front of the general's staff and,
looking the old officer straight in the eye, brusquely
said:

"'If I should kill Zucarraga, would you give me
whatever I might ask you for?'

"'Who are you?' said Garrido.

"'Juan Araquil, a lad of this neighborhood. A
man who is not afraid of death, but who has sworn
that he will be rich.'

"The general eyed the man from head to foot.
'You are from Guipuzcoa? How is it that you are not
with the army of Don Carlos?'

"'Because there is nothing that I care for in this
world, excepting a woman whom I love.'

"'A fiancée?'

"'Ah! I wish it were a fiancée! No, a farmer's daughter, with too much wealth for me, who am too poor and want to get money to win her.'

"He was well known throughout the countryside, was this Araquil, and we were all acquainted with his history, his love for the daughter of old Chegaray, a warm Guipuzcoa farmer, controlling four or five farms in this neighborhood and owner of hillsides where the apple trees bent beneath their weight of fruit and yielded cider in quantities—oh! it would have done you good to see. I have never tasted your French cider that they talk so much about, but isn't it true that it is not as good as our cider of Guipuzcoa?—It is not I who make the assertion.

"Father Chegaray lived between Hernani and fort Santa Barbara, which you may have seen on your way here from Saint Sebastian. Old Chegaray was as proud of Pepa, his daughter, as an Andalusian woman is of her jewels. He would hold his head very erect when he conducted his little girl to vespers or to the *romerias*, at our season of merrymaking. It is at the romerias that the young folks become engaged to one another, frequently without the parents being consulted. How quickly it comes about, in the midst of laughter and the dance! A heart is captured and a life is given in exchange.

"Down yonder in the valley at Loyola, not very far from here, there lived in those days a tall, good-looking young scapegrace who was eternally fluttering about the pretty girls, and who had all the qualities, faith, which find favor in the eyes of young women, but not a single one of those that are regarded kindly

by the young women's parents. It was that same
Araquil who had come to old General Garrido to tell
the tale of his aspirations. A lively youth, this youngster was, always ready for some mad frolic; first in the
game of tennis, strong as a horse and agile as a
monkey, devil-may-care, prone to fisticuffs; killing his
bulls in their impromptu *novilladas* as deftly as a professional *espada* and quite willing to get a broken head
or a perforated hide upon any pretext, or upon none
at all, for that matter. And bearing himself like a
king, withal, with the air of a cavalier and a chin that
was always freshly shaven, with the form of a Hercu-
les and the hand of a woman. In addition to all this
he had not a sou to his name, living from hand to
mouth, now on the stakes of a tennis-match won from
the lads of Bilbao or Tolosa, now on the proceeds of
a bet made with the *toreros*, whom he braved—oh! so
arrogantly!—in the bull-ring and in the combat with
knives. At Saint Sebastian one day, when the bewildered *cuadrilla* could not dispose of the bull, a furious
black brute with flanks specked with great spots of red
foam, slavering at the mouth with blood and froth,
Juan Araquil begins to hiss, and the people in the
circus, spectators and toreros, shout: 'Well, then,
into the ring with you, into the ring!' Ah! Juan
did not hesitate, sir. He rises, he leaps over the railing, he takes from the astounded espada—perhaps
he was pleased with the prospect of soon seeing this
great fool impaled on the bull's horns—he takes the
short-handled sword, you know, he takes it like that,
and planting himself squarely before the animal, he
looks him in the face, he laughs in his nostrils, he
makes a forward thrust with the point,—that way,—

just as el Tato or Lagartijo might have done, and bam, boum, the bull falls all in a lump, while Juan Araquil turns to the toreros and says to them, laughing all the while: 'You see, you fellows—it is easy enough!'

"But that is not the whole of the story. It made the toreros furious, wild with anger, to hear the shouts of the crowd, the bravos with which they saluted Araquil and the hisses that they visited upon the espada; they get together and surround Araquil, intending to take him to task for his audacity and perhaps, eh! parbleu, play him some nasty trick. Ah! well, very good! Araquil gives a look at this circle of enraged men. He gathers himself up, jumps clean over the head of the torero who is in front of him and makes his escape to the benches, leaving unbroken the circle that was about to close in on him and kill him. That evening he and one of the toreros fought with knives behind the circus and the torero buried his knife right in his chest. Juan Araquil kept his bed for two weeks, but when the two weeks were up he was as sound as ever. He was ready to kill another bull, and a torero as well, this time, should there be need of it.

"When our toreros are wounded, you know, they don't regard it as a matter of much consequence. Their skin unites again, their flesh heals quickly. They are carried off riddled with wounds from the bulls' horns, they are given up for dead—a sign of the cross, well, *requiescat!*—and at the month's end there they are, back again, with the espada or the banderilla in their hand. That was the kind of clay that Juan Araquil was made of! A slash of a knife or a blow from a tennis-racket—nothing hurt him. He was a man of iron, a genuine Basque.

"Then, besides, he had remedies for wounds, for he dabbled a little in almost everything and had associated with the bone-setters and the folks who make drugs and ointments out of the herbs that grow on the mountain to set you on your feet when there is anything wrong with you. He had even caused to be compounded for himself a sort of extract of some malignant plants or other, I don't know exactly what— flowers of aconite, or something of that description— which he carried about with him in a ring on his finger, saying that a man should always have it in his power to be master of his own life, and that sometimes, when one wishes to make an end of it, he fails to find his knife ready at hand. A knife, that may be taken from you; a ring, no—and by a simple movement of the finger to the lips, you are free. There! He was a man, was that Araquil.

"So one day (it was Easter Monday), at the romeria of Loyola, this handsome young fellow of twenty-five, who had been loved but had never loved, met a young girl whom he invited to dance with him, even as he had invited many another. It was Pepa Chegaray. A waltz-tune has the effect of turning young folks' brains, and the *guitarero* is the grand-master of the art of love—that is the way I feel about it, at least. It was fated that neither Juan nor Pepa were to forget that first interview, that dance in the open air, the music accompanied by smiles and song, more intoxicating than our cider.

> In the morning there rises a beautiful star,
> They say there is none more beautiful in the heavens;
> But here on earth, Oh, my loved one, there is one that is
>   brighter

And which has not its equal in the blue sky,
And to that one my heart goes forth
As the water flows, seeking its level.

"Ever since that Easter Monday Juan Araquil, usually so cheerful, had been morose and very gloomy, having but little to say, and there was never a smile to be seen on the face of Father Tiburcio Chegaray down there in his home. The reason of it was that that good-for-nothing urchin Love had passed that way.

"Oh! it was an absorbing, an engrossing love, that fell on them as swiftly as a thunder-clap. It happens that way, sometimes. She dreamed of him; he could think of nothing but her. He was as melancholy as a garden where there are no flowers, and his love did not improve his temper. Why? Because he had not a douro in his pocket, and Pepa was rich, and, what was worse yet, Father Tiburcio, that man of iron, had told his daughter that never, never would he give his Pepa to a man whose sole fortune was his tennis-ball.

"'But after all,' Araquil said to Father Chegaray one day, 'Pepa loves me; she has told me that she does.'

"'She has told me so, too,' replied the father.

"'I adore her. I am mad with love for her. I shall kill myself unless you give her to me. What must I do to obtain her for my wife?'

"'Do what I have always done,' replied the farmer, 'work, and bring home the wherewithal to buy bread for the children. I have not toiled all my life long to throw away my money and my daughter on a man who does nothing but hang around the romerias. When you can come to me and tell me that you have

saved up a little something and can supply your share
of bread and salt, you shall have Pepa, since she loves
you.'

"'And the share that I must contribute is—how
much?' Juan asked.

"'Two thousand douros!'

"'That's equal to ten thousand francs of your money.

"'Two thousand douros!' said Araquil, very pale.
'Where can I look to find such a sum as that?'

"'I found it in the ground, I did,' the farmer answered. 'Seek it there!'

"And Tiburcio was not a man to go back on his
word when he had once said a thing, not he! All that
was left for Araquil to do was to kill himself, as he
had threatened, or else go to work with pick and spade
and earn the money. Pepa, like a good girl, would
not disobey her father, but she was very much in love
with the good-looking youngster and would subdue her
impatience and wait until Juan had collected the required sum. In their furtive meetings, however, as
well as in their conversations in presence of the old
man, she did not attempt to conceal from Araquil that
her feeling for him was of that nature that forms an
indissoluble tie between two beings until it is sancti-
fied by the last sacrament. She had even sworn to
him—she had sworn it on the mass-book of her dead
mother—that she would never be another's if she
could not be his. Such a vow, uttered by a creature
as beautiful as the stars in heaven, was well calculated
to inspire courage in the heart of a bold man. Juan
said to himself: 'Well! yes; yes, I will get them, those
two thousand douros! I don't see how I am to get
them, but I will get them!'

"And how he cudgeled his brains with cogitating over different projects, and how he strove and toiled! He was near dashing his head against the wall of the tennis-ground at Saint Sebastian one day in his fury at having lost a game with the champion of Tolosa by a point. The betting was heavy. It would have been a nest-egg for him had he won. And Araquil was beaten by a point, by a miserable point, and the boys of Hernani with him! He tore his hair, he thumped himself on the forehead, he was beside himself with rage.

"He *must* have those two thousand douros, and he kept repeating to himself what Pepa had said to him:

"'Life with you or with no one, Araquil. But I shall obey my father while he is alive, and I shall always respect my father's wishes when he is dead.'

"He had reached such a state, poor Juan, that he thought of going far away. He had been told that the Basques who emigrated sometimes made their fortune out there at La Plata, in America. Yes, sir, it seems that the tennis-players of our country are able to pick up dollars by the handful at Buenos Ayres. The pretty house that you will see to the right of the road as you go back to Saint Sebastian belongs to a young fellow of Hernani who made his money in that way in the southern part of the New World. If it had not been for the idea of leaving Pepa, of never seeing her, even from a distance, at mass or at vespers, at the bull-fights, or even at her window when he passed the farmhouse, Araquil would certainly have gone away. Yes, he would have gone away. And then, a trapper or a gold-hunter, as the occasion offered, he would have sought wealth, since the old man had said to

him: 'Seek!' It would have been better for him had
he done so.

"But while matters were in this condition, along
comes the war, the last war, and sets the land on fire,
—there is no other way of expressing it than that,—
and the things that I have been telling you of happened before Bilbao. So, then, to resume my story,
this tall young adventurer comes and posts himself
before General Garrido, who is in a despairing mood,
and briefly relates his history, and while the old vet-
eran of Morocco, now beaten by the Carlists, looks at
him with frowning eyes, Juan Araquil adds:

" 'If the life of Zucarraga is worth a fortune, as you
say, general, I will win that fortune!'

" 'The life of Zucarraga is worth more than a fortune,' Garrido replied. 'It counterbalances the lives
of thousands of my poor boys. The name Zucarraga
means resistance, it means the key that will unlock
Bilbao for us, it means a continuation of slaughter,
that is all. You are not a soldier. I have no orders
to give you, but if you do what you say you will do,
remind me of what I have said!'

" 'Very well!' said Juan. 'We shall meet soon
again, general!'

"Old Garrido shrugged his shoulders and wondered for a moment if the man was not a spy.

"Araquil, for his part, allowed his mind to dwell on
only one thing: Zucarraga's life was worth a fortune!
And that fortune, for which he cared as much as he
cared for a raw onion, he longed for it only because it
would give him his Pepa. He left Hernani, he disappeared from sight. Nothing was heard of him for several days. The general said: 'I have been dealing

with a crazy man,' and went on to make preparation
for a night attack, intending to surprise Zucarraga and
carry the pass in the darkness, with only the flashes
of his musketry to light him.

"In the meantime Araquil was roaming about the
Carlist intrenchments. With his knife in his pocket,
that knife that at need he could hurl with the force of
a ball from a musket and plant unerringly in the remote target, he waited, sleeping by the light of the
stars, wherever he chanced to be, for an opportunity
of approaching Zucarraga and ridding old Garrido of
the Carlist chieftain. What was the life of that partisan commander to him? War with artillery, war with
the knife, it is war all the same. One has the right to
kill when he stakes his own life at the same time. He
kept repeating these arguments to himself and was on
the alert, watching his chance. One night when he
had come too near to the half-wrecked farmhouse in
which Zucarraga had his quarters among the ruins, a
sentry's bullet whistled close to Araquil's head, so
close that it carried away a little of the flesh from his
left ear. He paid not the slightest attention to it, and
regretted only one circumstance, that the Carlist sentinel had caught sight of him. Had it not been for
that he would have leaped the wall and been at Zucarraga's side! Now it was all to do over again.

"Very well, then; he would begin again on the morrow. But that morrow was the very day that Garrido
had selected for the night attack. Juan Araquil,
lying in a ditch, like a wild beast crouching in his
lair, was forming his plans for reaching Zucarraga,
this time, at every risk, at the very moment when old
Garrido was sending out an attacking column against

the Carlists. Araquil was surprised when the first shots of the engagement reached his ears, the succeeding ones delighted him. As there was a battle on, Zucarraga would come forth, would lead his troops into the firing. If Juan could slip up to him it would soon be done: the knife to his heart, and in open conflict, this time, not in a cowardly ambush. Ah! so Zucarraga's blood was worth a fortune? Father Chegaray should have his two thousand douros—and so much the worse for the Carlists!

"It was a plucky fight that was fought that night. Garrido's troops were in earnest, they came up to the assault of the intrenchments with bayonets fixed and struck up against the Carlists, whom they thought to surprise, but who were on the alert. The murdering, the killing went on under the cover of the darkness of night. Breasts were pierced by bayonets, heads were broken by revolvers. The work of slaughter was carried on by men who were invisible to one another. And I say again, what a pity it is that such things should happen among Spaniards!

"And the bloody work went on for a long time. At early dawn the soldiers of the army were once again retreating, poor devils, and what frightful loss their attempt had cost them! The attack had been fruitless. A night of slaughter that only added another to their series of defeats. Old Garrido, down there in his camp, would shed fresh tears of rage. The Carlists, on the other hand, after having fought all night, saluted the dawn with their joyful shouts: *Harri! Harri!* Then all at once their shouts, their glee subsided, and a black silence fell upon them. Their invincible chieftain—he whose voice had been heard that night in every quarter of the field animating his men: 'Come, courage, my children! Stand up to the enemy!' Zucarraga—had been brought in, wounded in the leg, the bone shattered, so it was said. It was in front of the gutted, empty house where he usually slept. The prisoners of the army of Madrid—the Carlists had made many prisoners during the night— saw this superb, lofty young man, his face as pale as his white *beret*, with his black beard, surrounded by his officers. Zucarraga could no longer stand erect; his friends were sustaining him, holding him under the armpits. Some of his men brought a bench and he was placed upon it with his leg extended at full length.

"Araquil was among the onlookers.

"He had been captured with Garrido's men and with them placed in the general herd, and now Carlist sentries, with loaded muskets, were standing guard over him, together with the others. His knife, his famous knife, had been of no use to him. When, swept away by the prevailing disorder, he had seen himself captured and included among the number of the prisoners, he had thrown it away, saying to himself: 'It will be to do over again!' And now, doomed as he probably was to be shot, since he alone among the prisoners was not in uniform, he said to himself that it was all over, all over, and that Pepa would marry another or would die a maid; and he shot a bitter, envenomed glance toward that human victim who was escaping him, toward that Zucarraga, whom he was beginning to hate, he could not tell why —or because, rather, while Zucarraga lived, his, Ara- quil's, life was a barren one, Pepa was lost to him.

The Carlist officers were bustling anxiously about Zucarraga. Some of them were down on their knees examining the wound. One of them was calling for a surgeon.

"'The surgeon! The surgeon, *valgame Dios!* Where is Urrabieta, then? Where is he?'

"Urrabieta was the surgeon of the Carlist detachment. Men were looking for him in every direction. The officers were beginning to become impatient. Zucarraga, smiling, made a motion with his hand and said, very gently: 'Wait. Perhaps Urrabieta has fallen asleep. He must have had so much to do, last night!'

"All at once a sergeant came running up toward the officers, very pale and with tears in his eyes. Urrabieta, the surgeon, had just been found among the dead, where he had fallen, laid low by a bullet, upon the corpse of a Naverrese whose wound he had been looking to. It had happened in the darkness, like all the rest of it. A stray bullet. Those bits of lead, they bring death just as surely to those who cure as to those who kill!

"Then there was consternation among the Carlists. Zucarraga's wound might be serious; nay, it *was* serious. And no surgeon to attend to it! Waiting to summon those of the adjacent army-corps, that would be a proceeding fraught with danger. He was losing blood freely. Then one of his officers walked straight up to the group of prisoners and asked in a loud voice:

"'Is there a surgeon among you?'

"Garrido's men looked one another in the face. No, there was no surgeon. They were all soldiers.

"'No one who can dress a wound?'

"Thereupon a man made answer: 'Yes, I can!'

" 'Step forward, you!'

"The man came forth from the drove of poor, de-jected creatures, wounded, some of them. He ad-vanced with head proudly erect. It was Araquil.

" 'You are not a soldier?' said the officer.

" 'No.'

" 'Why are you here?'

" 'Because they put me here. I am not a combat-ant, I am not. I was going to Bilbao to visit my re-lations, and the battle blocked my way. That is how it was.'

" 'And you know something of medicine?'

" 'No. But I know how to treat wounds. I am a bit of a torero at odd times.'

"The officer was distrustful and brought Araquil up to Zucarraga, who allowed his big black eyes to rest on the handsome young fellow. Then the Carlist chief called on him for an explanation. Araquil in-vented a story: he was longing to embrace his old parents, who were shut up in Bilbao. It was not his fault if the civil war separated families like that. He went his way, leading his usual life among the firing of the hostile armies.

" 'You belong to the Basque country? Why are you not with the legitimist Pretender?' Zucarraga asked in turn.

" 'Because I take sides with no one.'

"The officers had been examining and scrutinizing the young man rather doubtfully. His answer elicited some murmurs among them, which Zucarraga checked.

" 'Every one is free to do as he pleases,' he gently said. Then, bending his limpid glance straight into

Juan's eyes: 'You say that you know something of the healing art? Can you, at least, alleviate my pain? I am suffering greatly.'

"He pointed to his bare, bloodstained leg beneath the trousers that had been turned up and that were stiff with the red fluid.

"Araquil took off his jacket, impetuously tore off the left sleeve of his shirt and on the improvised bandage, unseen of all, all the time manipulating the bit of linen, he slowly poured a few drops of a liquid—that which he had in his ring on his finger—and then, pale as a sheet, took two steps forward toward Zucarraga, who had never, taken his eyes off him for a moment.

"There was no tremor in Araquil's hand as it held that piece of linen, marked with a small yellow stain. As he was about to kneel before Zucarraga to bind up his wound, one of the officers said to the Carlist leader:

"'We know nothing of this man!'

"The other replied, still with a smile on his face:

"'True, but neither do we know the physician, nor the priest.'

"And he stretched his leg out toward Juan Araquil with a painful effort.

"'But what causes that yellow spot?' a captain inquired.

"'A remedy of my own, for the wound of the *corrida*,' Juan replied.

"'Nonsense!'

"During all the operation Zucarraga never once took his great black eye away from that of Juan, and scarcely had the bandage been applied to the wound

when the partisan said: 'I feel better already!'
Then, addressing Juan: 'You are free.'

" 'But, general——,' interjected an officer.

"Zucarraga raised his head. 'The least that I can
do, sir,' said he, 'for this good youth is to repay his
service by another.' Then, addressing Araquil:
'What will you have beside?'

" 'Nothing,' answered the other.

"Zucarraga took from the pocket of his tunic a little
cigarette case of Manilla straw and handed it to Juan:
'In remembrance of me!'

" 'No,' said Juan.

" 'Oh! oh!'—and Zucarraga smiled—'I fear that
you don't cherish very kindly feelings toward the servants of Don Carlos. Will you accept nothing from
me?'

" 'Yes, a cigarette.'

"Araquil selected a *papelito* from the cigarette case
and was looking at it and turning it about in his fingers in a mechanical sort of way before putting it in
his pocket, when Zucarraga asked him:

" 'Your name?'

" 'Juan Araquil.'

" 'Well! Araquil, go, and God be with you! And
if you want to see your relations, wait until we make
our entry into Bilbao. It won't be long!—Give me
your hand!'

"Araquil, who was very pale, shook the hand that
the wounded man held out to him, put on his jacket,
and with a salute to the officers and a salute to the
prisoners, forthwith took himself off, very leisurely,
without hurrying, followed still by the penetrating
look of the Carlist hero.

"That same evening, in the little inn-parlor at Hernani that served as headquarters, old Garrido beheld the tall young man with whom he had conversed six days before on the Place de l'Ayuntamiento brought in under guard of some soldiers.

"The general was beside himself, he was ill, was threatened with congestion of the brain; since the disaster of the previous night he had been talking of shooting himself. He received Araquil as he would have received a dog.

" 'What do you want here, fellow? What assurance have I that you did not put those miserable Carlists on their guard?'

" 'You ask me what I want, general? I want to talk to you—to you, alone! Yes, alone!'

"And the lad spoke in such a distinct tone that old Garrido saw that he had something of importance to say and signed to his officers to leave them, the man and him.

" 'Well! what is it?' he asked, when Juan's request had been complied with and they were alone.

"Araquil waited a moment before speaking, as if the saliva had retreated from his mouth and left it parched and dry; then all at once he blurted out:

" 'You told me, general, that Zucarraga's life was worth a fortune?' And as Garrido made no answer: 'I am here to claim that fortune; I have earned it!'

"The general looked at him, knitting his eyebrows, wondering if he could have heard aright, and Araquil stood there, facing him, pale as death.

" 'What do you mean? How, earned it?' said Garrido after a moment's silence. 'I do not understand you.'

"'It is very simple, nevertheless,' Juan answered. 'Zucarraga will never again give the command to fire on your troops.'

"'He is dead?'

"'He ought to be, by this time. If it is not all over to-night, it will be by to-morrow.'

"Old Garrido was deeply moved, and his face was as white as his mustache. He wished to know more, not understanding Araquil's 'it will be by to-morrow,' and the lad told him everything: how he had tracked the Carlist chief, how he had endeavored to plant his knife in his breast, and, finally, how he had poured upon the raw flesh of the wounded man the poison of that ring that he had been keeping for himself.

"It seemed to the general as if he were choking, strangling, in the clutches of some hideous nightmare. Beneath his snowy locks his black eyes blazed like balls of fire. He only allowed himself to say:

"'You did that, you? You did that? To a wounded man?'

"Then Juan, speaking as a madman might speak, went on to tell how he would have done a great deal more than that for the sake of winning Pepa, and that as Father Chegaray had insisted on a portion of two thousand douros, he had taken those two thousand douros where he could find them. And besides—and the general himself had said it—he had caused the death of many men, and was continually causing their death, and brave men, too, this Zucarraga!

"'In battle, yes!' said Garrido hotly. 'In battle!'

"But that was an argument that had no force for Araquil; the only justification that he offered for what he had done was his passion for Pepa. He *wanted*

Pepa.   He could purchase her with the blood of
Zucarraga.   It was well.   That was all there was of it.

"Garrido had promised; Araquil came there, de-
manding payment of the debt.   The general said:

"'It is no more than just.'

"He asked where Pepa lived, summoned an aid-
de-camp, gave him the address and, pointing to Araquil, said:

"'You will lodge that man in the Fonda del Sol.
And to-morrow you will have the chaplain in readiness.   Yes, for a marriage.   Go!'

"Juan's night in the *fonda* that had been trans-
formed into a guardhouse seemed to him to pass
very slowly.   A long, long night it was, that seemed
as if it would never end, with the distant barking of
dogs—those howls that tell of coming death—and the
sound of firing down there in the direction of the
Carlist advanced posts.

"With the approach of morning he fell into a light
slumber, dreaming of Pepa and, in his dream, placing
gold coins in old Chegaray's skinny hand, the portion
of a living woman, the money received for a corpse.

"It was broad day when a detachment of soldiers,
headed by a sergeant, came to take Juan from the
guardhouse.   Who was it that wanted him?   The
general.   More than this, in reply to Araquil's questions, the sergeant would not answer.   They ascended
the main street of Hernani, the little, narrow street
where the houses were crowded and bunched closely
together, with ancient escutcheons carved on their
sandstone walls and those blue and yellow mouchara-
bies that struck you as so pretty awhile ago, until at
last they halted on the Grande Place.   The weather

was splendid; a brilliant sun was gilding the red walls of the old church and the shattered ruins, blackened by fire, of the Hôtel de Ville. The square was crowded with people; troops were drawn up in line, and near the church steps stood Garrido in full uniform, very pale, with his officers about him, while a few steps away, beautiful as a saint in the black veils of her holiday attire, was Pepa, with old Chegaray standing at her side.

"Araquil beheld all that at a glance: the assembled troops with their bayonets gleaming in the sunlight, the general, the beautiful girl, and through the open doors of the church, down there at the bottom of the scene, a *chapelle ardente*, the great chapel all streaming with light and gold.

"They conducted him before Garrido.

"Araquil cast a searching look upon Pepa, and she regarded him with a strange air from out her black eyes beneath their fringe of long lashes, and it seemed to Juan that the gilded mass-book that she held in her hand—the book upon which she had sworn to be his wife—was trembling in the clasp of her black-gloved fingers.

" 'Bring hither the priest!' said the general.

"The holy man appeared upon the steps of stone as if he had been awaiting the general's order—a white-robed priest, who stopped upon the threshold, motionless as a statue—the while the great bells in the campanile were pealing forth from their wide mouths, wide-gaping mouths like those of great siege-guns, their festal hosannah, the merry marriage hymn, the hymn of the happy!

" 'Tiburcio Chegaray,' said the general, then, addressing the old farmer, 'here is Juan Araquil with the portion of two thousand douros that you demanded as the condition of giving him your daughter. That which is promised should be performed. Do you consent to the marriage of Juan Araquil and your child?'

"Old Chegaray answered in a hoarse voice: ·

"'Yes!'

"'Juan Araquil,' said Garrido, 'you consent to receive Pepa Chegaray as your wife?'

"'Yes,' replied Juan, in a tone of deep feeling.

"He had thrown into that *yes* the very essence of his being. The priest stood waiting, ready to give them his benediction.

"'Pepa Chegaray,' demanded Garrido, turning to the young woman, 'do you consent to receive Juan Araquil, who stands before you, as your husband?'

"Pepa advanced two steps toward Juan, cast her handsome black eyes upon him, and made answer:

"'No!'

"There was a stifled outcry among the crowd that filled the space behind the line of soldiers, an ominous *oh!* The soldiers stood motionless, watching the scene.

"'No,' repeated the young girl, raising her voice, 'I have sworn that I would marry no one but you, and having made that vow, I will marry no one. But never will I be the wife of a dastard!'

"Juan Araquil might have been taken for one bereft of reason, as he stood there looking at her; his face was haggard and drawn and as white as the priest's cope. Far, very far in the distance, from the depths of the valley, the assemblage could now hear the mournful sound of a bell as it rose and rose and swelled over the intervening hills, the sound of the funeral knell, the long-drawn, wailing lament of the bell mourning the dead. The Carlists were ringing the knell of the dying, and the poison had done its work.

"The bells of Hernani, too, as if wishing in their turn to do honor to the dying man, had gradually ceased ringing; they were silent, up there in their tower, and all that was heard was the tolling of the knell, the distant knell.

"Then, all at once, the knell, too, ceased tolling and a silence settled down upon the crowded *place*, as if the wind had whispered to all those ears the news that all was over down there in the valley.

" 'Zucarraga is dead!' said old Garrido.

"Araquil cast a burning glance toward Pepa, as if beseeching her to read his thoughts.

" 'It is for thy sake! It was for thy sake!' he said to her reproachfully.

"Pepa turned away her head.

"Then the general, addressing Juan, coldly said:

" 'Araquil, what disposition do you wish made of your two thousand douros?'

" 'The money?' Araquil had understood. 'Let it be given to the poor. I want nothing for myself, not even a cross in the graveyard.' Pointing to the platoon that had acted as guard to him, he added: 'That is for me, I suppose?'

" 'Araquil, no man takes a soldier's life by poison,' replied Garrido.

"Then Juan Araquil made the sign of the cross, kneeled before the priest and said aloud: 'God have mercy on my soul!' And now the bells of Hernani were tolling the knell for the dying, even as those of the plain had done, down beneath the hill of Santa Barbara.

"Juan arose, took from the pocket of his jacket a cigarette, the cigarette that Zucarraga had given him, and asked the sergeant for a light. When the papelito was alight he placed it between his lips, turned and gave a last look at Pepa, who made a movement as if she would have gone to him, but nerved herself and remained where she was, and the tall, handsome lad, with a melancholy smile upon his face, lifted his head proudly and was lost to sight among the soldiers, who moved off in obedience to a sign from Garrido.

"Pepa turned, endeavoring to see him, to catch one last glimpse of him; she could not distinguish him in the circle of muskets that was receding along the church wall; all that she could make out was a little cloud of smoke, a thin blue smoke that rose above the heads of the men, among the flashing bayonets, and floated away in the clear sky.

"And chants were begun, and prayers were put up, there in the church, while Juan Araquil, passing along that red wall, in the bright sunlight, was taking the last pull at his cigarette.

"Then, amid the silence as of death that reigned over the *place*, Pepa heard a command given in the distance and a rattling as of arms shifted, and then there came to her ears, distinctly audible, this word: 'Fire!'

"She fell upon her knees, heartbroken, and was beginning to recite aloud: 'Our Father, which art in heaven,—' but the crash of the discharge that ensued immediately brought her prayer to an abrupt end.

"At the same instant Juan Araquil, who until then had remained erect against the wall of the parsonage, his breast streaming with blood, sank, face downward, lifeless to the ground.

"When the sergeant approached the body to fire the 'shot of mercy' into the ear, the cigarette that Juan was holding in his fingers was still emitting a little thread of blue smoke—Zucarraga's cigarette! And that smoke outlived Zucarraga the hero, and Araquil the murderer."

THE ATTACK ON THE MILL.

ÉMILE ZOLA.

I

IT was high holiday at Father Merlier's mill on that pleasant summer afternoon. Three tables had been brought out into the garden and placed end to end in the shade of the great elm, and now they were awaiting the arrival of the guests. It was known throughout the length and breadth of the land that that day was to witness the betrothal of old Merlier's daughter, Françoise, to Dominique, a young man who was said to be not overfond of work, but whom never a woman for three leagues of the country around could look at without sparkling eyes, such a well-favored young fellow was he.

That mill of Father Merlier's was truly a very pleasant spot. It was situated right in the heart of Rocreuse, at the place where the main road makes a sharp bend. The village has but a single street, bordered on either side by a row of low, whitened cottages, but just there, where the road curves, there are broad stretches of meadow-land, and huge trees, which follow the course of the Morelle, cover the low grounds

of the valley with a most delicious shade. All Lor-
raine has no more charming bit of nature to show.
To right and left dense forests, great monarchs of the
wood, centuries old, rise from the gentle slopes and fill
the horizon with a sea of waving, trembling verdure,
while away toward the south extends the plain, of
wondrous fertility and checkered almost to infinity
with its small inclosures, divided off from one another
by their live hedges. But what makes the crowning
glory of Rocreuse is the coolness of this verdurous
nook, even in the hottest days of July and August.
The Morelle comes down from the woods of Gagny,
and it would seem as if it gathered to itself on the way
all the delicious freshness of the foliage beneath which
it glides for many a league; it brings down with it the
murmuring sounds, the glacial, solemn shadows of the
forest. And that is not the only source of coolness;
there are running waters of all sorts singing among the
copses; one cannot take a step without coming on a
gushing spring, and as he makes his way along the
narrow paths seems to be treading above subterrene
lakes that seek the air and sunshine through the moss
above and profit by every smallest crevice, at the roots
of trees or among the chinks and crannies of the
rocks, to burst forth in fountains of crystalline clear-
ness. So numerous and so loud are the whispering
voices of these streams that they silence the song of
the bullfinches. It is as if one were in an enchanted
park, with cascades falling and flashing on every side.

The meadows below are never athirst. The shadows beneath the gigantic chestnut trees are of inky
blackness, and along the edges of the fields long rows

of poplars stand like walls of rustling foliage.   There
is a double avenue of huge plane trees ascending across
the fields toward the ancient castle of Gagny, now
gone to rack and ruin.   In this region, where drought
is never known, vegetation of all kinds is wonderfully
rank; it is like a flower garden down there in the low
ground between those two wooded hills, a natural
garden, where the lawns are broad meadows and the
giant trees represent colossal beds.   When the noon-
day sun pours down his scorching rays the shadows
lie blue upon the ground, vegetation slumbers in the
genial warmth, while every now and then a breath of
almost icy coldness rustles the foliage.

Such was the spot where Father Merlier's mill enliv-
ened nature run riot with its cheerful clack.   The
building itself, constructed of wood and plaster,
looked as if it might be coeval with our planet.   Its
foundations were in part laved by the Morelle, which
here expands into a clear pool.   A dam, a few feet
in height, afforded sufficient head of water to drive the
old wheel, which creaked and groaned as it revolved,
with the asthmatic wheezing of a faithful servant who
has grown old in her place.   Whenever Father Merlier
was advised to change it, he would shake his head and
say that like as not a young wheel would be lazier and
not so well acquainted with its duties, and then he
would set to work and patch up the old one with anything that came to hand, old hogshead-staves, bits of
rusty iron, zinc, or lead.   The old wheel only seemed
the gayer for it, with its odd, round countenance, all
plumed and feathered with tufts of moss and grass,
and when the water poured over it in a silvery tide its

gaunt black skeleton was decked out with a gorgeous
display of pearls and diamonds.

That portion of the mill which was bathed by the
Morelle had something of the look of a Moorish arch
that had been dropped down there by chance. A
good half of the structure was built on piles; the
water came in under the floor, and there were deep
holes, famous throughout the whole country for the
eels and the huge crawfish that were to be caught
there. Below the fall the pool was as clear as a look.
ing-glass, and when it was not clouded by foam from
the wheel one could see great fish swimming about
in it with the slow, majestic movements of a fleet.
There was a broken stairway leading down to the
stream, near a stake to which a boat was fastened, and
over the wheel was a gallery of wood. Such windows
as there were were arranged without any attempt at
order. The whole was a quaint conglomeration of
nooks and corners, bits of wall, additions made here
and there as afterthoughts, beams and roofs, that gave
the mill the aspect of an old dismantled citadel, but
ivy and all sorts of creeping plants had grown luxuri-
antly and kindly covered up such crevices as were too
unsightly, casting a mantle of green over the old dwelling. Young ladies who passed that way used to stop
and sketch Father Merlier's mill in their albums.

The side of the house that faced the road was less
irregular. A gateway in stone afforded access to the
principal courtyard, on the right and left hand of
which were sheds and stables. Beside a well stood an
immense elm that threw its shade over half the court.
At the further end, opposite the gate, stood the

house, surmounted by a dovecote, the four windows of its first floor symmetrically aligned. The only manifestation of pride that Father Merlier ever allowed himself was to paint this façade every ten years. It had just been freshly whitened at the time of our story, and dazzled the eyes of all the village when the sun lighted it up in the middle of the day.

For twenty years had Father Merlier been mayor of Rocreuse. He was held in great consideration on account of his fortune; he was supposed to be worth something like eighty thousand francs, the result of patient saving. When he married Madeleine Guilliard, who brought him the mill as her dowry, his entire capital lay in his two strong arms, but Madeleine had never repented of her choice, so manfully had he conducted their joint affairs. Now his wife was dead, and he was left a widower with his daughter Françoise. Doubtless he might have sat himself down to take his rest and suffered the old mill-wheel to sleep among its moss, but he would have found the occupation too irksome and the house would have seemed dead to him, so he kept on working still, for the pleasure of it. In those days Father Merlier was a tall old man, with a long, unspeaking face, on which a laugh was never seen, but beneath which there lay, none the less, a large fund of good-humor. He had been elected mayor on account of his money, and also for the impressive air that he knew how to assume when it devolved on him to marry a couple.

Françoise Merlier had just completed her eighteenth year. She was small, and for that reason was not accounted one of the beauties of the country. Until she reached the age of fifteen she was even homely; the good folks of Rocreuse could not see how it was that the daughter of Father and Mother Merlier, such a hale, vigorous couple, had such a hard time of it in getting her growth. When she was fifteen, however, though still remaining delicate, a change came over her and she took on the prettiest little face imaginable. She had black eyes, black hair, and was red as a rose withal; her little mouth was always graced with a charming smile, there were delicious dimples in her cheeks, and a crown of sunshine seemed to be ever resting on her fair, candid forehead. Although small as girls went in that region she was far from being slender; she might not have been able to raise a sack of wheat to her shoulder, but she became quite plump with age and gave promise of becoming eventually as well-rounded and appetizing as a partridge. Her father's habits of taciturnity had made her reflective while yet a young girl; if she always had a smile on her lips it was in order to give pleasure to others. Her natural disposition was serious.

As was no more than to be expected, she had every young man in the countryside at her heels as a suitor, more even for her money than for her attractiveness, and she had made a choice at last, a choice that had been the talk and scandal of the entire neighborhood. On the other side of the Morelle lived a strapping young fellow who went by the name of Dominique Penquer. He was not to the manor born; ten years previously he had come to Rocreuse from Belgium to receive the inheritance of an uncle who had owned a small property on the very borders of the forest of Gagny, just

facing the mill and distant from it only a few musket-
shots. His object in coming was to sell the property,
so he said, and return to his own home again; but he
must have found the land to his liking for he made no
move to go away. He was seen cultivating his bit of
a field and gathering the few vegetables that afforded
him an existence. He hunted, he fished; more than
once he was near coming in contact with the law
through the intervention of the keepers. This inde-
pendent way of living, of which the peasants could not
very clearly see the resources, had in the end given
him a bad name. He was vaguely looked on as nothing better than a poacher. At all events he was lazy,
for he was frequently found sleeping in the grass at
hours when he should have been at work. Then, too,
the hut in which he lived, in the shade of the last
trees of the forest, did not seem like the abode of an
honest young man; the old women would not have
been surprised at any time to hear that he was on
friendly terms with the wolves in the ruins of Gagny.
Still, the young girls would now and then venture to
stand up for him, for he was altogether a splendid
specimen of manhood, was this individual of doubtful
antecedents, tall and straight as a young poplar, with
a milk-white skin and ruddy hair and beard that
seemed to be of gold when the sun shone on them.
Now one fine morning it came to pass that Françoise
told Father Merlier that she loved Dominique and that
never, never would she consent to marry any other
young man.

It may be imagined what a knockdown blow it was
that Father Merlier received that day! As was his

wont, he said never a word; his countenance wore its
usual reflective look, only the fun that used to bubble
up from within no longer shone in his eyes. Françoise, too, was very serious, and for a week father and
daughter scarcely spoke to each other. What troubled
Father Merlier was to know how that rascal of a
poacher had succeeded in bewitching his daughter.
Dominique had never shown himself at the mill. The
miller played the spy a little, and was rewarded by
catching sight of the gallant, on the other side of the
Morelle, lying among the grass and pretending to be
asleep. Françoise could see him from her chamber
window. The thing was clear enough; they had been
making sheep's eyes at each other over the old mill-
wheel, and so had fallen in love.

A week slipped by; Françoise became more and
more serious. Father Merlier still continued to say
nothing. Then, one evening, of his own accord, he
brought Dominique to the house, without a word.
Françoise was just setting the table. She made no
demonstration of surprise; all she did was to add another plate, but her laugh had come back to her and
the little dimples appeared again upon her cheeks.
Father Merlier had gone that morning to look for
Dominique at his hut on the edge of the forest, and
there the two men had had a conference, with closed
doors and windows, that lasted three hours. No one
ever knew what they said to each other; the only
thing certain is that when Father Merlier left the hut
he already treated Dominique as a son. Doubtless
the old man had discovered that he whom he had
gone to visit was a worthy young man, even though

he did lie in the grass to gain the love of young
girls.

All Rocreuse was up in arms. The women gathered at their doors and could not find words strong
enough to characterize Father Merlier's folly in thus
receiving a ne'er-do-well into his family. He let them
talk. Perhaps he thought of his own marriage.
Neither had he possessed a penny to his name at the
time when he married Madeleine and her mill, and yet
that had not prevented him from being a good husband
to her. Moreover Dominique put an end to their
tittle-tattle by setting to work in such strenuous fashion that all the countryside was amazed. It so happened just then that the boy of the mill drew an
unlucky number and had to go for a soldier, and
Dominique would not hear to their engaging another.
He lifted sacks, drove the cart, wrestled with the old
wheel when it took an obstinate fit and refused to turn,
and all so pluckily and cheerfully that people came
from far and near merely for the pleasure of seeing
him Father Merlier laughed his silent laugh. He
was highly elated that he had read the youngster
aright. There is nothing like love to hearten up
young men.

In the midst of all that laborious toil Françoise
and Dominique fairly worshiped each other. They
had not much to say, but their tender smiles conveyed
a world of meaning. Father Merlier had not said a
word thus far on the subject of their marriage, and
they had both respected his silence, waiting until the
old man should see fit to give expression to his will.
At last, one day along toward the middle of July, he

had had three tables laid in the courtyard, in the shade
of the big elm, and had invited his friends of Rocreuse
to come that afternoon and drink a glass of wine with
him. When the courtyard was filled with people and
every one there had a full glass in his hand, Father
Merlier raised his own high above his head and said:

"I have the pleasure of announcing to you that
Françoise and this stripling will be married in a month
from now, on Saint Louis' fête-day."

Then there was a universal touching of glasses,
attended by a tremendous uproar; every one was laughing. But Father Merlier, raising his voice above the
din, again spoke:

"Dominique, kiss your wife that is to be. It is no
more than customary."

And they kissed, very red in the face, both of them,
while the company laughed louder still. It was a
regular fête; they emptied a small cask. Then, when
only the intimate friends of the house remained, conversation went on in a calmer strain. Night had
fallen, a starlit night and very clear. Dominique and
Françoise sat on a bench, side by side, and said nothing. An old peasant spoke of the war that the emperor had declared against Prussia. All the lads of the
village were already gone off to the army. Troops
had passed through the place only the night before.
There were going to be hard knocks.

"Bah!" said Father Merlier, with the selfishness of
a man who is quite happy, "Dominique is a foreigner,
he won't have to go—and if the Prussians come this
way, he will be here to defend his wife."

The idea of the Prussians coming there seemed to

the company an exceedingly good joke. The army
would give them one good, conscientious thrashing
and the affair would be quickly ended.

"I have seen them, I have seen them," the old
peasant repeated in a low voice.

There was silence for a little, then they all touched
glasses once again. Françoise and Dominique had
heard nothing; they had managed to clasp hands
behind the bench in such a way as not to be seen by the
others, and this condition of affairs seemed so beatific
to them that they sat there, mute, their gaze lost in the
darkness of the night.

What a magnificent, balmy night! The village lay
slumbering on either side of the white road as peace-
fully as a little child. The deep silence was undisturbed save by the occasional crow of a cock in some
distant barnyard, acting on a mistaken impression that
dawn was at hand. Perfumed breaths of air, like
long-drawn sighs, almost, came down from the great
woods that lay around and above, sweeping softly over
the roofs, as if caressing them. The meadows, with
their black intensity of shadow, took on a dim, mysterious majesty of their own, while all the springs, all
the brooks and water courses that gurgled and trickled
in the darkness, might have been taken for the cool
and rhythmical breathing of the sleeping country.
Every now and then the old dozing mill-wheel,
like a watchdog that barks uneasily in his slumber,
seemed to be dreaming as if it were endowed with
some strange form of life; it creaked, it groaned, it
talked to itself, rocked by the fall of the Morelle,
whose current gave forth the deep, sustained music of

an organ pipe. Never was there a more charming or happier nook, never did more entire or deeper peace come down to cover it.

II

ONE month later to a day, on the eve of the fête of Saint Louis, Rocreuse was in a state of alarm and dismay. The Prussians had beaten the emperor and were advancing on the village by forced marches. For a week past people passing along the road had brought tidings of the enemy: "They are at Lormières, they are at Novelles;" and by dint of hearing so many stories of the rapidity of their advance, Rocreuse woke up every morning in the full expectation of seeing them swarming down out of Gagny wood. They did not come, however, and that only served to make the affright the greater. They would certainly fall upon the village in the night-time, and put every soul to the sword.

There had been an alarm the night before, a little before daybreak. The inhabitants had been aroused by a great noise of men tramping upon the road. The women were already throwing themselves upon their knees and making the sign of the cross when some one, to whom it happily occurred to peep through a half-opened window, caught sight of red trousers. It was a French detachment. The captain had forthwith asked for the mayor, and, after a long conversation with Father Merlier, had remained at the mill.

The sun rose bright and clear that morning, giving promise of a warm day. There was a golden light floating over the woodland, while in the low grounds

white mists were rising from the meadows. The
pretty village, so neat and trim, awoke in the cool
dawning, and the country, with its stream and its
fountains, was as gracious as a freshly plucked bouquet. But the beauty of the day brought gladness to
the face of no one; the villagers had watched the
captain and seen him circle round and round the old
mill, examine the adjacent houses, then pass to the
other bank of the Morelle and from thence scan the
country with a field-glass; Father Merlier, who accompanied him, appeared to be giving explanations.
After that the captain had posted some of his men
behind walls, behind trees, or in hollows. The main
body of the detachment had encamped in the courtyard of the mill. So there was going to be a fight,
then? And when Father Merlier returned, they questioned him. He spoke no word, but slowly and sor-
rowfully nodded his head. Yes, there was going to
be a fight.

Françoise and Dominique were there in the courtyard, watching him. He finally took his pipe from
his lips and gave utterance to these few words:

"Ah! my poor children, I shall not be able to
marry you to-day!"

Dominique, with lips tight set and an angry frown
upon his forehead, raised himself on tiptoe from time
to time and stood with eyes bent on Gagny wood, as if
he would have been glad to see the Prussians appear
and end the suspense they were in. Françoise, whose
face was grave and very pale, was constantly passing
back and forth, supplying the needs of the soldiers.
They were preparing their soup in a corner of the

courtyard, joking and chaffing one another while awaiting their meal.

The captain appeared to be highly pleased. He
had visited the chambers and the great hall of the
mill that looked out on the stream. Now, seated
beside the well, he was conversing with Father
Merlier.

"You have a regular fortress here," he was saying.
"We shall have no trouble in holding it until evening.
The bandits are late; they ought to be here by this
time."

The miller looked very grave. He saw his beloved
mill going up in flame and smoke, but uttered no word
of remonstrance or complaint, considering that it
would be useless. He only opened his mouth to say:

"You ought to take steps to hide the boat; there is
a hole behind the wheel fitted to hold it. Perhaps
you may find it of use to you."

The captain gave an order to one of his men. This
captain was a tall, fine-looking man of about forty, with
an agreeable expression of countenance. The sight of
Dominique and Françoise seemed to afford him much
pleasure; he watched them as if he had forgotten all
about the approaching conflict. He followed Françoise with his eyes as she moved about the courtyard,
and his manner showed clearly enough that he thought
her charming. Then, turning to Dominique:

"You are not with the army, I see, my boy?" he
abruptly asked.

"I am a foreigner," the young man replied.

The captain did not seem particularly pleased with
the answer; he winked his eyes and smiled. Fran-

çoise was doubtless a more agreeable companion than
a musket would have been. Dominique, noticing his
smile, made haste to add:

"I am a foreigner, but I can lodge a rifle-bullet in
an apple at five hundred yards. See, there's my
rifle, behind you."

"You may find use for it," the captain dryly answered.

Françoise had drawn near; she was trembling a
little, and Dominique, regardless of the bystanders,
took and held firmly clasped in his own the two hands
that she held forth to him, as if committing herself to
his protection. The captain smiled again, but said
nothing more. He remained seated, his sword between his legs, his eyes fixed on space, apparently lost
in dreamy reverie.

It was ten o'clock. The heat was already oppressive. A deep silence prevailed. The soldiers had
sat down in the shade of the sheds in the courtyard
and begun to eat their soup. Not a sound came from
the village, where the inhabitants had all barricaded
their houses, doors and windows. A dog, abandoned
by his master, howled mournfully upon the road.
From the woods and the near by meadows, that lay
fainting in the heat, came a long-drawn, whispering,
soughing sound, produced by the union of what wandering breaths of air there were. A cuckoo sang.
Then the silence became deeper still.

And all at once, upon that lazy, sleepy air, a shot
rang out. The captain rose quickly to his feet, the
soldiers left their half-emptied plates. In a few seconds all were at their posts; the mill was occupied

from top to bottom. And yet the captain, who had
gone out through the gate, saw nothing; to right and
left the road stretched away, desolate and blindingly
white in the fierce sunshine. A second report was
heard, and still nothing to be seen, not even so much
as a shadow; but just as he was turning to re-enter he
chanced to look over toward Gagny and there beheld
a little puff of smoke, floating away on the tranquil
air, like thistle-down. The deep peace of the forest
was apparently unbroken.

"The rascals have occupied the wood," the officer
murmured. "They know we are here."

Then the firing went on, and became more and
more continuous, between the French soldiers posted
about the mill and the Prussians concealed among the
trees. The bullets whistled over the Morelle without
doing any mischief on either side. The firing was
irregular; every bush seemed to have its marksman,
and nothing was to be seen save those bluish smoke
wreaths that hung for a moment on the wind before
they vanished. It lasted thus for nearly two hours.
The officer hummed a tune with a careless air. Françoise and Dominique, who had remained in the courtyard, raised themselves to look out over a low wall.
They were more particularly interested in a little soldier
who had his post on the bank of the Morelle, behind
the hull of an old boat; he would lie face downward
on the ground, watch his chance, deliver his fire, then
slip back into a ditch a few steps in his rear to reload,
and his movements were so comical, he displayed such
cunning and activity, that it was difficult for any one
watching him to refrain from smiling. . He must have

caught sight of a Prussian, for he rose quickly and
brought his piece to the shoulder, but before he could
discharge it he uttered a loud cry, whirled completely
around in his tracks and fell backward into the ditch,
where for an instant his legs moved convulsively, just
as the claws of a fowl do when it is beheaded. The
little soldier had received a bullet directly through
his heart. It was the first casualty of the day. Françoise instinctively seized Dominique's hand and held
it tight in a convulsive grasp.

"Come away from there," said the captain. "The
bullets reach us here."

As if to confirm his words a slight, sharp sound was
heard up in the old elm, and the end of a branch came
to the ground, turning over and over as it fell, but the
two young people never stirred, riveted to the spot as
they were by the interest of the spectacle. On the
edge of the wood a Prussian had suddenly emerged
from behind a tree, as an actor comes upon the stage
from the wings, beating the air with his arms and falling over upon his back. And beyond that there was
no movement; the two dead men appeared to be
sleeping in the bright sunshine; there was not a soul
to be seen in the fields on which the heat lay heavy.
Even the sharp rattle of the musketry had ceased.
Only the Morelle kept on whispering to itself with
its low, musical murmur.

Father Merlier looked at the captain with an astonished air, as if to inquire whether that were the end
of it.

"Here comes their attack," the officer murmured.
"Look out for yourself! Don't stand there!"

The words were scarcely out of his mouth when a terrible discharge of musketry ensued. The great elm was riddled, its leaves came eddying down as thick as snowflakes. Fortunately the Prussians had aimed too high. Dominique dragged, almost carried Françoise from the spot, while Father Merlier followed them, shouting:

"Get into the small cellar, the walls are thicker there."

But they paid no attention to him; they made their way to the main hall, where ten or a dozen soldiers were silently waiting, watching events outside through the chinks of the closed shutters. The captain was left alone in the courtyard, where he sheltered himself behind the low wall, while the furious fire was maintained uninterruptedly. The soldiers whom he had posted outside only yielded their ground inch by inch; they came crawling in, however, one after another, as the enemy dislodged them from their positions. Their instructions were to gain all the time they could, taking care not to show themselves, in order that the Prussians might remain in ignorance of the force they had opposed to them. Another hour passed, and as a sergeant came in, reporting that there were now only two or three men left outside, the officer took his watch from his pocket, murmuring:

"Half-past two. Come, we must hold out for four hours yet."

He caused the great gate of the courtyard to be tightly secured and everything was made ready for an energetic defense. The Prussians were on the other side of the Morelle, consequently there was no reason to fear an assault at the moment. There was a bridge, indeed, a mile and a quarter away, but they were probably unaware of its existence, and it was hardly to be supposed that they would attempt to cross the stream by fording. The officer therefore simply caused the road to be watched; the attack, when it came, was to be looked for from the direction of the fields.

The firing had ceased again. The mill appeared to lie there in the sunlight, void of all life. Not a shutter was open, not a sound came from within. Gradually, however, the Prussians began to show themselves at the edge of Gagny wood. Heads were protruded here and there; they seemed to be mustering up their courage. Several of the soldiers within the mill brought up their pieces to an aim, but the captain shouted:

"No, no; not yet; wait. Let them come nearer."

They displayed a great deal of prudence in their advance, looking at the mill with a distrustful air; they seemed hardly to know what to make of the old structure, so lifeless and gloomy, with its curtains of ivy. Still, they kept on advancing. When there were fifty of them or so in the open, directly opposite, the officer uttered one word:

"Now!"

A crashing, tearing discharge burst from the position, succeeded by an irregular, dropping fire. Françoise, trembling violently, involuntarily raised her hands to her ears. Dominique, from his position behind the soldiers, peered out upon the field, and when the smoke drifted away a little, counted three Prussians extended on their backs in the middle of the

meadow. The others had sought shelter among the
willows and the poplars. And then commenced the
siege.

For more than an hour the mill was riddled with
bullets; they beat and rattled on its old walls like hail.
The noise they made was plainly audible as they
struck the stonework, were flattened, and fell back into
the water; they buried themselves in the woodwork
with a dull thud. Occasionally a creaking sound
would announce that the wheel had been hit. Within
the building the soldiers husbanded their ammunition,
firing only when they could see something to aim at.
The captain kept consulting his watch every few minutes, and as a ball split one of the shutters in halves
and then lodged in the ceiling:

"Four o'clock," he murmured. "We shall never
be able to hold the position."

The old mill, in truth, was gradually going to
pieces beneath that terrific fire. A shutter that had
been perforated again and again until it looked like a
piece of lace, fell off its hinges into the water and had
to be replaced by a mattress. Every moment, almost,
Father Merlier exposed himself to the fire in order to
take account of the damage sustained by his poor
wheel, every wound of which was like a bullet in his
own heart. Its period of usefulness was ended this
time, for certain; he would never be able to patch it
up again. Dominique had besought Françoise to
retire to a place of safety, but she was determined to
remain with him; she had taken a seat behind a great
oaken clothes-press, which afforded her protection. A
ball struck the press, however, the sides of which gave

out a dull, hollow sound, whereupon Dominique stationed himself in front of Françoise. He had as yet
taken no part in the firing, although he had his rifle in
his hand; the soldiers occupied the whole breadth of
the windows, so that he could not get near them. At
every discharge the floor trembled.

"Look out! look out!" the captain suddenly
shouted.

He had just descried a dark mass emerging from
the wood. As soon as they gained the open they set
up a telling platoon fire. It struck the mill like a tor-
nado. Another shutter parted company and the bullets came whistling in through the yawning aperture.
Two soldiers rolled upon the floor; one lay where he
fell and never moved a limb; his comrades pushed
him up against the wall because he was in their way.
The other writhed and twisted, beseeching some one
to end his agony, but no one had ears for the poor
wretch; the bullets were still pouring in and every one
was looking out for himself and searching for a loop-
hole whence he might answer the enemy's fire. A
third soldier was wounded; that one said not a word,
but with staring, haggard eyes sank down beneath a
table. Françoise, horror-stricken by the dreadful
spectacle of the dead and dying men, mechanically
pushed away her chair and seated herself on the floor,
against the wall; it seemed to her that she would
be smaller there and less exposed. In the meantime
men had gone and secured all the mattresses in the
house; the opening of the window was partially closed
again. The hall was filled with débris of every description, broken weapons, dislocated furniture.

"Five o'clock," said the captain. "Stand fast, boys. They are going to make an attempt to pass the stream."

Just then Françoise gave a shriek. A bullet had struck the floor and, rebounding, grazed her forehead on the ricochet. A few drops of blood appeared. Dominique looked at her, then went to the window and fired his first shot, and from that time kept on firing uninterruptedly. He kept on loading and discharging his piece mechanically, paying no attention to what was passing at his side, only pausing from time to time to cast a look at Françoise. He did not fire hurriedly or at random, moreover, but took deliberate aim. As the captain had predicted, the Prussians were skirting the belt of poplars and attempting the passage of the Morelle, but each time that one of them showed himself he fell with one of Dominique's bullets in his brain. The captain, who was watching the performance, was amazed; he complimented the young man, telling him that he would like to have many more marksmen of his skill. Dominique did not hear a word he said. A ball struck him in the shoulder, another raised a contusion on his arm. And still he kept on firing.

There were two more deaths. The mattresses were torn to shreds and no longer availed to stop the windows. The last volley that was poured in seemed as if it would carry away the mill bodily, so fierce it was. The position was no longer tenable. Still, the officer kept repeating:

"Stand fast. Another half-hour yet."

He was counting the minutes, one by one, now. He

had promised his commanders that he would hold
the enemy there until nightfall, and he would not
budge a hair's-breadth before the moment that he
had fixed on for his withdrawal. He maintained his
pleasant air of good-humor, smiling at Françoise by
way of reassuring her. He had picked up the musket
of one of the dead soldiers and was firing away with
the rest.

There were but four soldiers left in the room. The
Prussians were showing themselves *en masse* on the
other bank of the Morelle, and it was evident that they
might now pass the stream at any moment. A few
moments more elapsed; the captain was as determined
as ever and would not give the order to retreat, when
a sergeant came running into the room, saying:

"They are on the road; they are going to take us
in rear."

The Prussians must have discovered the bridge.
The captain drew out his watch again.

"Five minutes more," he said. "They won't be
here within five minutes."

Then exactly at six o'clock, he at last withdrew his
men through a little postern that opened on a narrow
lane, whence they threw themselves into the ditch and
in that way reached the forest of Sauval. The captain
took leave of Father Merlier with much politeness,
apologizing profusely for the trouble he had caused.
He even added:

"Try to keep them occupied for a while. We shall
return."

While this was occurring Dominique had remained
alone in the hall. He was still firing away, hearing

nothing, conscious of nothing; his sole thought was to
defend Françoise.   The soldiers were all gone and he
had not the remotest idea of the fact; he aimed and
brought down his man at every shot.   All at once
there was a great tumult.   The Prussians had entered
the courtyard from the rear.   He fired his last shot,
and they fell upon him with his weapon still smoking
in his hand.

It required four men to hold him; the rest of them
swarmed about him, vociferating like madmen in their
horrible dialect. . Françoise rushed forward to inter-
cede with her prayers.   They were on the point of
killing him on the spot, but an officer came in and
made them turn the prisoner over to him.   After ex-
changing a few words in German with his men he
turned to Dominique and said to him roughly, in very
good French:

"You will be shot in two hours from now."

III

It was the standing regulation, laid down by the
German staff, that every Frenchman, not belonging to
the regular army, taken with arms in his hands, should
be shot.   Even the *compagnies franches* were not
recognized as belligerents.   It was the intention of
the Germans, in making such terrible examples of the
peasants who attempted to defend their firesides, to
prevent a rising *en masse*, which they greatly dreaded.

The officer, a tall, spare man about fifty years old,
subjected Dominique to a brief examination.   Although he spoke French fluently, he was unmistakably
Prussian in the stiffness of his manner.

"You are a native of this country?"

"No, I am a Belgian."

"Why did you take up arms? These are matters with which you have no concern."

Dominique made no reply. At this moment the officer caught sight of Françoise where she stood listening, very pale; her slight wound had marked her white forehead with a streak of red. He looked from one to the other of the young people and appeared to understand the situation; he merely added:

"You do not deny having fired on my men?"

"I fired as long as I was able to do so," Dominique quietly replied.

The admission was scarcely necessary, for he was black with powder, wet with sweat, and the blood from the wound in his shoulder had trickled down and stained his clothing.

"Very well," the officer repeated. "You will be shot two hours hence."

Françoise uttered no cry. She clasped her hands and raised them above her head in a gesture of mute despair. Her action was not lost upon the officer. Two soldiers had led Dominique away to an adjacent room where their orders were to guard him and not lose sight of him. The girl had sunk upon a chair; her strength had failed her, her legs refused to support her; she was denied the relief of tears, it seemed as if her emotion was strangling her. The officer continued to examine her attentively and finally addressed her:

"Is that young man your brother?" he inquired.

She shook her head in negation. He was as rigid and unbending as ever, without the suspicion of a

smile on his face.   Then, after an interval of silence,
he spoke again:

"Has he been living in the neighborhood long?"

She answered yes, by another motion of the head.

"Then he must be well acquainted with the woods
about here?"

This time she made a verbal answer.   "Yes, sir,"
she said, looking at him with some astonishment.

He said nothing more, but turned on his heel, requesting that the mayor of the village should be brought
before him.   But Françoise had risen from her chair, a
faint tinge of color on her cheeks, believing that she
had caught the significance of his questions, and with
renewed hope she ran off to look for her father.

As soon as the firing had ceased Father Merlier had
hurriedly descended by the wooden gallery to have a
look at his wheel.   He adored his daughter and had
a strong feeling of affection for Dominique, his son-
in-law who was to be; but his wheel also occupied a
large space in his heart.   Now that the two little ones,
as he called them, had come safe and sound out of the
fray, he thought of his other love, which must have
suffered sorely, poor thing, and bending over the great
wooden skeleton he was scrutinizing its wounds with
a heartbroken air.   Five of the buckets were reduced
to splinters, the central framework was honeycombed.
He was thrusting his fingers into the cavities that the
bullets had made to see how deep they were, and reflecting how he was ever to repair all that damage.
When Françoise found him he was already plugging
up the crevices with moss and such debris as he could
lay hands on.

"They are asking for you, father," said she.

And at last she wept as she told him what she had just heard. Father Merlier shook his head. It was not customary to shoot people like that. He would have to look into the matter. And he re-entered the mill with his usual placid, silent air. When the officer made his demand for supplies for his men, he answered that the people of Rocreuse were not accustomed to be ridden roughshod and that nothing would be obtained from them through violence; he was willing to assume all the responsibility, but only on condition that he was allowed to act independently. The officer at first appeared to take umbrage at this easy way of viewing matters, but finally gave way before the old man's brief and distinct representations. As the latter was leaving the room the other recalled him to ask:

"Those woods there, opposite, what do you call them?"

"The woods of Sauval."

"And how far do they extend?"

The miller looked him straight in the face. "I do not know," he replied.

And he withdrew. An hour later the subvention in money and provisions that the officer had demanded was in the courtyard of the mill. Night was closing in; Françoise followed every movement of the soldiers with an anxious eye. She never once left the vicinity of the room in which Dominique was imprisoned. About seven o'clock she had a harrowing emotion; she saw the officer enter the prisoner's apartment and for a quarter of an hour heard their voices raised in

violent discussion.   The officer came to the door for
a moment and gave an order in German which she did
not understand, but when twelve men came and
formed in the courtyard with shouldered muskets, she
was seized with a fit of trembling and felt as if she
should die.   It was all over, then; the execution was
about to take place.   The twelve men remained there
ten minutes; Dominique's voice kept rising higher and
higher in a tone of vehement denial.   Finally the
officer came out, closing the door behind him with a
vicious bang and saying:

"Very well; think it over.   I give you until to-
morrow morning."

And he ordered the twelve men to break ranks by a
motion of his hand.   Françoise was stupefied.   Father
Merlier, who had continued to puff away at his pipe
while watching the platoon with a simple, curious air,
came and took her by the arm with fatherly gentleness.   He led her to her chamber.

"Don't fret," he said to her; "try to get some
sleep.   To-morrow it will be light and we shall see
more clearly."

He locked the door behind him as he left the room.
It was a fixed principle with him that women are good
for nothing and that they spoil everything whenever
they meddle in important matters.   Françoise did not
retire to her couch, however; she remained a long
time seated on her bed, listening to the various noises
in the house.   The German soldiers quartered in the
courtyard were singing and laughing; they must have
kept up their eating and drinking until eleven o'clock,
for the riot never ceased for an instant.   Heavy foot-

steps resounded from time to time through the mill
itself, doubtless the tramp of the guards as they were
relieved. What had most interest for her was the
sounds that she could catch in the room that lay
directly under her own; several times she threw herself prone upon the floor and applied her ear to the
boards. That room was the one in which they had
locked up Dominique. He must have been pacing
the apartment, for she could hear for a long time his
regular, cadenced tread passing from the wall to the
window and back again; then there was a deep
silence; doubtless he had seated himself. The other
sounds ceased, too; everything was still. When it
seemed to her that the house was sunk in slumber she
raised her window as noiselessly as possible and leaned
out.

Without, the night was serene and balmy. The
slender crescent of the moon, which was just setting
behind Sauval wood, cast a dim radiance over the
landscape. The lengthening shadows of the great
trees stretched far athwart the fields in bands of blackness, while in such spots as were unobscured the grass
appeared of a tender green, soft as velvet. But Françoise did not stop to consider the mysterious charm of
night. She was scrutinizing the country and looking
to see where the Germans had posted their sentinels.
She could clearly distinguish their dark forms outlined
along the course of the Morelle. There was only one
stationed opposite the mill, on the far bank of the
stream, by a willow whose branches dipped in the
water. Françoise had an excellent view of him; he
was a tall young man, standing quite motionless with

face upturned toward the sky, with the meditative air
of a shepherd.

When she had completed her careful inspection of
localities she returned and took her former seat upon
the bed. She remained there an hour, absorbed in
deep thought. Then she listened again; there was
not a breath to be heard in the house. She went
again to the window and took another look outside, but
one of the moon's horns was still hanging above the
edge of the forest and this circumstance doubtless
appeared to her unpropitious, for she resumed her
waiting. At last the moment seemed to have arrived;
the night was now quite dark; she could no longer dis-
cern the sentinel opposite her, the landscape lay
before her black as a sea of ink. She listened intently
for a moment, then formed her resolve. Close beside
her window was an iron ladder made of bars set in the
wall, which ascended from the mill-wheel to the gran-
ary at the top of the building and had formerly served
the miller as a means of inspecting certain portions of
the gearing, but a change having been made in the
machinery the ladder had long since become lost to
sight beneath the thick ivy that covered all that side
of the mill.

Françoise bravely climbed over the balustrade of
the little balcony in front of her window, grasped one
of the iron bars and found herself suspended in space.
She commenced the descent; her skirts were a great
hindrance to her. Suddenly a stone became loosened
from the wall and fell into the Morelle with a loud
splash. She stopped, benumbed with fear, but reflection quickly told her that the waterfall, with its contin-

uous roar, was sufficient to deaden any noise that she could make, and then she descended more boldly, putting aside the ivy with her foot, testing each round of her ladder.   When she was on a level with the room that had been converted into a prison for her lover she stopped.   An unforeseen difficulty came near depriving her of all her courage: the window of the room beneath was not situated directly under the window of her bedroom, there was a wide space between it and the ladder, and when she extended her hand it only encountered the naked wall.

Would she have to go back the way she came and leave her project unaccomplished?   Her arms were growing very tired, the murmuring of the Morelle, far down below, was beginning to make her dizzy.   Then she broke off bits of plaster from the wall and threw them against Dominique's window.   He did not hear; perhaps he was asleep.   Again she crumbled fragments from the wall, until the skin was peeled from her fingers.   Her strength was exhausted, she felt that she was about to fall backward into the stream, when at last Dominique softly raised his sash.

"It is I," she murmured.   "Take me quick; I am about to fall."   Leaning from the window he grasped her and drew her into the room, where she had a paroxysm of weeping, stifling her sobs in order that she might not be heard.   Then, by a supreme effort of the will, she overcame her emotion.

"Are you guarded?" she asked, in a low voice.

Dominique, not yet recovered from his stupefaction at seeing her there, made answer by simply pointing toward his door.   There was a sound of snoring audi-

ble on the **outside**; it was evident that the sentinel
had **been overpowered by** sleep and had thrown himself
upon the floor close against the door in such a **way**
that it could **not be** opened without arousing
him.

"You must fly," she **continued** earnestly. "I came
here to bid you fly and say **farewell.**"

But he seemed not to hear her. He kept repeating:
"What, is it you, is it you? Oh, what a fright you
gave me! You might **have killed** yourself." He
took her hands, he kissed them again and again.
"How I love you, Françoise! You are as courageous
as you are good. The only thing I feared was that I
might **die** without seeing you again, but **you** are here,
and now they may shoot me **when** they will. Let me
but have a quarter of an hour with **you and I am**
ready."

He had gradually drawn her to him; her head was
resting on his shoulder. The peril that **was so** near at
hand brought them closer to each other, **and** they forgot everything in that long embrace.

"Ah, Françoise!" Dominique went on in low, caressing tones, "to-day is the **fête of** Saint Louis, our
wedding-day, that we **have been waiting** for so long.
Nothing has been able to keep us apart, for we are both
here, faithful to our appointment, are we not? It **is**
now our wedding morning."

"Yes, yes," she repeated **after him,** "our wedding
morning."

They **shuddered as they exchanged a** kiss. But
suddenly she **tore herself** from **his arms;** the terrible
reality arose before her eyes.

"You must fly, you must fly," she murmured breathlessly. "There is not a moment to lose." And as he stretched out his arms in the darkness to draw her to him again, she went on in tender, beseeching tones: "Oh! listen to me, I entreat you. If you die, I shall die. In an hour it will be daylight. Go, go at once; I command you to go."

Then she rapidly explained her plan to him. The iron ladder extended downward to the wheel; once he had got that far he could climb down by means of the buckets and get into the boat, which was hidden in a recess. Then it would be an easy matter for him to reach the other bank of the stream and make his escape.

"But are there no sentinels?" said he.

"Only one, directly opposite here, at the foot of the first willow."

"And if he sees me, if he gives the alarm?"

Françoise shuddered. She placed in his hand a knife that she had brought down with her. They were silent.

"And your father—and you?" Dominique continued. "But no, it is not to be thought of; I must not fly. When I am no longer here those soldiers are capable of murdering you. You do not know them. They offered to spare my life if I would guide them into Sauval forest. When they discover that I have escaped their fury will be such that they will be ready for every atrocity."

The girl did not stop to argue the question. To all the considerations that he adduced, her one simple answer was: "Fly. For love of me, fly. If you love

me, Dominique, do not linger here a single moment
longer.''

She promised that she would return to her bedroom; no one should know that she had assisted him.
She concluded by folding him in her arms and smoth-
ering him with kisses, in an extravagant outburst of
passion.   He was vanquished.   He put only one more
question to her:

"Will you swear to me that your father knows what
you are doing and that he counsels my flight?''

"It was my father who sent me to you,'' Françoise
unhesitatingly replied.

She told a falsehood.   At that moment she had but
one great, overmastering longing, to know that he was
in safety, to escape from the horrible thought that the
morning's sun was to be the signal for his death.
When he should be far away, then calamity and evil
might burst upon her head; whatever fate might be in
store for her would seem endurable, so that only his
life might be spared.   Before and above all other considerations, the selfishness of her love demanded that
he should be saved.

"It is well,'' said Dominique; "I will do as you
desire.''

No further word was spoken.   Dominique went to
the window to raise it again.   But suddenly there was
a noise that chilled them with affright.   The door
was shaken violently, they thought that some one was
about to open it; it was evidently a party going the
rounds who had heard their voices.   They stood by
the window, close locked in each other's arms, awaiting the event with anguish unspeakable.   Again there

came the rattling at the door, but it did not open.
Each of them drew a deep sigh of relief; they saw
how it was; the soldier lying across the threshold had
turned over in his sleep.   Silence was restored, indeed, and presently the snoring commenced again,
sounding like sweetest music in their ears.

Dominique insisted that Françoise should return to
her room first of all.   He took her in his arms, he
bade her a silent farewell, then assisted her to grasp
the ladder, and himself climbed out on it in turn.   He
refused to descend a single step, however, until he
knew that she was in her chamber.   When she was
safe in her room she let fall, in a voice scarce louder
than the whispering breeze, the words:

"*Au revoir*, I love you!"

She kneeled at the window, resting her elbows on
the sill, straining her eyes to follow Dominique.   The
night was still very dark.   She looked for the sentinel,
but could see nothing of him; the willow alone was
dimly visible, a pale spot upon the surrounding blackness.   For a moment she heard the rustling of the ivy
as Dominique descended, then the wheel creaked, and
there was a faint plash which told that the young man
had found the boat.   This was confirmed when, a
minute later, she descried the shadowy outline of the
skiff on the gray bosom of the Morelle.   Then a horrible feeling of dread seemed to clutch her by the
throat and deprive her of power to breathe; she mo-
mently expected to hear the sentry give the alarm;
every faintest sound among the dusky shadows seemed
to her overwrought imagination to be the hurrying
tread of soldiers, the clash of steel, the click of mus-

ket-locks.   The seconds slipped by, however, the
landscape still preserved its solemn peace.   Dominique
must have landed safely on the other bank.   Françoise
no longer had eyes for anything.   The silence was
oppressive.   And she heard the sound of trampling
feet, a hoarse cry, the dull thud of a heavy body falling.   This was followed by another silence, even
deeper than that which had gone before.   Then, as if
conscious that Death had passed that way, she became
very cold in presence of the impenetrable night.

IV

AT early daybreak the repose of the mill was disturbed by the clamor of angry voices.   Father Merlier
had gone and unlocked Françoise's door.   She descended to the courtyard, pale and very calm, but
when there could not repress a shudder upon being
brought face to face with the body of a Prussian soldier that lay on the ground beside the well, stretched
out upon a cloak.

Soldiers were shouting and gesticulating angrily
about the corpse.   Several of them shook their fists
threateningly in the direction of the village.   The
officer had just sent a summons to Father Merlier to
appear before him in his capacity as mayor of the
commune.

"Here is one of our men," he said, in a voice that
was almost unintelligible from anger, "who was found
murdered on the bank of the stream.   The murderer
must be found, so that we may make a salutary example of him, and I shall expect you to co-operate with
us in finding him."

"Whatever you **desire**," the miller replied, with his customary impassiveness. "**Only** it will be no easy matter."

The officer stooped **down** and **drew aside** the skirt of the cloak which concealed the dead man's face, disclosing as he did so a frightful **wound**. The sentinel had been struck in the throat and the weapon had not been withdrawn from the wound. It was a common kitchen-knife, with a black handle.

"Look at that knife," the officer said to Father Merlier. "Perhaps it will assist us in our investigation."

The old man had started violently, but recovered himself at once; not a muscle of his face moved as he replied:

"Every one about here has knives like that. Like enough your man was tired of **fighting and did the business himself.** Such things have **happened before** now."

"Be silent!" the officer shouted in a fury. "I don't know what it is that keeps me from applying the torch to the four corners of your village."

His rage fortunately kept him from noticing the great change that had come over Françoise's countenance. Her feelings had compelled her to sit down upon the stone bench beside the well. Do what she would she could not remove her eyes from the body that lay stretched upon the ground, almost at her feet. He had been a tall, handsome young man in life, very like Dominique in appearance, with blue eyes and golden hair. The resemblance went to her heart. She thought that perhaps the dead man had left behind him in his German home some loved one who would weep for his loss. And she recognized her knife in the dead man's throat. She had killed him.

The officer, meantime, was talking of visiting Ro-creuse with some terrible punishment, when two or three soldiers came running in. The guard had just that moment ascertained the fact of Dominique's escape. The agitation caused by the tidings was extreme. The officer went to inspect the locality, looked out through the still open window, saw at once how the event had happened, and returned in a state of exasperation.

Father Merlier appeared greatly vexed by Dominique's flight. "The idiot!" he murmured; "he has upset everything."

Françoise heard him, and was in an agony of suffering. Her father, moreover, had no suspicion of her complicity. He shook his head, saying to her in an undertone:

"We are in a nice box, now!"

"It was that scoundrel! it was that scoundrel!" cried the officer. "He has got away to the woods; but he must be found, or by ——, the village shall stand the consequences." And addressing himself to the miller: "Come, you must know where he is hiding?"

Father Merlier laughed in his silent way and pointed to the wide stretch of wooded hills.

"How can you expect to find a man in that wilderness?" he asked.

"Oh! there are plenty of hiding-places that you are

acquainted with. I am going to give you ten men;
you shall act as guide to them."

"I am perfectly willing. But it will take a week to
beat up all the woods of the neighborhood."

The old man's serenity enraged the officer; he saw,
indeed, what a ridiculous proceeding such a hunt
would be. It was at that moment that he caught
sight of Françoise where she sat, pale and trembling,
on her bench. His attention was aroused by the girl's
anxious attitude. He was silent for a moment, glanc-
ing suspiciously from father to daughter and back
again.

"Is not this man," he at last coarsely asked the old
man, "your daughter's lover?"

Father Merlier's face became ashy pale, and he
appeared for a moment as if about to throw himself on
the officer and throttle him. He straightened himself
up and made no reply. Françoise had hidden her
face in her hands.

"Yes, that is how it is," the Prussian continued;
"you or your daughter have assisted him to escape.
You are his accomplices. For the last time, will you
surrender him?"

The miller did not answer. He had turned away
and was looking at the distant landscape with an air
of supreme indifference, just as if the officer were talking to some other person. That put the finishing
touch to the latter's wrath.

"Very well, then!" he declared, "you shall be shot
in his stead."

And again he ordered out the firing-party. Father
Merlier was as imperturbable as ever. He scarcely

did so much as shrug his shoulders; the whole drama appeared to him to be in very doubtful taste. He probably believed that they would not take a man's life in that unceremonious manner. When the platoon was on the ground he gravely said:

"So, then, you are in earnest?—Very well, I am willing it should be so. If you feel you must have a victim, it may as well be I as another."

But Françoise arose, greatly troubled, stammering: "Have mercy, good sir; do not harm my father. Take my life instead of his. It was I who assisted Dominique to escape; I am the only guilty one."

"Hold your tongue, my girl," Father Merlier exclaimed. "Why do you tell such a falsehood? She passed the night locked in her room, monsieur; I assure you that she does not speak the truth."

"I *am* speaking the truth," the girl eagerly replied. "I left my room by the window, I incited Dominique to fly. It is the truth, the whole truth."

The old man's face was very white. He could read in her eyes that she was not lying and her story terrified him. Ah, those children, those children! how they spoiled everything, with their hearts and their feelings! Then he said angrily:

"She is crazy; do not listen to her. It is a lot of trash she is giving you. Come, let us get through with this business."

She persisted in her protestations; she kneeled, she raised her clasped hands in supplication. The officer stood tranquilly by and watched the harrowing scene.

"*Mon Dieu*," he said at last, "I take your father because the other has escaped me. Bring me back

the other man and your father shall have his
liberty.''

She looked at him for a moment with eyes dilated
by the horror which his proposal inspired in her.

"It is dreadful," she murmured. "Where can I
look for Dominique now? He is gone; I know nothing beyond that."

"Well, make your choice between them; him or
your father."

"Oh! my God! how can I choose? Even if I
knew where to find Dominique I could not choose.
You are breaking my heart. I would rather die at
once. Yes, it would be more quickly ended thus.
Kill me, I beseech you, kill me——"

The officer finally became weary of this scene of
despair and tears. He cried:

"Enough of this! I wish to treat you kindly, I will
give you two hours. If your lover is not here within
two hours, your father shall pay the penalty that he has
incurred."

And he ordered Father Merlier away to the room
that had served as a prison for Dominique. The old
man asked for tobacco and began to smoke. There
was no trace of emotion to be descried on his impas-
sive face. Only when he was alone he wept two big
tears that coursed slowly down his cheeks as he
smoked his solitary pipe. His poor, dear child, what
a fearful trial she was enduring!

Françoise remained in the courtyard. Prussian
soldiers passed back and forth, laughing. Some of
them addressed her with coarse pleasantries which she
did not understand. Her gaze was bent upon the door

through which her father had disappeared, and with a slow movement she raised her hand to her forehead, as if to keep it from bursting. The officer turned sharply and said to her:

"You have two hours. Try to make good use of them."

She had two hours. The words kept buzzing, buzzing in her ears. Then she went forth mechanically from the courtyard; she walked straight ahead with no definite end. Where was she to go? what was she to do? She did not even endeavor to arrive at any decision, for she felt how utterly useless were her efforts. And yet she would have liked to see Dominique; they could have come to some understanding together, perhaps they might have hit on some plan to extricate them from their difficulties. And so, amid the confusion of her whirling thoughts, she took her way downward to the bank of the Morelle, which she crossed below the dam by means of some stepping-stones which were there. Proceeding onward, still involuntarily, she came to the first willow, at the corner of the meadow, and stooping down, beheld a sight that made her grow deathly pale—a pool of blood. It was the spot. And she followed the trace that Dominique had left in the tall grass; it was evident that he had run, for the footsteps that crossed the meadow in a diagonal line were separated from one another by wide intervals. Then, beyond that point, she lost the trace, but thought she had discovered it again in an adjoining field. It led her onward to the border of the forest, where the trail came abruptly to an end.

Though conscious of the futility of the proceeding,

Françoise penetrated into the wood. It was a comfort to her to be alone. She sat down for a moment,
then, reflecting that time was passing, rose again to
her feet. How long was it since she left the mill?
Five minutes? or a half-hour? She had lost all idea of
time. Perhaps Dominique had sought concealment in
a clearing that she knew of, where they had gone
together one afternoon and eaten hazel-nuts. She
directed her steps toward the clearing, she searched it
thoroughly. A blackbird flew out, whistling his sweet
and melancholy note; that was all. Then she thought
that he might have taken refuge in a hollow among
the rocks where he went sometimes with his gun to
secure a bird or a rabbit, but the spot was untenanted.
What use was there in looking for him? She would
never find him, and little by little the desire to discover his hiding-place became a passionate longing.
She proceeded at a more rapid pace. The idea suddenly took possession of her that he had climbed into
a tree, and thenceforth she went along with eyes
raised aloft and called him by name every fifteen or
twenty steps, so that he might know she was near him.
The cuckoos answered her; a breath of air that
rustled the leaves made her think that he was there and
was coming down to her. Once she even imagined
that she saw him; she stopped, with a sense of suffo-
cation, with a desire to run away. What was she to
say to him? Had she come there to take him back
with her and have him shot? Oh! no, she would not
mention those things; she would tell him that he must
fly, that he must not remain in the neighborhood.
Then she thought of her father awaiting her return,

and the reflection caused her most bitter anguish.
She sank upon the turf, weeping hot tears, crying
aloud:

"My God! My God! why am I here!"

It was a mad thing for her to have come. And as
if seized with sudden panic, she ran hither and thither,
she sought to make her way out of the forest. Three
times she lost her way, and had begun to think she
was never to see the mill again, when she came out into
a meadow, directly opposite Rocreuse. As soon as
she caught sight of the village she stopped. Was she
going to return alone?

She was standing there when she heard a voice calling her by name, softly:

"Françoise! Françoise!"

And she beheld Dominique, raising his head above
the edge of a ditch. Just God! she had found him!

Could it be, then, that heaven willed his death?
She suppressed a cry that rose to her lips and slipped
into the ditch beside him.

"You were looking for me?" he asked.

"Yes," she replied bewilderedly, scarce knowing
what she was saying.

"Ah! what has happened?"

She stammered, with eyes downcast: "Why, nothing; I was anxious, I wanted to see you."

Thereupon, his fears alleviated, he went on to tell
her how it was that he had remained in the vicinity.
He was alarmed for them. Those rascally Prussians
were not above wreaking their vengeance on women
and old men. All had ended well, however, and he
added, laughing:

"The wedding will be deferred for a week, that's all."

He became serious, however, upon noticing that her dejection did not pass away.

"But what is the matter? You are concealing something from me."

"No, I give you my word I am not. I am tired; I ran all the way here."

He kissed her, saying it was imprudent for them both to remain there longer, and was about to climb out of the ditch in order to return to the forest. She stopped him; she was trembling violently.

"Listen, Dominique; perhaps it will be as well for you to remain here, after all. There is no one looking for you, you have nothing to fear."

"Françoise, you are concealing something from me," he said again.

Again she protested that she was concealing nothing. She only liked to know that he was near her. And there were other reasons still that she gave in stammering accents. Her manner was so strange that no consideration could now have induced him to go away. He believed, moreover, that the French would return presently. Troops had been seen over toward Sauval.

"Ah! let them make haste; let them come as quickly as possible," she murmured fervently.

At that moment the clock of the church at Rocreuse struck eleven; the strokes reached them, clear and distinct. She arose in terror; it was two hours since she had left the mill.

"Listen," she said, with feverish rapidity, "should

we need you I will go up to my room and wave my handkerchief from the window.''

And she started off homeward on a run, while Dominique, greatly disturbed in mind, stretched himself at length beside the ditch to watch the mill. Just as she was about to enter the village Françoise encountered an old beggarman, Father Bontemps, who knew every one and everything in that part of the country. He saluted her; he had just seen the miller, he said, surrounded by a crowd of Prussians; then, making numerous signs of the cross and mumbling some inarticulate words, he went his way.

''The two hours are up,'' the officer said, when Françoise made her appearance.

Father Merlier was there, seated on the bench beside the well. He was smoking still. The young girl again proffered her supplication, kneeling before the officer and weeping. Her wish was to gain time. The hope that she might yet behold the return of the French had been gaining strength in her bosom, and amid her tears and sobs she thought she could distinguish in the distance the cadenced tramp of an advancing army. Oh! if they would but come and deliver them all from their fearful trouble!

''Hear me, sir; grant us an hour, just one little hour. Surely you will not refuse to grant us an hour!''

But the officer was inflexible. He even ordered two men to lay hold of her and take her away, in order that they might proceed undisturbed with the execution of the old man. Then a dreadful conflict took place in Françoise's heart. She could not allow her father to be murdered in that manner; no, no, she

would die in company with Dominique rather, and she
was just darting away in the direction of her room in
order to signal her *fiancé*, when Dominique himself
entered the courtyard.

The officer and his soldiers gave a great shout of
triumph, but he, as if there had been no soul there
but Françoise, walked straight up to her; he was perfectly calm, and his face wore a slight expression of
sternness.

"You did wrong," he said. "Why did you not
bring me back with you? Had it not been for Father
Bontemps I should have known nothing of all this.
Well, I am here, at all events."

V

It was three o'clock. The heavens were piled high
with great black clouds, the tail-end of a storm that
had been raging somewhere in the vicinity. Beneath
the coppery sky and ragged scud the valley of Rocreuse, so bright and smiling in the sunlight, became a
grim chasm, full of sinister shadows. The Prussian
officer had done nothing with Dominique beyond placing him in confinement, giving no indication of his
ultimate purpose in regard to him. Françoise, since
noon, had been suffering unendurable agony; notwithstanding her father's entreaties she would not
leave the courtyard. She was waiting for the French
troops to appear, but the hours slipped by, night was
approaching, and she suffered all the more since it
appeared as if the time thus gained would have no
effect on the final result.

About three o'clock, however, the Prussians began
to make their preparations for departure. The officer
had gone to Dominique's room and remained closeted
with him for some minutes, as he had done the day
before. Françoise knew that the young man's life was
hanging in the balance; she clasped her hands and
put up fervent prayers. Beside her sat Father Merlier, rigid and silent, declining, like the true peasant
he was, to attempt any interference with accomplished
facts.

"Oh! my God! my God!" Françoise exclaimed,
"they are going to kill him!"

The miller drew her to him and took her on his lap
as if she had been a little child. At this juncture the
officer came from the room, followed by two men conducting Dominique between them.

"Never, never!" the latter exclaimed. "I am
ready to die."

"You had better think the matter over," the officer
replied. "I shall have no trouble in finding some one
else to render us the service which you refuse. I am
generous with you; I offer you your life. It is simply
a matter of guiding us across the forest to Montredon;
there must be paths."

Dominique made no answer.

"Then you persist in your obstinacy?"

"Shoot me, and have done with the matter," he
replied.

Françoise, in the distance, entreated her lover with
clasped hands; she was forgetful of all considerations
save one, she would have had him commit a treason.
But Father Merlier seized her hands that the Prus-

sians might not see the wild gestures of a woman whose
mind was disordered by her distress.

''He is right,'' he murmured, ''it is best for him to
die.''

The firing-party was in readiness. The officer still
had hopes of bringing Dominique over, and was waiting to see him exhibit some signs of weakness. Deep
silence prevailed. Heavy peals of thunder were
heard in the distance, the fields and woods lay lifeless
beneath the sweltering heat. And it was in the midst
of this oppressive silence that suddenly the cry arose:

''The French! the French!''

It was a fact; they were coming. The line of red
trousers could be seen advancing along the Sauval
road, at the edge of the forest. In the mill the confusion was extreme; the Prussian soldiers ran to and
fro, giving vent to guttural cries. Not a shot had
been fired as yet.

''The French! the French!'' cried Françoise, clap-
ping her hands for joy. She was like a woman possessed. She had escaped from her father's embrace
and was laughing boisterously, her arms raised high in
air. They had come at last, then, and had come in
time, since Dominique was still there, alive!

A crash of musketry that rang in her ears like a
thunder-clap caused her to suddenly turn her head.
The officer had muttered: ''We will finish this business first,'' and with his own hands pushing Dominique
up against the wall of a shed, had given the command to the squad to fire. When Françoise turned
Dominique was lying on the ground, pierced by a
dozen bullets.

She did not shed a tear, she stood there like one suddenly rendered senseless. Her eyes were fixed and staring, and she went and seated herself beneath the shed, a few steps from the lifeless body. She looked at it wistfully; now and then she would make a movement with her hand in an aimless, childish way. The Prussians had seized Father Merlier as a hostage.

It was a pretty fight. The officer, perceiving that he could not retreat without being cut to pieces, rapidly made the best disposition possible of his men; it was as well to sell their lives dearly. The Prussians were now the defenders of the mill and the French were the attacking party. The musketry fire began with unparalleled fury; for half an hour there was no lull in the storm. Then a deep report was heard and a ball carried away a large branch of the old elm. The French had artillery; a battery, in position just beyond the ditch where Dominique had concealed himself, commanded the main street of Rocreuse. The conflict could not last long after that.

Ah! the poor old mill! The cannon-balls raked it from wall to wall. Half the roof was carried away; two of the walls fell in. But it was on the side toward the Morelle that the damage was greatest. The ivy, torn from the tottering walls, hung in tatters, débris of every description floated away upon the bosom of the stream, and through a great breach Françoise's chamber was visible with its little bed, the snow-white curtains of which were carefully drawn. Two balls struck the old wheel in quick succession and it gave one parting groan; the buckets were carried away down stream, the frame was crushed into a shapeless mass. It was the soul of the stout old mill, parting from the body.

Then the French came forward to carry the place by storm. There was a mad hand-to-hand conflict with the bayonet. Under the dull sky the pretty valley became a huge slaughter-pen; the broad meadows looked on affrightedly, with their great isolated trees and their rows of poplars, dotting them with shade, while to right and left the forest was like the walls of a tilting-ground inclosing the combatants, and in nature's universal panic the gentle murmur of the springs and water-courses sounded like sobs and wails.

Françoise had not stirred from the shed, where she remained hanging over Dominique's body. Father Merlier had met his death from a stray bullet. Then the French captain, the Prussians being exterminated and the mill on fire, entered the courtyard at the head of his men. It was the first success that he had gained since the breaking out of the war, so, all afire with enthusiasm, drawing himself up to the full height of his lofty stature, he laughed pleasantly, as a handsome cavalier like him might laugh, and perceiving poor idiotic Françoise where she crouched between the corpses of her father and her husband, among the smoking ruins of the mill, he saluted her gallantly with his sword and shouted:

"Victory! victory!"

THE END.

www.ingramcontent.com/pod-product-compliance
Lightning Source LLC
Chambersburg PA
CBHW021049030726
47496CB00006B/1759